"LOOK, CLAY, THE GAME IS OVER."

"Game?"

"Sure, the I-care-for-you-despite-your-flaws game."

His hazel eyes locked onto hers with a fierce insistency. "It's no game, Shelby. I do care."

She waved away his declaration, even though his words were what she most wanted to hear. "I'll sell you the land. Isn't that what you want? I'm . . . not sure I want to stick around."

He scanned her face in confusion. "This isn't about the land."

She could no longer meet his gaze. Swallowing thickly, she said, "Sometimes I feel like I'm in a triangle, with the land as your true love and me as a temporary mistress—fun for a while, but much too imperfect for real love." Clay belonged with Louisville royalty. His consort should be from among the fold.

His frustration boiled over. He took her by the waist and pulled her to him. "How can I convince you? Your land is just a plot of earth. People mean much more to me. Do you want to know what means a lot to me? You on a sunny day."

Shelby twisted to break his hold, but his warm hands, so gentle yet so firm, would not let her go. In his eyes she saw that he could not let her go.

LINDA GUSS
Hot Spell

ZEBRA BOOKS
KENSINGTON PUBLISHING CORP.

ZEBRA BOOKS

are published by

Kensington Publishing Corp.
475 Park Avenue South
New York, NY 10016

First Printing: December, 1992

Printed in the United States of America

To the memory of my mother, Gloria
— who would have gotten such a kick out of this

And special thanks to Richard,
brother-in-law, lawyer extraordinaire

Chapter One

Shelby Langstaff looked up from the May issue of *Louisville Today* magazine and was astonished to see Clay Trask walk into the reception area of the law firm Fisk and Fisk. Clay Trask—the boy voted "most likely to succeed in the back seat of a Mustang convertible" by Shelby's high school senior class twelve years ago. Although Shelby had been voted "most likely to break the bell curve," she had had a decidedly unintellectual crush on Clay, frustrated by the fact that they moved in different circles. Much different. Soon after graduation she'd left Kentucky for New York City. On her brief visits back to see her great-aunt Desiree, she'd managed to avoid running into acquaintances from her unlamented high school days—until now. And ironically this was to be her last visit.

She'd just gotten back from the funeral of her great-aunt Desiree, the woman who had raised her. The service had been a sad affair, attended by only three people, which wasn't surprising considering Desiree's penchant for solitude. The mourners had consisted of Shelby, her cousin, Logan, and Bryant Fisk, Desiree's attorney.

A kind man, Bryant had called Shelby two days ago in New York and told her about Desiree's fatal heart attack. He then helped with the funeral arrangements. After the interment, however, he startled Shelby with the information that a "situation" concerning Desiree's will needed her attention, and asked her to go to his office today.

Sitting now in Bryant's small waiting room, Shelby's emotions were in a tangle. Bryant had told her that she was Desiree's sole beneficiary, which meant that Shelby stood to inherit an ancient, broken-down Victorian house and not much else. So what was the mysterious new "situation" that he wanted her to hear about? Desiree's death had unleashed a flood of ambivalent memories about her odd aunt and Shelby's even odder upbringing.

Not that her aunt had been cruel or abusive. She'd welcomed Shelby, her late brother's grandchild, into her home with as much kindness as she could muster after Shelby's parents died in a car accident when Shelby was six. The problem was that Aunt Desiree seemed to live in the past and had dealt with the present reluctantly. Her remote, eccentric nature remained frozen in a gentler era of Southern ladies and gentlemen, and she wanted everyone to join her there.

But Shelby could never get the hang of this "lady" business. The effortless grace and unfazed calm so necessary to a lady's character was alien to Shelby's.

8

Her intensity had always alarmed Desiree, especially during Shelby's teen years, when Desiree feared that Shelby's rebellious nature would jeopardize her scholarship to the prestigious Breckinridge Preparatory School. How ironic, Shelby thought, that the very forthrightness that had made her so different from the belles at Breck Prep now served her so well in her present career as lifestyle reporter for *Courant* magazine.

Yes, having been an outsider at a fancy prep school turned out to be perfect training for her incisive, unawed portraits of the rich and powerful. Now she gazed at the quintessential Louisville insider. Seeing Clay Trask momentarily distracted Shelby from thoughts about Desiree.

He spoke to the receptionist in tones too low for Shelby to hear, but the elderly woman's face left no doubt as to her reaction to him. The barest pink color suffused her complexion, and she took off her glasses as she said, "If you'll just have a seat, Mr. Trask."

He walked into the waiting room. As Clay passed her, Shelby glanced up, making eye contact with him. He gazed briefly and sat down. He pulled a file out of his briefcase and started reading.

Oh, well, Shelby thought with an inward shrug. What else did she expect? Twelve years was a long time, and they'd just been acquaintances.

But, oh, how those features had made her teen-aged heart pound! Clay was handsome in that uniquely Louisville way that worships the square jaw, the straight nose, and the chiseled cheek-bones—bold features but in an eternally youthful face.

But Clay was all man now. Shelby could see that. His hazel eyes still held that elusive quality that had intrigued her so. Ringed by dark lashes, Clay's eyes were a curious mixture of light green and pale brown. Recessed slightly, they drew you in but revealed little. His wavy blond hair was slightly long, demonstrating his indifference for barbers or the current short styles. Clay's body still looked lean in a gray herringbone suit, although she remembered a more lanky build. The increased muscular definition gave his body a controlled power that a teenager could never possess.

High school heroes rarely kept the aura of "winner" about them when they faced the rigors of adult life. Not Clay. His athletic body, his expensive suit, his gleaming soft leather shoes combined with his slightly-unconventional hair showed a man confident in himself and his place in the world.

Shelby forced her attention back to a riveting article on bourbon candy. She was reading how important using *good* bourbon was when she heard, "Shelby? Shelby Langstaff?"

She felt a small inner stab of pleasure. "Yes?"

He put down his file. "Perhaps you don't remember me, but we went to school together? Breckinridge Prep?"

"Sure, you're . . ."

"Clay Trask."

His quick reply was disarming, as if he assumed she wouldn't remember the most popular boy in the class. "I remember you, Clay," she said. "You haven't changed much."

She'd meant the remark as a compliment, but his reaction was a subdued "thank you," an almost rueful resignation. Her eyes followed the line of his body as his broad shoulders met his chest, and then the line tapered to his narrow waist and hips. His physical presence still exuded a sense of imminent action and sinewy strength. Perhaps having a body this fine made one take it for granted.

"I'm sorry about your aunt."

His unexpected condolence touched her. "Thank you."

"I saw the obituary in the paper. 'Desiree Langstaff, survived by a niece, Shelby.' I thought there could be only one."

"Yes, there was only one Desiree Langstaff."

She spoke in a neutral tone, although internally she felt her age-old confusion over Desiree. One side of Shelby had deeply loved her aunt, but another side remembered the lonely, isolated childhood she'd had with her.

Clay's hazel eyes suddenly intensified, as if he understood immediately the ambiguity of her remark and was searching her eyes now for hidden feelings. She met his gaze with forced composure, blinking back the shiny glaze of sorrow that thinking of Desiree had brought. Clay's intuitive reaction, however, unsettled her.

"No, I meant there could only be one Shelby Langstaff."

"Oh," Shelby managed to say, surprised by his emphasis.

"But I almost didn't recognize you."

"Well, it's been twelve years."

Clay shook his head, the overhead light bouncing off the blond waves of his hair. "No, you don't understand. I remember you clearly, but in seeing you today, I realized that I had been expecting the *look* of the Shelby Langstaff in high school. That's why I didn't recognize you right off."

Shelby sat up in her chair. Clay had remembered her *look?* Her surprise deepened when she recalled another part of his comment. "You were expecting to see me today?"

His handsome face closed slightly. "Not exactly. I was hoping that we might meet, but I thought I would have to go through Bryant first."

"I'm here about my aunt's estate."

"So am I. I'd like to buy it."

Shelby was rarely rendered speechless. Clay's statement, however, left her with her mouth half open, an expression Aunt Desiree would have deemed ill-mannered.

"You would?" she finally said. "That du—" she caught herself before she said "dump." Despite what she privately thought of Desiree's large old Victorian, it would never do to run it down in front of a prospective buyer, possibly the *only* prospective buyer. Besides, the house was run down

12

enough. Originally the Langstaff family home, it was built on several acres at the turn of the century in the Queen Anne style. But years of neglect put it far past its prime. Shelby had found all the turrets and drafty rooms spooky as a child, and the plumbing hadn't been upgraded since Harry Truman took office. And now here was Clay Trask offering to buy it.

"That might be possible," she stammered. "I'm the beneficiary. I live in New York now, and the house is—" Again she stopped herself from saying "a white elephant." But, hell, if she knew the defects, didn't he? The Trask fortune had originally been made in real estate, so presumably he could spot a lemon. Why look a gift horse in the mouth? Shelby chided herself. Especially such a nice mouth. Still, her reporter's curiosity demanded an answer.

"Why do you want this house, Clay? It's . . . unique, yes, very nearly a historical landmark, but it's also a tad . . . decrepit." She couldn't lie.

He half-smiled and leaned closer. Shelby picked up a subtle scent that momentarily pushed Desiree's estate out of her mind. "It's not really the house we want, but the land around it. Your aunt's estate borders Trask property, and it would be prudent to add it to our holdings."

The "we" and "our" Shelby took to mean the Trask family, who owned not just considerable property in the Louisville area, but also a chain of discount stores called Tramarts.

"We'd like to make what I think is a fair offer for

it," Clay said. "I went over some figures this morning, and I'd be prepared to offer you . . . one hundred thousand dollars."

One hundred thousand dollars! Shelby had been expecting, at the most, fifty thousand for the land. What was under that mausoleum, oil? Shelby's face must have shown her surprise and delight.

"I hoped you'd be pleased," Clay said in a light drawl, as smooth as the best bourbon. "Perhaps after you talk to Bryant, I could join you and the three of us can discuss it." He smiled, but Shelby thought she detected definite relief over this mere "prudent buy." Only her reporter's training caught that relaxation of his body, as if all the muscles in his taut frame had uncoiled. What a coincidence running into him. What fortuitous happenstance. What a crock.

Clay Trask had always been a cool customer, difficult to read. Something was going on here—one hundred thousand dollars for a piece of land not even in the city, but east of it. Why? Shelby started to ask the question, then stopped herself. Why did *she* care? Shouldn't she just take the money and go back to New York? After all, now that Desiree was gone, what reason did she have to come back to Louisville? Wasn't a lucrative offer what she wanted so that she could divest herself of this final reminder of her unhappy past?

If so, why did she suddenly have a sad, empty feeling? Everything was happening so fast. Shelby looked at Clay, and for the second time she had the unsettling feeling that he could see into her heart.

His eyes, now a soft, mossy green, lost their detachment and seemed to offer balm to her troubled thoughts.

"I imagine you're anxious to get back to New York," he said, "although there's always a tie to the place you grew up in."

How strange that this man seemed to guess her thoughts. She couldn't read his. But she'd always been fascinated by Clay. Perhaps because she was more rambunctious compared to his legendary cool.

Shelby ran her hand through her long curly red hair, letting the tendrils glide through her fingers. "Well, yes and no," she said. "My job actually takes me all over the country, wherever there's a good story. Who knows, maybe there's a family of bluegrass blue bloods just ripe for my kind of slant."

His clear eyes locked onto hers. She'd touched a nerve. Obviously he was aware of her work as a chronicler of the rich and powerful. "Is that your plan?"

"No, no, I was just speculating." But his reaction made Shelby curious.

He relaxed a little, his lean body returning to its original lazy grace. "I've read several of your articles."

"I'm flattered. Is it easy to get *Courant* here?" Somehow the question came out too incredulous.

"Oh, we can get it," he said smoothly. "Next to the Sears catalogue, it's my favorite form of reading."

15

"If I remember school gossip, your favorite form of reading stayed hidden in paper bags in your locker."

"I had no choice. *War and Peace* was *so* heavy to carry around."

Shelby grinned. "A magazine is much lighter. Are you really familiar with my work?"

He nodded, one side of his mouth tilting upward. "You have an almost surgical ability to cut to the heart of any matter—and the confidence to take on any subject."

Shelby hadn't expected such a specific opinion. "I'm glad you like it."

He paused. The glint in his eye told Shelby that a gauntlet was about to be thrown down. "Your writing is fearless, but I don't always like it."

Now they were getting to it, Shelby thought with an inward smile. The rich tended to close ranks against outsiders, especially an outsider who wrote articles exposing the side of them that their publicists tried to hide. "Okay," she said, straightening her black skirt, "which one of your friends have I wrongly profiled?"

He smiled, almost, it seemed, in spite of himself. Shelby remembered that smile. Filled with a boyish zest, Clay's smile counterbalanced the more rugged aspects of his cheekbones and jaw. "I don't know if 'wrongly profiled' is accurate, but your article on the Blackwood family went . . . one step too far in discussing their private lives."

"Too far? Mason Blackwood, the elderly baby food magnate, married for the fourth time a girl

16

almost young enough to need his products. He had a heart attack on their honeymoon. Rumor has it that he died with a smile on his face, but Mason forgot to change his will to include his child bride. Major lawsuits ensued between the young wife and Mason's children, who claimed that the wife tricked a faltering old man into marrying her. Clay, I didn't sensationalize this story—I just reported it."

Clay leaned back, the increased physical distance a statement of his doubt. "His children were very embarrassed by your revelation about Mason's obsession with remaining virile. One of them is an old college friend, and he had no idea that to remain, um, active, Mason had had a . . ."

"Penile implant?" Shelby watched with amusement as Clay nodded and at the same time crossed his legs. Every man she'd told had the same reaction. "I don't know what the fuss was about. Thousands of men have the procedure when an illness—diabetes, for example—renders them unable to maintain an erec—"

"Yes, I know why the implant is done," Clay said, "but you wrote that Mason didn't *have* a physical problem."

"He didn't, other than being seventy. He had the implant to increase his stamina—to achieve peak performance, shall we say."

Clay uncrossed his legs and leaned forward. For a crazy second Shelby wondered what his peak performance would feel like.

"You're straying off the subject," Clay said.

17

"The subject was privacy. Mason may have chosen a high profile, but his children didn't."

"I only wrote about his children in connection with the suit. I didn't delve into their personal lives."

"The exposure of Mason's follies hit them all privately. We can't disconnect ourselves from the people who raise us, no matter what they've done."

Again Shelby had the feeling that he was addressing her inner thoughts. But what about his? The Trask family had made their wealth in a little more than one generation. Clay's grandfather had been a farmer. There was usually a story behind so much wealth attained so quickly.

"If you've read my pieces," she said, "then you know that I'm not so petty as to write an article merely to reveal the sad obsessions of a rich man, but to show how his actions could destroy a company and a family."

"All the more reason not to write about it! Look, I'm not naive. I know the public loves to read about the dark side of fame and wealth, and you do it with as much real reporting flair as any I've read—"

"Damned with faint praise."

"But where is the limit? Does wealth automatically make any family fair game for one of your personal invasions?"

"Of course not! Don't relegate my career to that of a common scold. I write about fame and money because those who possess them have abnormal power over others." Shelby sat back in her chair.

18

She hadn't realized that the exchange had brought her to the edge of her seat. "But don't worry. As I said, I'm not interested in your family."

"That's a relief."

"*You* maybe."

His eyes widened as his face struggled to remain unruffled. He was powerless, however, to keep his smooth skin from coloring a little. *Gotcha,* Shelby thought. His further reaction was unfortunately checked by the arrival of Bryant's secretary. "Ms Langstaff, Mr. Fisk will see you now. Mr. Trask, he'll see you in a few minutes."

Shelby got up. Clay had stiffened at her remark, but his irritation, Shelby sensed, was mixed with another emotion. The heightened color in his face and the snap of his replies bespoke a certain fascination, albeit grudging.

Clay Trask probably didn't talk to too many people like her. His wealth—and naked ring finger—probably created circumstances where people fawned over him, or at least tried to please him. Shelby had no intention of doing either, although sparring with him had recharged her entire body from its weariness.

She followed Bryant's secretary out of the waiting room. She took one last glance at Clay. He was still looking at her.

Clay watched Shelby's lithe figure disappear into the hallway. What a firecracker she was, so different from the women he usually met who were too polite to ever tell you an honest thought. Her directness was refreshing. Her coltish legs and wild red hair were . . . inviting, but her reputation for journalistic snooping definitely unsettled him.

In Clay's most optimistic scenario Shelby Langstaff would sell him her aunt's property and then return quickly to New York. Minimal contact with him, and *no* contact with his family. After the bombshell that had exploded that morning, his parents, John and Mary-Alice Trask, were in a state. John had stood at the door of Park View, the family home, and in a speech reminiscent of General Lee to the troops before Gettysburg, commanded Clay to "get that land!"

Clay understood the importance, but he was not as flappable as his parents. John and Mary-Alice Trask always saw disaster lurking. They were convinced that one social faux pas would knock the nouveau riche Trasks from their precarious toehold in Louisville society.

Clay never gave two hoots about society, but he cared deeply about his family. So when a mysterious letter had been hand-delivered to his grandfather that morning, he'd been concerned. After the contents upset the frail old man so much that he'd needed oxygen, Clay was frightened. He read the letter and immediately knew one thing: he had to have Desiree Langstaff's estate.

The key was Shelby Langstaff. Mmmm, the full lips, the creamy skin, the strong face—he'd remembered Shelby.

She hadn't remembered him, he thought ruefully. But then, Shelby had never been impressed with his crowd in high school. Shallow charmers—

that's what she'd called his friends, and she was probably half right. That *he* might be different had probably never occurred to her.

Clay had found that once people have an impression of you, they're loath to give it up. Louisville was so sure it had him pegged. From high school on success had been expected, *assumed* from him. He started the Tramart discount stores on a gamble, but when they prospered, no one was surprised but him. Successful, rich, and eligible — why, he had everything. *So you think,* Clay mused. The image Louisville admired often seemed like a stranger to him.

But the river city was his home; he belonged here. His family had given him more opportunities at thirty than most people got their whole lives. He loved his family, and now that he basically ran Trask Industries, he felt responsible for protecting them. That obligation never seemed more acute than today. As much as Shelby Langstaff intrigued him, with her passionate, vibrant personality, he could not indulge his desire to see her again. Shelby could be very dangerous to him.

Bryant Fisk's office was like his waiting room, Shelby thought, conservative, Early American, prosperous but not ostentatious. As she sat down in a wing chair, she felt a nervous flutter in her stomach. The air conditioning did little to cool her nerves.

What was the problem with Desiree's estate?

What had her aunt done? Wouldn't it be ironic, Shelby thought, that in death she might learn more about her aunt than in life? For behind Desiree's dissembling countenance, Shelby had always sensed an inner turmoil, a mysterious but real desolation. Shelby had never known the cause, but now she wondered if this restless unease was a family trait.

For despite her spirited defense of her writing with Clay, Shelby had been feeling a growing disconnection with her present life, as exciting as it was at times. The fame and the satisfaction her work provided were, of course, the plus side. The down side was that a writer had to remain distanced from her subjects to be objective. Even a confessed outsider like herself would like to belong somewhere, with someone. Now with the loss of Desiree, Shelby was feeling more alone than ever.

Bryant's face was not reassuring. His bushy white brows were knit in a worried frown. "Thank you for coming, Shelby. I wanted to speak to you as soon as possible about your aunt's affairs, but I didn't feel it was proper to discuss it at the funeral."

"You mean in front of Logan, right?"

Bryant adjusted his tie clasp. "I mean in front of anyone. Your aunt's business is confidential."

Shelby agreed, although she thought her first suspicion had merit. Logan Langstaff was her last living relative. He was a good-looking blond in his early thirties who was perpetually one "deal" away from easy street. Logan had thought it unfair that he should have an old, respected name, but not a fortune to go along with it. Shelby had always liked him. As children they'd played together, whispering confidences and dreams. She was touched that he'd come to the funeral today.

"Of course my aunt's business is private, but you and Auntie were always so hard on Logan. He's trustworthy in his way. You just don't know him as I do."

Bryant nodded absently in an ever-so-polite way of saying he wished to move on. "Let us not dwell on him. You know, Shelby, Desiree left her entire estate to you."

"Yes, I know."

"Well, your aunt accrued some debts, especially after her first heart attack."

Shelby shot up in her chair. "What first heart attack!"

Bryant turned a mottled shade of pink. "I was sworn not to tell you. Desiree didn't want to worry you."

"I thought she had mild angina! If I'd known—"

"You'd have come back to take care of her. Desiree didn't want you to leave your life in New York. She just rested at home. You know she never liked going out anyway."

"Still . . ."

"She hid the heart attack from you, yes. Desiree was always so private. I will tell you, Shelby, that, during my last phone call with her, Desiree confided in me that the heart attack had made her re-evaluate her life. Since she'd become a virtual shut-in, I sent my law clerk out to her, just to make sure all her legal papers were in order. He said she was positively gay. He said she sorted through the papers — adding some, weeding out others — as happy as a clam. And that was but one week before she died."

A happy Desiree? Shelby pondered this unusual concept.

"As I say," Bryant went on, "she accrued some debts. In fact, she was in danger of losing the house before she died."

The frigid blasts of air conditioning didn't keep Shelby from suddenly feeling hot. "I would never have let that happen."

Ever the considerate host, Bryant moved a box of tissues in front of Shelby. "I know and, fortunately, Desiree did not have to go through that. But the debts have mounted."

"Then I'll sell the house." Shelby had come to Louisville prepared to do just that. But now, with the incredibly quick loss of everything that meant family to her, she felt oddly distraught.

Bryant pursed his lips and rubbed his hand over the few silver strands of hair he had left. "That might not be enough, but don't worry, the creditors can't come after you."

Shelby had no intention of stiffing people who had lent credit to Desiree in her last months. "I'll pay out of my own pocket!"

"I wonder if you have that much cash. Desiree had a number of doctor bills. Her debts may exceed the value of the house, which I estimate is about fifty thousand, by as much as twenty."

Shelby pulled a tissue out of the box and pressed it to her forehead. Southern women never perspired, Desiree had always told her, they *glowed*. Shelby was definitely glowing. "I don't have that kind of money," she said softly. "I make a good salary at *Courant,* but New York is expensive. I don't even own my own apartment."

Bryant nodded gravely. "Well, there is a grace period while claims against the estate are investigated and evaluated. No creditor can force you to do anything during this time. But I imagine—"

"Wait, Bryant!" Shelby interrupted. "I have a solution, or rather, a solution just presented itself."

"Come again?"

"You'll never guess who I ran into in your waiting room."

"My guess would be little old ladies, but I'll wager I'm wrong."

Shelby smiled. "Clay Trask."

Bryant slapped his blotter. "My secretary told me he was out there! Is that why he's here? Does he want to make an offer on the house?"

"Yes, and Bryant, you'll never guess what he offered. One hundred thousand dollars!"

Bryant's bushy white eyebrows shot so high that they would have hit his hairline, if he had still had one. "One hundred thousand dollars! That's mighty generous, mighty generous!" Generous came out "genrus." "Why, you could pay off all the debts and, even with taxes, have a tidy nest egg left over. That would be perfect."

25

"Yes, it would," Shelby said, breathing normally again. Despite her relief, a tiny voice whispered "too perfect."

"Well, let's get that boy in here!" He buzzed his secretary. "Lillian, ask Mr. Trask to come in here. Well, this is the best news I've heard all day!"

Clay came in, shook hands with Bryant, told the venerable old lawyer to call him Clay, and sat down next to Shelby. His finely-sculpted face had regained its composure. He looked like a man whose plan had come together.

"Now, Clay," Bryant began, "Miss Langstaff tells me that you have made an offer for the property. Is that correct?"

Clay nodded. "Yes, I've made an offer of one hundred thousand dollars."

Bryant beamed. "Miss Langstaff has — " He was interrupted by his intercom. Picking up the phone, he listened intently, frowned, and hung up. "Could you pardon me for a moment? There is a conference call I must take in another office." He got up and moved to the door. "My apologies. I won't be long."

As the office door closed, Shelby remembered one unusual comment that Clay had made in the waiting room. This might be her last chance to ask him about it. "What did you mean when you said that you didn't recognize me right off because my *look* was so different? I think I rather look the same. I haven't gotten any taller."

He smiled at her mild jest about her height. In Kentucky, where the feminine ideal was dainty, doe-eyed, and demure, Shelby had always stood out. She'd reached her adult height of five feet nine inches by the time she was thirteen, a fact that had made her self-conscious. Shelby's face was unconventional, too, having a long oval shape, high cheekbones, full lips, and an aquiline nose. But none of these features had changed in the last twelve years. What did he mean?

"No, you haven't gotten any taller," Clay said, "and your hair is just as red, but your *look* is different. In high school you seemed to . . ." He stopped, as if musing over the old days was distasteful. "Well, that was then. How we appear in high school often bears little resemblance to who we are."

Shelby wondered if he was referring to her or himself. At Breck Prep Shelby had been determinedly offbeat, never really aligning herself with any group. At the time she'd claimed it was a protest against conformity, but twelve years of perspective had further conceded that she'd also been scared of rejection. *I was offbeat,* she thought, with a mixture of pride and pain. *And here I am talking to a man who's never had to worry about acceptance anywhere.* "I think you're right, Clay, it was very hard to be different from the group. That's why I left this place after high school."

"Oh, Louisville was to blame? You were angry at the whole city?"

"I wasn't angry. I was just annoyed at the inflexible social rules at Breck Prep."

"You know a Langstaff helped found the

school."

"How could I forget when the principal reminded me every year that this fact accounted for my scholarship," she said quietly.

"That and your high grades," Clay added.

"Yes," she admitted, oddly pleased that he remembered how smart she was, "but I never fit in there. Never, but at least I wasn't a sheep."

She'd surprised him with that response, but he looked as if he expected her to be blunt, even enjoyed it. "A sheep?"

"Yes, a blind slave to fashion—a clone, or clonette, as the case may be."

"I follow you," Clay said and then snapped his fingers. "I guess that sounded sheeplike. I mean, I understand."

Shelby had to laugh.

"Let's see," he continued, shifting his six-foot frame in the small chair, "a Breck Prep clonette, circa 1980 would have . . . ?"

"A layered Farrah Fawcett hairdo with cascades of sun-tipped hair falling past her perfect complexion and landing on her perfect shoulders," Shelby recited.

"I don't remember such perfection," Clay said.

"She'd wear dresses with big floral prints, and at least one set of the holes in her ears would have real pearl earrings. In the winter she'd wear tassel loafers, and in the summer espadrilles, and always, always her add-a-bead necklace."

"And we know what each bead stood for!" Clay interjected.

28

Shelby stopped dead in her recitation. "No, what?"

Clay's lightly-tanned face suddenly showed a faint blush. It was so unexpected, so boyishly appealing, that Shelby was thrown. "What, Clay, what did it mean?"

"Ahhh, each bead was supposed to have commemorated . . . a romantic experience."

Shelby had never had an add-a-bead necklace. Considering her dating life at Breck Prep, she obviously hadn't needed one. "I see my knowledge of clonettes wasn't total. I bow to your more extensive experience."

He seemed more abashed than complimented. "Reports of my exploits were greatly exaggerated."

"Not from what I heard. But are we describing clones now?"

His hazel eyes accepted her challenge. "Okay, chinos, oxford-cloth shirts, loafers with no socks, anything from Brooks Brothers."

"Preferably worn by your father or grandfather," Shelby interjected. "The older, the better."

"Well, in my case, that would have been barely a generation."

Clay's family was nouveau riche, but he'd never been embarrassed by his rural roots, Shelby remembered, nor pretended a bogus genealogy that went back to Daniel Boone.

"So you bought it new and had the maid run it through the washer twenty times."

"Are you implying that I was a sheep?"

"You were their idol."

He lifted his chin, a bare smile on his lips. "And you looked down on us."

His response astonished her. "You looked down on *me*."

"Not true!"

"Yes!"

He leaned forward, and Shelby felt a wave of energy go through his body. He looked as if he wanted to touch her. "I thought you were . . . different."

"Odd."

"Original," he shot back, and Shelby saw in a flash that he was telling the truth. "You always spoke your mind. And you always dressed . . . uniquely. I especially liked your punk phase, although I thought dyeing your red hair platinum and then spiking it didn't exactly flatter you. But the fishnet stockings under your uniform were a real bonus."

Shelby felt her cheeks grow hot. Clay *had* remembered her, and in such detail! The trouble was . . . "I don't remember you or anyone else praising my orange lipstick in those days."

"You didn't let people in."

"No one tried."

"So you left Louisville and found fame in New York."

"Yes, I guess I did," Shelby said with satisfaction.

"And you're anxious to get back."

"Brother, am I!" But at that moment Shelby realized that she'd felt more alive in the past hour than

30

she had in the past few months. Clay's unexpected recollection of her had her in a state of pleasant confusion. Her body lost its weary stiffness as she drank in the spicy scent of his after-shave and the look of intense interest in his eyes.

She'd gotten all wound up, literally forgetting Desiree. But Clay had touched on an area still sensitive to her. How did she really feel about Louisville? And was her anger springing from scars of adolescence or from unresolved questions about her relationship with Desiree?

"Well, then I hope we can conclude this sale as quickly as possible so you can leave."

Oh, so that's where this stroll down memory lane is leading, Shelby thought with a jolt. *Nicely done, Clay. Guide the conversation so that you're performing a real service for me by buying my land.*

She could appreciate his finesse, even as she wondered if all his words were calculated. Had he really remembered her fishnet stockings? Was Clay just flattering her, and why did she care? Here was a man ready to solve all her problems. So what if he looked through a couple of old yearbooks to reacquaint himself with her "look." He'd done his research, figured out a pitch, and made his offer.

For double what the land was worth. Somehow this whole scenario was playing too cleanly. The rich don't make "prudent" buys. They always expect a return on their investment—that's how they got to be rich.

Bryant's reappearance interrupted her thoughts. "I'm sorry I was so long," he said, lowering his

31

bulk back into his chair. "Now, where were we? Oh, yes, Miss Langstaff was just telling me about your offer, and she —"

"Would like to think about it."

Surprise flickered over Clay's face. And alarm.

"Uh, excuse me, Shelby?" Poor Bryant looked at her as if she'd just dyed her hair platinum and spiked it.

"I said I'd like to think about it."

"Oh, well . . ." Bryant was speechless.

"I thought you liked the deal," Clay said quietly. He now looked mildly puzzled, but not condescending. In fact, he looked as if he were reassessing her.

"It's a generous offer," Bryant added hopefully.

"Yes, it is, but it wouldn't be prudent to make a decision so quickly." *Especially not when my curiosity is up,* she thought.

Clay's eyes narrowed at the word "prudent." He got up and extended his hand. "I really hadn't thought that I would meet you today, so take your time. The offer will stand until you make a decision. Bryant, I'll be at Park View for the rest of the afternoon."

His hand was strong and warm. His words seemed sincere. Why did Shelby want to doubt him? Because he was rich? Or because they had discussed *her* vulnerabilities in high school, not his.

Did he even have them? Could the boy voted Prom King by his peers ever have a problem with his golden boy image?

The moment the door closed, Bryant started sputtering. "What in tarnation made you hesitate, Shelby?"

She straightened her black skirt. "I don't know. Something's not right about this. He's offering a lot of money—too much."

"Should I ask him to lower his price?"

Shelby smiled. "No, but what I'd like you to do is call one of your colleagues. You handle wills, Bryant, not real estate. Call one of your counterparts in real estate and ask if there has been any talk about Desiree's land."

It took a few minutes to convince Bryant to call his friend, Duddy, a real estate lawyer. Even after he did, his initial demeanor was half apologetic. Then his face began to change. Midway through his conversation, his eyebrows began to rise, and when he hung up the phone, he looked astonished.

"Well, bless my buttons, I never would have thought it."

"What, Bryant, what?"

"Well, Shelby, you may not know this, but Louisville is growing to the east."

"So?"

"Well, for years Desiree's land was considered in the country, but now the city's practically at her doorstep."

"Meaning?" Bryant's leisurely way of getting to things had her on the edge of her seat.

"It looks like Desiree's land is now prime real estate. Duddy told me that the word at the Fairview Country Club is that there will probably be more offers. People are waiting out of respect, this being the day of the funeral and all."

"But not Clay Trask."

"Uh, no. There's a rumor that his family needs this acreage badly as part of a new Tramart."

So it wasn't just a prudent buy! "I knew it," she whispered.

"And, Shelby, the land is worth more than one hundred thousand dollars. A lot more."

Chapter Two

Shelby felt tiny prickles at her hairline. "How much more?"

Bryant threw up his hands. "Difficult to say. If there are several offers, then the price could rise with the competition."

"How about a ballpark figure?"

"Oh, maybe as much as five hundred thousand, maybe more."

Five hundred thousand dollars! That wasn't a nest egg—that was freedom! With half a million dollars Shelby could take only the assignments she wanted, or take a leave of absence to write that book she'd had percolating in her brain. Five hundred thousand dollars meant living on the *interest* generated by her inheritance—like the rich did.

"You're going to need some tax shelters," Bryant said, already acting matter-of-factly about this miracle. But Shelby was still in a daze.

"I can't believe it," she said.

"Well, believe it, honey," Bryant said with a chuckle.

"I'm just sorry Aunt Desiree didn't benefit from her land."

Bryant shook his head. "She would never have left that house, Shelby. Never. You know that. You tried to get her to move years ago. Desiree once told me that the house was her penance. I never *did* know what she meant by that." He sighed. "She told me that she'd gotten an offer for the place a few months ago but turned it down flat. She wanted to leave you something that meant family."

Shelby felt her throat tighten. This concern so late in life—why hadn't Desiree shown this before? Shelby's sorrow slowly turned to anger.

"Who made her the offer, Bryant?"

"I don't know. I asked, but she waved me off."

"It wouldn't, by any chance, have been Clay Trask?"

"Shelby, I don't know."

But Shelby did, or rather she suspected. Clay had had his sights on Desiree's property all along. Her land probably "bordered" Trask property because they'd *bought* all the other land around it. And when Desiree had rebuffed him, he'd waited, waited until she was dead and then popped up on the day of the funeral with an offer big enough to impress Shelby so that she'd agree quickly and leave before ever finding out how much the land was really worth. What nerve. What bad taste.

"What a liar!"

"Now, you don't know who made the offer!"

Shelby stood up. Her hands felt slick and

36

clammy. "Yes, I do, and I'm going to make sure Clay Trask knows just exactly why he will never get that land!"

Within seconds Bryant was at Shelby's side putting a calming hand on hers.

"Don't be hasty. Clay Trask may ultimately make the best offer. The man is innocent until proven guilty."

"Oh, he's guilty, all right."

"Why? Because he made the offer today? He was coming to see me, not you. Clay Trask may be a little unorthodox, but he has a reputation for honesty. Don't laugh. Clay never said this was his final offer. And one hundred thousand dollars *was* a generous price. This is business, Shelby, but you're taking it personally."

Shelby gently lifted Bryant's hand from hers. She fumbled for her purse and took out her car keys. "The rich always say it's just business when they hoodwink the poor. Well, I'm going to tell one robber baron that he's been found out. Now how do I get to the Trask estate? What's it called?"

"Park View." Bryant sighed and opened the door. "You can get the address from my secretary. But, Shelby, think about this as you rush off to tell Clay Trask to go to hell. You're going to be one wealthy woman after this. It's very easy to criticize the rich and how they handle their affairs until suddenly you have money. Your perspective will change. You'll see."

Shelby got the Trask address from Bryant's secretary. She nearly laughed when she read "Park

View on Park Lane." Of course they'd have a private road. And naturally they lived east of Brownsboro Road. Only the very wealthy lived east of this thoroughfare, in such exclusive enclaves as Indian Hills and Glenview.

As Shelby steered her rented car east, she thought about Bryant's admonition. Money wouldn't change her, she told herself. All that this windfall meant was that now she'd have a chance to really contribute to the charities and causes she believed in. Of course, that hadn't been her *first* reaction, she admitted. Her first response had been to think about herself, but wasn't that natural? After years of paying her dues, she was just beginning to tap her potential as a writer. The money would free her artistically.

Shelby settled comfortably into this rationale until she realized that her inheritance now put her in the position of being one of the rich that she wrote so scathingly about. Would she lose her edge? Would her perspective change?

Desiree had always said that you didn't really know folks until you walked a mile in their shoes. Would being one of the rich so acquaint her with their problems that she'd no longer see them clearly? Would familiarity breed understanding rather than the healthy contempt she had now?

She found Park Lane with some difficulty. The small sign was nearly obscured by the foliage that hid the estate entrance from the casual passerby. She turned into the private road. Her troubled thoughts were interrupted by the dazzling beauty of the grounds for which the house was named. Here, nature and a sure hand had conspired to create a lush playground for the senses. The velvety green lawn was being cut, filling the air with the faint smell of tarragon. The warm May sun sparkled off charming ponds, while a variety of colorful spring flowers proclaimed the earth's renewal. Every tree looked as if it had been there for generations. Although the grounds were certainly planned, the whole effect had a spontaneous feel, as if the designer knew instinctively where to put each plant. It was a lovely display of restrained taste.

Park View was another story. Three stories, actually, of white brick and pillars. Shelby guessed that the basic design was Greek revival, with massive Corinthian columns and a two-story portico. The structure, however, had elements of the federal style, with a veranda that screamed New Orleans, and a Victorian cupola on the roof.

To carp about Park View's inconsistencies was to miss the point, she thought. The house didn't reach for architectural integrity—it reached for grandeur. It was an antebellum plantation house built by people who'd never been in one.

This was where Clay Trask grew up and apparently still lived. Shelby parked her car in the semicircular driveway, right behind a maroon Cadillac and a vintage red Mustang convertible.

"Toto, I don't think we're in Kansas anymore," she said, getting out of her car.

Shelby rang the bell. After a minute or two the

massive front door swung open, and a gust of cool air hit Shelby's warm face. A tall, portly man in an elaborate butler's uniform greeted her.

"Yes?"

"Is Clay Trask home?"

"Do you have an appointment?"

"No, but—"

"You must make an appointment. His business number is—"

"I think he'll see me."

The butler almost sniffed. Obviously he'd heard that before. "Who, may I ask, is calling?"

"Shelby Langstaff."

Upon hearing her name, the butler's expression changed from dismissive to cautious. There were so many folds and lines on his ancient face that it wasn't easy to tell, but his eyes gave him away. They turned as hard as flint and twice as sharp. Why he regarded her with unease Shelby didn't know. But she was not mistaken.

"Mr. Clay did . . . mention you." He paused, pondering some unknown dilemma.

"Look, may I come in? It's hotter than usual for May."

"No!"

Instinctively Shelby took one step back. This butler was definitely spooked. "I promise I won't steal the silver," she joked, trying to lighten the situation.

He looked furious at having lost his composure. "Oh, uh, I'm sorry, but what I meant to say is that you wouldn't want to come in because Mr. Clay isn't here."

Shelby was becoming impatient. "Where is he?"

The butler started to answer when a voice — old, tired, and brittle — called out. "Who is it, Mapes?"

Shelby tried to peer in, but Mapes stepped into her line of sight.

"Just a visitor for Mr. Clay."

"Well, don't leave them standing outside. Where's your manners?" The accent was rural Kentucky. Shelby saw the shadow of a figure in a wheelchair.

"I was just telling her that Mr. Clay's on the grounds," Mapes called back. He turned to her and said urgently, "Go past that arbor of maples to your left and you'll come to a small stream. He's there." Mapes closed the door before she had a chance to reply.

How odd, Shelby thought as she trudged through the grove. Mapes seemed to be petrified that she would see the shadowy figure inside. Who was he? She must remember to ask Clay — after she told him off, of course.

Shelby came to the stream Mapes had described, but the only person there was a gardener, bending over several plants.

"Excuse me," she called out, "I'm looking for Clay Trask."

"Well, you've found him." The figure straightened and turned around.

Shelby didn't know who was more surprised. Clay's hazel eyes widened and he instinctively wiped his soiled hands on his jeans. "Why, Shelby"

41

was all he said.

Before her stood a rougher, earthier man than the immaculately-tailored young executive that Shelby had met earlier. Perhaps this was the true Clay Trask. In any case, he was an arresting sight. His jeans, worn to a faded pale blue, outlined strong thighs, slender hips, and a flat stomach. The thin cotton of his navy T-shirt inadequately concealed his lightly-muscled chest and powerful forearms. Yes, Clay was definitely all man now.

In a suit Clay radiated power due to his position and the force of his personality. Here, he radiated a different power, more primitive and elemental, rising from the sheer strength of his body. As determined as she was to confront him, Shelby couldn't deny the impact of his splendid form on her tired brain.

She lived so much of her life in her mind, thinking of stories, planning her research, and writing her thoughts. Frequently she saw the power of the written word but rarely the power of the human physique. Clay's body consumed her with curiosity.

What would it look like in its raw simplicity? How would it feel to touch, to kiss, to be under? Shelby noticed for the first time tiny lines of age — or experience — at the edges of his eyes. This man probably had a lot of experience, she thought. The spring sun glanced off his high cheekbones and played light and shadow with his wavy blond hair, giving it a shimmering quality. His face was slightly flushed from the sun, but he wasn't perspiring.

Such a cool character. Shelby wondered what it would take to put a glaze of sweat on his face.

The first possibility that came to mind almost made her forget her original purpose in being there. Perhaps it was the grass, as soft as a blanket beneath her feet, or the warm late-afternoon sun, or the smell of the earth's annual rebirth that set her mind on lovemaking. Or perhaps it was just Clay Trask.

"What can I do for you?" he asked.

Embarrassed by her daydream, Shelby willed herself to remember just who she was talking to. "Frankly, Clay, I came here to tell you that there is *nothing* you can do for me—ever." She turned around and then stopped. "Oh, there's one small thing you can do. Go to hell."

She started to walk away, but Clay was quickly in front of her. Small beads of sweat had formed on his brow.

"What do you mean? What are you talking about?" he demanded. He braced her shoulders with his strong hands. Shelby saw genuine confusion in his eyes, but at that moment she couldn't trust her feelings where Clay Trask was concerned.

"Bafflement doesn't become you, Clay, so I'll put you out of your misery. There's nothing you can do for me since I wouldn't sell my land to you if you were the last man on earth!"

His grip tightened. "Why?"

"Because you're a liar and a sneak! Not two minutes after you left, Bryant learned that your 'prudent' buy was actually a *necessity,* and that the land is worth five times what you offered!"

Stunned, he let her go. His body tensed as he drew a quick breath. Shelby could still feel his fingers on her shoulders. "Do you deny that you lied about the land?"

His eyes turned a pale green. "Of course I deny it."

"You never mentioned Tramart."

"No, but keeping it a secret was *not* a business ploy! Tramart plans are always held close to the vest. Do you tell your writing friends who you're planning to profile before you have the subject nailed down?"

Shelby never revealed her subjects until well into her research on a project. It was simply imprudent to show her hand.

"All right, I don't! But, Clay, the rumor is all over the Fairview Country Club."

"And that's why the land has risen in value! We want it. And so now others are eager to bid because they think we know where the next commercial boom will be."

Shelby ran a nervous hand through a red curl. Her scalp near her hairline was damp. "Louisville is growing to the east."

"Yes, but no one knows exactly where. Look, I never meant to offer you anything less than what the land was worth. In fact, I offered you double, based on *my* knowledge of its value."

Shelby's estimate had been the same, too, she had to admit.

"I don't intend to be underbid. Tell me your

highest offer and I'll top it."

Now Shelby was the one confused. What Clay said made sense. Still, the question of Desiree's recent offer lingered in her mind. "I have no idea what the highest offer will be. Most people are waiting out of respect."

Clay's gaze dropped. When he spoke again, his voice had an odd tone, almost a tenderness. "As I said in the office, I had no idea that I would see you today." He looked straight into her eyes. "I'm sorry if I upset you. You must feel almost bruised after this morning. I know I would if I lost any of my family."

This admission, so gently stated, touched Shelby in that part of her still so troubled over Desiree's death. Why could he read her so well?

"Yes, it's been difficult."

He rested his hand on her shoulder. The pressure this time conveyed a soothing warmth. "My grandfather is the same generation as your aunt. As old as he is, I can't bear to think — I mean, I wouldn't be prepared to say goodbye."

Shelby thought of the courteous but tired voice that she'd heard from the foyer at Park View. "I almost met your grandfather today."

Anxiety flashed across his face. "You did?"

"Yes, at least I think it was him. The butler seemed intent on blocking any introduction."

Shelby definitely saw it. For a brief second Clay was relieved.

He looked beyond her, to the white house still partly visible. "Well, Mapes is a bit protective.

Grandpa Ford is not well."

So the courtly voice belonged to Ford Trask, the patriarch who'd started the Trask fortune from a humble farm. "I'm sorry about your grandfather. My aunt was ill for quite some time. And would you believe someone pestered her to sell her home not more than a few months ago?"

His eyes immediately met hers. "Who was it?" he asked, his tone more a demand than a question.

"I don't know. She wouldn't say."

Shelby had expected his reaction to be relief that this secret died with Desiree. Now no one would know of his crass attempt to get the land. Instead, he looked nettled.

"As I said," he repeated, "I'll top any offer."

"You're obsessed with the Tramarts!" Shelby exclaimed. "I believe you want one in every town in Kentucky."

His tense expression relaxed a little. "What's wrong with that?"

"Nothing, but does the world need more discount stores?"

"Does the world need more scandal magazines?"

Her black heels raised Shelby nearly eye to eye with Clay. She fixed him with an icy stare. "*Courant* isn't like that, and you know it!"

"The items we carry may be inexpensive, but they're not shoddy."

"Hmmm," Shelby mused, "I'm well aware of your clothing line. Does superstar Lana Niles really design them?"

"She has artistic input," he said breezily, reaching down for a sapling that had fallen over. Several young trees waited to be planted.

"Yes, I loved her artistry in that TV show, 'I Married An Alien.' "

Clay gently removed the burlap that covered the tree's roots and attached soil. Wavy strands of blond hair fell on his cheek. "You were always an elitist."

The notion shocked her. "Me? That's incredible. My clothes never had designer labels. I don't even own a car."

He straightened, brushing the errant stands back with his hand. "I don't mean financial snobbery or even social snobbery. I just remember your rather lethal letters to the editor in high school about the low-brow taste of the student body. Your crowd—"

"My crowd? You mean my two friends? The principal called you 'the prince.' He called me 'the pest.' My 'crowd' was no match for your group of clones and clonettes."

He half-smiled, refusing to be provoked. "You know, you ought to be a writer."

"Are you making fun of me?"

His light eyes narrowed so that the dark lashes emphasized their transparent qualities. He reached out and moved a tendril of hair from where it had fallen over her forehead to the side. The gentle motion, and the dry, warm hand on her flushed cheek made Shelby start a little from surprise and pleasure. "No," he said, softly.

Shelby felt awkward and shy—two unaccustomed feelings. "I believed in all the things I

47

wrote about. That rebel really was me, just like being the Prom King really was you."

His eyes lost their liquid glow. "Was that really me?" He picked up a spade. Thump! The blade hit the earth, sinking in several inches.

"You gave a good imitation of someone extremely popular, not to mention confident, affable, and good-looking."

"Don't forget my add-a-bead reputation." Thump! Clay hit the soil again, loosening it.

"I thought you said it was exaggerated."

Clay lifted a mound of dirt, his powerful forearms straining. "Then how could I be the Prom King?" he asked, dumping the soil next to the hole he was digging. "The Prom King was perfect. He always dated the cutest girls."

Thump!

"He never lost at sports," he added.

Thump!

"He made good grades but pretended not to care."

Thump! His voice had taken on an element of contempt.

"And never showed the strain," Shelby finished. But it was showing now. "Must have been lonely at the top."

Clay stopped abruptly and gazed deep into Shelby's blue eyes. When he realized that she hadn't been mocking him, his face lost some of its detachment. He half-smiled, almost shyly. Shelby fought an irresistible urge to put her arms around him. "I wouldn't exactly feel sorry for me," he said, leaning on the shovel. "It's just that I've had that Prom King label on my back for twelve years. Someone at the Fairview Country Club mentioned it last week."

"You go there often?"

"Just to play tennis. Why?"

"You seem more at home here."

Clay glanced around. "I love working on the grounds. Not just designing them, but actually planting a tree or putting in tomatoes." He laughed. "Must be my peasant background. I like to see things grow."

Clay's beautifully-chiseled body did seem more comfortable in faded jeans than a business suit. Watching his taut muscles contend with the soil was almost a sensual experience. For the first time Shelby noticed his hands—broad and strong. Perfect hands for plowing a field or chopping wood. The grounds at Park View reflected his love. But Prom Kings weren't farmers. Where did the young executive channel his need to see things grow? The answer was obvious—those concrete Tramarts.

She walked closer to him. He smiled, that maddening smile that lightened the intensity of his face. She found herself smiling back. How odd, Shelby thought. She'd come here to tell him off but was now actually considering selling the land to him. "So you'll fertilize your offer, so to speak, and hope that I'll help you grow another Tramart?"

He laughed. "Just let me know how much manure I have to add."

His handsome face drew her closer. "I'm not sure

49

when I'll know, but—ahhh!" Her right shoe sunk into the ground he'd been loosening. Shelby lost her balance, but immediately Clay stopped her fall. It only took one arm to guide her upright, but another found its way around her waist. Such presumption called for a wisecrack, but Shelby remained silent. She was enveloped by Clay Trask, and it felt good.

She didn't tower over him as she did with so many men. The warmth of his fingers penetrated the thin silk of her blouse. In the moment that he held her, she saw his eyes appreciate what his hands could touch—her lithe body. Never before had Shelby met her match physically, but Clay Trask's body next to hers was a perfect fit.

"I can't have you sinking in fertilizer just yet," he said, guiding her to more solid ground.

Shelby looked at her muddy shoe and foot. "Being at one with nature is somewhat overrated."

"I can fix that." Clay stripped off his T-shirt and bent to remove Shelby's shoe so that he could wipe her foot and shoe with his shirt. Shelby gazed at his smooth, broad chest. The setting sun caught the firm ridges. She'd come to Park View to wipe her feet on Clay Trask. The actual experience was far more unnerving.

"There," he said, dropping his T-shirt next to the shovel when he was done. "If you have another pair of shoes, I'll take these and have them cleaned and polished for you."

"Oh, no, I have to be going. I want to settle in at Aunt Desiree's and unpack. I'll clean them there."

"You're staying at her house?" His voice an edge to it.

"Yes, why not? It's my home, and I will have to dispose of Desiree's possessions."

Clay tensed. Being half-naked, he had a hard time hiding the momentary stiffness of his body. Shelby wondered why Desiree's old things should interest him.

"How long do you plan to be in Louisville?" he said.

Two days ago the answer to that question would have been "as short a time as possible." Even this morning she had told her office that she'd be back in a week, tops. Now, however, with the possibility of multiple bids coming in for her aunt's land, Shelby didn't know how long the process would take. She could have Bryant handle everything, but somehow that didn't seem right. Desiree had hung on to the house so that Shelby could inherit something that meant "family." The Langstaff home was her heritage, her responsibility. Perhaps sorting through Desiree's possessions would give Shelby a clearer picture of her aunt. Certainly this would be the last time she could try.

And what would she be returning to? Her editor would want new ideas for an article. Spring would fade in a haze of work. Not that she noticed spring much in New York City. She could only detect seasonal change by the rise and fall in temperature. The city's principal fragrance was eau de auto exhaust.

Louisville was so lovely this time of year. In her

brief walk to find Clay she'd spotted crocuses, daffodils, forsythia, even lilies — spring flowers she remembered from her childhood. Shelby missed the connection to the land and the relaxed feeling this bonding had given her as a child. New York was exciting, yes, but not relaxing.

"I really don't know, Clay. I've decided not to rush things." In fact, she had just decided this.

He wasn't happy at this pronouncement, but he asked in a friendly tone, "What about your work?"

She waved her hand. "Oh, I can continue my work here," she boasted with a confidence she didn't feel. To stay on top, you had to produce. Eventually she would have to go back — or find a family in Kentucky to profile. "Louisville is so pretty right now."

Clay's body relaxed, and he considered Shelby with bemusement. "Perhaps you can, but I'm surprised at your sudden affection for Louisville. Earlier you seemed somewhat at odds with the city."

He had her there. She didn't feel at home in Louisville, but increasingly she'd been feeling disconnected from New York. This was hardly something she could confide in a man so sure of his place in the world. She envied Clay that certainty. Louisville was *his* town.

"I thought I'd rediscover Louisville," she retorted, "and perhaps find a reapproachment."

"Oh." He nodded solemnly, but his eyes were disbelieving. Then he gazed at her hard, his face lighting up. "Why not start rediscovering it this week-end?"

"What?"

"Yes, this weekend is a unique opportunity to re-acquaint yourself with the natives."

Shelby was trying to dodge the pull of his smile. "What unique opportunity?"

"The Kentucky Derby is tomorrow—"

"And you want me to sit in your box. Clay, how thoughtful."

He rubbed one eyebrow with his index finger as he bit back a laugh. "No, that would be too pri-vate. You'd only be there with my parents."

"Aren't you going?"

"I'm spending the day with my grandfather. We plan the grounds of Park View together."

Shelby would have honestly enjoyed seeing that.

"What I had in mind was the Roses Ball tomor-row night. Would you like to go?"

The Roses Ball was *the* party of the year. It was where the upper crust broke bread and ate brie. Each year at this gala a Run for the Roses Princess was named from all the belles who'd come out. After being named, the tearful winner walked down a long aisle and received a bou-quet and a rhinestone crown in the shape of a horseshoe.

Since every member of Louisville's elite attended this party, Shelby realized that to go would be tan-tamount to a high school reunion. She immediately regressed to the skinny, socially-inept teen that she used to be. "Ohhh, I don't know, Clay."

He took her hand, and his strong fingers warmed her increasingly clammy palm. "Come on, think of it as research. All those rich people in one room."

She glared at him, but he had a point.

"There will be a lovely buffet, and music and dancing."

"Don't you have a date?"

"Actually, I wasn't planning to go, but seeing how much you wanted to reacquaint yourself with Louisville, I'd be only too happy to be your escort. Pick you up at eight?"

Shelby caught the challenge in his face. She knew she had to say yes. A part of her was more than a little curious to accompany him to the ball. Life seemed in sharper focus around Clay. She wanted to get to know him, to compare her long-held perceptions about him with the Clay Trask of today. Perhaps his invitation was Clay's attempt to do the same.

"Okay, okay, you've convinced me," Shelby said. "Now where am I going to find a long floral dress with hot pink roses on it by tomorrow?"

"Try Tramart, the Lana Niles collection."

Shelby laughed a deep throaty laugh that Clay enjoyed. He had expected her to accept his invitation, even though her reception at the party was far less secure than his. The guests might not feel comfortable letting their hair down with a "lifestyle reporter" noticing every foible. Clay had dared her to come, however, and he knew she wouldn't back down. He admired her gutsiness and her refreshing lack of pretense.

He liked the way her pale skin flushed and her blue eyes glowed when she was sparring with him. Holding her, even briefly, had allowed him to feel her body against his, to touch the smooth skin of her arms and wonder if the rest of her was even softer. Up close, Clay could smell lilac mixed with the more intoxicating scent of clean skin.

He looked forward to the ball, where he could take her willowy figure in his arms and dance cheek to cheek. A long, sultry ballad would give him ample time to admire her azure eyes and full lips. No less tantalizing was her long, curly hair. The vibrant red proclaimed her uniqueness and her willingness to take on a challenge.

She'd come out to confront him directly about the land. He liked that. No middleman for Shelby. She'd asked him point-blank about the Tramart rumor, and this had given him a chance to explain. So he was still in the running, and he knew he would win. He had to.

For Clay's attraction to Shelby did not mitigate the unease he felt at her staying in Louisville. The longer she stayed, the greater the risk to his family.

His father would be distraught that the deal hadn't been struck today. The stress on his grandfather had already increased since this morning when that letter to Ford had unleashed a crisis involving the whole family.

Clay hadn't told Shelby the complete story about the land. What he'd said had been the truth, just not the whole truth. In fact, Clay had been relieved when Shelby confronted him with *only* the rumor about the land! Yes, the Trasks needed it for a new Tramart. Failure to get it would cost his family a lot of money. Failure to get her aunt's *house*, however, would cost them more than money.

For somewhere in that decrepit old Victorian was a secret that could jeopardize the Trask family name. What it was, Clay didn't know. The letter merely alluded to it. Grandpa knew but wouldn't tell, and this was aging him visibly. Clay stifled a sigh as he walked Shelby back to her car. His family's secret lay waiting to be discovered, perhaps by this wildly-attractive woman, who just happened to make her living revealing the secrets of the rich.

Chapter Three

The carved wooden door opened with the same creak she'd heard for over twenty years. Shelby steeled herself. Entering the Langstaff family home without Desiree there seemed so unnatural. Although Desiree had died in an ambulance, she had been born here and suffered her final heart attack in this house. Incredible, Shelby thought, an entire lifetime in one place.

Nothing would seem the same, and yet upon first glance everything was the same—the cracked and peeling plaster, the scuffed and splintered wood floors, and the musty smell of mildew.

The Victorian style believed that more was *more*, and Aunt Desiree had carried on this tradition started by her family when the house was built in 1890s.

The front parlor was stuffed with chairs, sofas, and ottomans, all in elaborately-carved frames with lumpy brocaded seats or wild paisley prints. Faded carpets and dusty velvet curtains added to the oppressive clutter.

Shelby had always felt suffocated by the excess, but now she looked beyond it to the basic lines of the parlor. The room had been grandly designed with high ceilings, intricate moldings, and a marble fireplace. With a little renovation and a mammoth yard sale this room could look — Shelby stopped herself. Could this home ever be *her* home? It would forever possess Desiree Langstaff's unsettled spirit.

Shelby couldn't bring herself to look in Desiree's bedroom. She went hastily to the bathroom and took some aspirin. Going through her aunt's belongings hadn't seemed so daunting earlier. Now, every memento, every letter, every piece of clothing would recall her aunt's reclusive life and their own imperfect relationship.

Aunt Desiree had always been so remote. She had existed happily in another era when the Langstaffs were society, before the Depression ruined it all. Dealing with the present had proved less desirable, and dealing with a child and then a hormonal teenager had been a disaster.

Shelby thought back to Clay's tender remarks about his grandfather. She suddenly realized that she was jealous of Clay, jealous of the love he had with his grandfather and the history of good times they shared. She'd wanted a relationship like that with Desiree.

Clay had something that she'd dreamed about. Shelby had always thought of him as a person who had everything, and it seemed strange that now she possessed something he needed. How ironic that

Desiree's broken-down legacy should have turned out to be so valuable, even with the debts she'd accrued. Despite the mild night, Shelby shivered. Out of death came . . .what? A rebirth in her own life? This windfall promised change, but any change propelled a person into new and unsettling territory.

Shelby was ready fifteen minutes early for her date. She'd spent Saturday morning buying an evening dress and a few items of apparel she might need for a longer stay.

Her decision to remain in Louisville past a few days had forced her to make a difficult call to her boss in New York. He'd sounded properly consoling until she told him that she planned to stay in Louisville "for a few weeks." He was just at the sputtering stage when she'd mollified him with the idea that she was researching Kentucky blue bloods for an article. After a less than warm goodbye Shelby called a friend who had a spare key to her apartment. Her friend promised to send some clothes and Shelby's mail.

The rest of the afternoon was spent preparing for the ball, and now Shelby checked her new dress in the front hall mirror. She'd bought a pale-turquoise gown with a double-flounced neckline she pulled down to bare her shoulders. The silk dress swirled down, glancing off every curve until it gently grazed her pumps. The look was delicate and romantic. With her image as a sophisticated

New York reporter, Clay might expect her to wear a severely-stylish dress. She wanted to surprise him.

The moment Clay saw her, he was glad he'd bought a wrist corsage. The delicate bodice of her gown couldn't hold the spray of tea roses that he'd purchased. Corsages may have been passé for the country-club set, but tonight's ball was a traditional affair, and he took a chance that she'd appreciate this.

Shelby looked so lovely. Her lithe figure suited the delicate folds of the dress perfectly. The pale turquoise contrasted with the creamy glow of her soft skin and the vibrant red of her hair. He was glad she hadn't put up her hair. He enjoyed the way the curls gently fell down her long, graceful neck and onto her bare shoulders. A single strand of pearls nestled where the swell of her breasts rose slightly above the bodice, giving notice that something beautiful lay hidden beneath the blue silk.

He suddenly didn't want to go to the Derby gala. He wanted to be alone with this refreshingly-different woman, with her blunt honesty and cheeky wit.

"You look lovely," he said. "This is for you."

A corsage. Shelby was undone. Clay couldn't possibly know that this was the first corsage she'd ever received. She'd skipped the senior prom, saying it was too bourgeois, when in fact no one had asked her. The corsage slipped easily around her wrist. She admired the reddish-pink roses and just hoped that her face wasn't the same shade.

Clay crooked his arm, and Shelby slipped her

other hand into it. She felt like a teenager again, only this time she was going to the prom in a swirling aqua dress. Escorting her was a dashingly-handsome man in black tie, the color a dramatic contrast with his blond good looks.

Why couldn't they just skip the party and find a quiet spot where they could dance alone? She saw herself loosening his tie and unbuttoning his jacket so that his hard body would be against hers. And after a sultry ballad she'd know the taste of his mouth and discover the playfulness of his tongue. The suggestion lingered in her mind, but she rode to the gala in silence. She definitely wanted Clay, but did she trust him?

Clay drove to the Seelbach Hotel in downtown Louisville. One of the oldest sections of the city, downtown had a stateliness, almost a grandeur, that was missing from the malls and the Tramarts of the suburbs. Tall brick buildings had been erected with an eye toward beauty, harmony, and longevity.

One of the loveliest of all the old buildings was the Seelbach Hotel. Not as huge as some of the newer hotels, the Seelbach nevertheless had a mellow beauty that the others could only envy. Shelby loved the foyer with its marble walls trimmed in brass and the beautiful wooden table in the center that always held an elaborate floral arrangement. Gracious, refined, the Seelbach was a paean to tradition, and although she disdained most traditions, she liked the Seelbach's style. It was an original.

Shelby and Clay entered the ballroom to the loud hum of people reacquainting themselves. Derby and horse motifs decorated the room, the most impressive being the huge wire figure of Pegasus, the Greek winged horse, hanging from the ceiling. Everyone looked as sleek and well groomed as the thoroughbreds who'd run for the roses that afternoon. Indeed, the room was bedecked with the flower, its scent perfuming the air.

Shelby watched people greet each other. What stories, she wondered, lay behind all the effusive y'alls and the gracious veneers of people bred to courtesy before candor?

One side of the ballroom featured hors d'oeuvres, and on both sides full bars displayed traditional Derby drinks like the mint julep, and punches of rum slush or pineapple ale.

Shelby and Clay remained anonymous for thirty seconds.

"Clay! Clay, boy!"

"Hey, Clay!"

Several men came up to slap him on the back.

"C'mon, Clay, is Tramart going public?"

"Hey, I hear you made it into the singles final at the club. Man, you've got a killer forehand."

Clay smiled and greeted everyone by name. He was courteous, but Shelby noticed that he deflected questions about Tramart. Several women joined the crowd and coolly looked Shelby over. Clay introduced her, but either they didn't remember her or they didn't seem particularly pleased that Clay had brought a date.

"Shelby! My God, is that you?"

She turned around. "Logan? What are you doing here?"

Her cousin's flushed face told her that he'd already sampled the punch, but he looked dashing in his white dinner jacket. Logan always did have style. Not a hair on his sandy-blond head was out of place, his trousers had a crease so crisp you could cut with it, and even his nails looked buffed. "Honey," he drawled, "I come to this shindig every year. What are *you* doing here? This isn't exactly your crowd."

Shelby hugged him. "I'm sort of here on a dare. Clay Trask invited me."

Logan moved her away from the crowd. "I know how much you like a challenge, Shelby, but be careful. Clay loves 'em and leaves 'em."

She was surprised at how much this comment pricked her ego. "You just don't like Clay because he bought up that warehouse business of yours that, um, floundered."

"And built his first Tramart on it." Logan's easy smile faded. "Man, everything always goes his way."

Poor Logan, Shelby thought. He never got a break. "Not totally, cousin. Clay wants to buy Desiree's land to build a new Tramart, but I'm not selling — at least not yet."

His face became alert. "Really? Desiree's land isn't big enough for a Tramart."

"Yes, but it borders Trask land. That's why they want it."

Logan smiled again. "Then get 'em for all the money you can, Shelby! Clay Trask's priority, other than his family, is those Tramarts. Just get everything in writing."

Shelby laughed, but she realized that Logan knew far more about Clay Trask than she did and obviously felt burned by the experience.

"By the way," he said, giving her dress the once-over, "you look like a million bucks."

Shelby was flattered. Logan had an eye for fashion. She couldn't resist saying, "I think half a million is more accurate."

"What?"

She chuckled. "Nothing. Just a private joke."

He narrowed one eye quizzically. "Well, however much you're worth, you look terrific."

Shelby started to thank him when she heard a shriek. She turned to see a blonde with butterscotch streaks in her hair throw herself into Clay's arms. The crowd roared its approval.

Logan muttered, "I need a drink." He kissed Shelby on her cheek. "Let's have lunch soon." He walked away, pulling a pack of cigarettes out of his pocket and quickly lighting one.

"The Prom King and Prom Queen, together again!" someone called out.

The butterscotch streaks belonged to Heather Scott. Heather had been the prettiest girl in their senior class at Breck Prep, an attribute helpful in her professed goal of marrying well. Heather's first husband, according to Desiree who'd read the society pages, had died when his espresso maker exploded. Unfortunately this was not before he lost most of his money trying to start a professional basketball team in Kentucky.

So Heather was between partners. She still looked great. She was one of those women whose panty hose never bagged, whose mascara was never smudged, and whose tan was always even. Too many hours baking by the Fairview pool were beginning to take their toll, however. *Idle hands are the devil's crow's-feet,* Shelby thought with amusement.

"Darling, you said at the club that you weren't coming."

Clay disentangled himself from Heather's arms. "I changed my mind. I'm here with Shelby Langstaff." He motioned for Shelby to join them.

The news that Clay had a date startled Heather, who peered closely at Shelby. "My God . . . I remember you from Breck Prep. You used to always break the bell curve. We called you the Duchess of Doom because you were always so depressed."

"I guess I thought people were talking behind my back."

Heather laughed insincerely, but Clay's smile was thoughtful.

A thin figure came up from behind Heather. "Hey, babe, where did you run off to?" Buzz Mathis looked at Clay. "Oh. Hello, Clay." Buzz put one arm territorially around Heather.

"Evening, Buzz."

Like Shelby, Buzz Mathis had been a scholarship student at Breck Prep. He'd been further stigmatized by being perceived as a nerd. Shelby had tried to sympathize back then, but Buzz's cold personality and his aggressive competitiveness had stopped her good intentions. The aggressiveness must have paid off. According to *Fortune* magazine, Buzz had amassed quite a fortune.

He kissed Heather on the cheek, giving notice to Clay that Heather belonged to him this evening. Clay seemed mildly annoyed. His attitude gave Heather smug satisfaction, Shelby observed. Heather had always thought of herself as a prize, to be fought over by men. She definitely preferred Clay, but didn't the Prom King *belong* with the Prom Queen? A rich man was her due. Shelby had envied Heather's confidence with men. She sensed, however, that Clay's barely-cordial demeanor had more to do with Buzz than with Heather. At least she hoped so.

Buzz tore his eyes off Heather long enough to notice Shelby. "Shelby Langstaff!" he cried. "I can't believe it!"

"Believe it, Buzz," she said in a friendly tone.

"Your *Courant* photo doesn't do you justice! I read you faithfully."

Shelby was touched. "Thank you, Buzz."

"Yes, I've always thought that you and I were cut from the same cloth. Two poor kids who succeeded on their own smarts."

Buzz had never been subtle. Clay ignored the dig entirely, but Shelby found herself annoyed on his behalf.

"I haven't quite succeeded like you, Buzz," she

said flatly.

"Oh, well." Buzz tried to shrug modestly, but his skinny frame accepted the compliment eagerly. "My success has been hard won. Nothing's come easy for me," he paused, looking at Heather, "but I'm a patient man. I set my sights on something, and then I work, slowly and steadily, until I get it." He glanced nonchalantly at Clay. "Like just being named the Chamber of Commerce's Man of the Year."

Clay's eyes widened for an instant. He was surprised. "Congratulations."

"Thank you. Youngest man to ever win it, did you know that, Shelby?"

"No, I didn't." Clay and Buzz were the same age, a fact that all four of them *did* know.

"Yes, work hard and you'll be rewarded," Buzz intoned.

"It doesn't hurt to be on the nominating committee."

"Now, Clay, I absented myself from voting."

"Ah, yes, of course you did, to ensure fairness."

Heather sighed dramatically. "Are you boys going to talk business?"

Buzz patted Heather on her behind. "Why don't you go powder your pretty nose. I have some business that I'd like to discuss with Shelby."

Heather seemed used to Buzz's manhandling, but she turned to see if Clay had minded. His face registered wary distaste. Heather considered this acceptable and walked away content. Shelby, however, suspected another reason for Clay's irritation.

"So, Shelby, let me extend to you my deepest condolences on the death of your aunt. Our loved ones never really leave us in spirit."

"Thank you, Buzz."

"I hope you don't think me too crass, but the word is out that you have come into a highly-desirable piece of land. If you're planning to sell it, I'd like to make you an offer."

Clay's eyes turned stormy, Shelby noticed, but he said nothing. How could he? He'd been no less crass.

"I'll certainly consider all offers."

"You've been approached already?" Buzz caught the quick glance she gave Clay. "Ahhh, I should have known. The Prom King's timing was always impeccable. Well, I can't offer you as smooth a line, but I can top anything he's offering."

"Buzz . . ." Clay's tone was deadly.

"What? Am I being too blunt?" Buzz shrugged. "I stopped competing with you in the polish department a long time ago, but I can compete where money is concerned." He shook his finger at Clay. "You overextended yourself with the Tramarts. You don't have the spare change I do!"

This was news to Shelby. She thought the Trasks were financially secure. Had Clay's business put the whole family in jeopardy?

Clay smiled at Buzz, but it wasn't friendly. "I'm touched that you care."

"I don't. But I do care about Shelby." He turned to her. "Shelby, you and I live in the real world. We've gotten where we are by our own moxie, not from what Mommy and Daddy have given us. This land may give you the money to belong to the Fairview Country Club, but tell me, do you want to? You and I will never fit into their la-de-da ways. Sell me the land. You'll at least get an honest buy, because if you believe *his line*, then he's just romancing the land out from under you!"

Buzz was nearly six feet tall, but Clay had surprisingly little difficulty lifting him up and slamming him against the wall. Shelby was stunned, but not half as stunned as Buzz.

"Help, let me down!"

Shelby touched Clay's arm. People were staring. "Clay," she said softly, "let him go." On his face she saw a controlled fury.

Clay slowly lowered Buzz until they were eye to eye. "Pandering to a prejudice is just as despicable as what you accused me of doing," he said in a hushed but lethal voice. "Shelby can go anywhere she wants. Shelby *belongs* everywhere. It's you who's trying to settle a score from twelve years ago. Don't drag Shelby into it."

Buzz's face glowed with perspiration. "I'll top any offer you make."

"So you can build another of your sweatshops? Why don't you tell Shelby why half your work force signed a petition against you?"

"Half didn't!"

"And those were the ones you didn't fire!"

"Why don't you hire those whiners for your Tramarts?"

"I have! And I'll hire more if—"

"You can build the new store," Buzz said. Clay released him. Despite his embarrassment, Buzz looked as if he'd scored a point. He straightened his tux, took out his handkerchief, and wiped his face. "I'd better find Heather. Shelby, I will contact you about an offer. Your lawyer is Bryant Fisk, right?"

"Right." Shelby wondered how he knew who her lawyer was, but then Clay had known. Gossip in upper-crust Louisville traveled at lightning speed.

"A lot is riding on your decision," Buzz continued. "I guess what it boils down to is who do you stand for? Us or them?" He motioned to Clay, who turned his back. "Think about it."

He walked off. Shelby pivoted to face Clay. He'd managed to regain his composure, but his lips were still set in a grim line. Clay was turning out to be more complex than she'd thought. Rich people usually took more than they gave, but Clay *cared*. He was protective of the people around him—his family and his employees. He'd even been protective of her.

"That . . . what you said to Buzz about me belonging everywhere . . . I appreciated it."

He looked into her eyes. "It was no line."

Shelby believed him, or rather she badly wanted to. The image she held of herself was the person Clay described—confident, at home anywhere with all kinds of people. An idealized view, perhaps, but she cherished Clay for ascribing it to her. A small stab of guilt pricked her. She was not immune to Buzz's prejudices. She often judged the rich by a

70

collective standard. Clay was different.

"I believe you, Clay."

His hazel eyes reflected emotions she hadn't seen before. Mingled with anger were flashes of frustration and hurt. "I work hard, Shelby, sometimes seven days a week. No one handed me the Tramarts—I started them. Every employee is important to me. Buzz Mathis, on the other hand, victimizes the very working folk that he says he's a part of! I worry about getting my people a good health plan, fair hours, and—"

He was cut off by the orchestra beginning "My Old Kentucky Home." Clay fell silent, but Shelby could sense the lingering tension in his body. To be misunderstood, misperceived . . . she knew those feelings. She looked around the room and saw several old schoolmates who'd dismissed her at Breck Prep because of her scholarship and secondhand clothes. Desiree had told her to hold her head high, but the rejection had hurt. Anger rose in her against those who were so quick to judge. Anger not just for herself, but also for Clay.

Shelby took his hand and found it to be trembling a little. He wrapped his long fingers tightly around hers. Yesterday his touch had given her a purely physical rush, his hard body promising sensuality and experience. Tonight his touch was charged with understanding. The body and the soul—it was a combination that made Clay even more attractive.

The thought of making love to him swept over Shelby like a fine rain. Her body responded to the fantasy with a pulsing warmth that started in her head and got hotter the farther south it traveled.

Clay's body promised passion, but Shelby's imagination caught fire at the thought of his gentleness. The loving way he talked about his grandfather showed a tender side. Men usually dwelled on the final explosive act of lovemaking, not realizing that women wanted the slow buildup of touch and caress. Foreplay with Clay might just last forever.

The beautiful but wistful state song played on.

"Weep no more, my lady,
weep no more today!
We will sing one song for my old Kentucky
home,
For my old Kentucky home far away."

Shelby sang the chorus with Clay. Kentucky had been her home, and now she was back.

Clay put his hands on her shoulders, his warm fingers lightly massaging her bare skin. "Buzz was right about one thing. Your *Courant* picture doesn't do you justice. You are beautiful tonight."

His compliment sent a wave of pure pleasure through her, as if she'd just eaten a rich chocolate. Shelby relaxed under the exquisite pressure of his fingers.

His hands dropped to her arms and he guided her to the dance floor. Cheek to cheek, Clay pressed her body to his. For a tall man he was graceful, making her feel fluid, delicate, and so very treasured.

"Are you saying that I'm the proper consort for the Prom King?" she teased.

He frowned. "Don't call me that. Besides, I got the impression you didn't think I was perfect."

"No, you're more interesting than that."

A slow smile spread across his face. "I'm glad you came tonight," he said.

Shelby was, too. Despite the intrusion of memories, the rest of the evening promised to be filled with music, dancing, and the company of this handsome, enigmatic man. Clay led her effortlessly, as if his body and hers melded perfectly as one unit.

Clay closed his eyes. He let the music and the feel of this beautiful woman's body wash his anger away. Buzz had touched a sore spot. While half the men in this room might be content to live off their stock dividends, he felt he had to earn his living.

Grandpa Ford had seen to that. His old-fashioned love and discipline had counterbalanced Clay's parents' mania to make him the perfect under par country-club gentleman. Besides, Clay liked tennis better than golf. The game was faster, with split-second timing. Clay liked the speed of tennis, just as he enjoyed driving his convertible a bit too fast. Sometimes he had to break out, do the unexpected. Grandpa Ford understood. Clay suspected—he hoped—that Shelby might understand, too.

As if reading his mind, she asked, "Are you okay now? I mean about Buzz."

He squeezed her hand. "Buzz who?"

She laughed, her body vibrating lightly against his. Shelby's flaming mass of hair, in all its naturalness, put to shame the lacquered hairdos in the room. Her face, so strong yet with such vulnerable lips, tantalized him with the paradox.

"You went a little crazy," she murmured.

He pulled his head back. "Did I scare you?"

She smiled. "No, but afterward I think you needed a hole to dig."

"Or wood to chop."

Her blue eyes twinkled. "Must be the peasant in you."

He laughed out loud. Heads turned. Clay didn't care. He was having fun for the first time that evening. They danced on, oblivious to anyone but each other.

A high-pitched drawl interrupted their reverie. "You two want to be alone?"

Surprised, Shelby lifted her head from Clay's shoulder. She wasn't in the mood for another Buzz or Heather.

A small crowd had formed near them. Shelby assumed it was another Clay Trask fan club.

"Uh, Miss Langstaff?" asked a woman with ropes of pearls around her neck. "You are Shelby Langstaff from *Courant* magazine, aren't you? That's what people are saying."

Clay reluctantly released her.

"Yes, I am."

"Could I have your autograph?"

"My autograph?"

74

"Yes." The matron seemed embarrassed but determined. She squared her shoulders, causing her pearls to click. "I just love those articles you write. They are so incisive."

Shelby was flattered. This crowd, she was amazed to discover, was for her.

"Absolutely!" chimed in another woman. "I especially loved the article you did on the New York jet set. Tell me, do you get invited to all their fabulous parties?"

"Um, no, I don't," Shelby answered. "That article was on a family that went broke trying to fit into the jet set. I'm not part of that crowd."

"Oh, pooh," an elderly woman said. She wore a typical Derby dress of flowered silk and had the bluest hair Shelby had ever seen. "You're just too modest. You have to know a subject to write about it. I bet you're like Barbara Walters—you know, a friend, but someone who can ask the tough questions, like who are you sleeping with, or when's the last time you cried?"

Shelby stifled an exasperated sigh. "I try to be more penetrating than that in my articles."

"How about skewering?" a man commented. "Wow, some of your victims are grease spots after you finish with them."

"I never skewer people," Shelby shot back, "but my writing doesn't shirk unpleasant truths, either."

"I like your articles," a distinguished-looking woman interjected. "I find them intelligent, thought-provoking, witty, and beautifully written."

Shelby was touched. "Why, thank you."

"You don't happen to know Kevin Costner, do you?" the woman added.

"Miss Langstaff has to leave now," Clay announced. He took her arm. "Yes, I'm sorry, but she's due in London tomorrow—Princess Di wants to put an end to all the rumors—and let's face it, the Concorde won't wait forever!"

The crowd sighed in envy.

Clay steered her to a terrace, its emptiness a refreshing break. He let go of her long enough to find two glasses of champagne. He handed her one, then raised the other. "To your impending trip."

Shelby laughed, but she was troubled. "These people have made all sorts of assumptions about me without ever having met me!"

Clay nodded. "And they don't want to hear the truth. They want their fantasy jet-setter, and you'd better not disappoint them."

Shelby sipped her drink and then set it on the terrace ledge. "To be pigeonholed that way, it's like being trapped. I felt it when I was in high school and was the 'brain.' "

"I felt it, too, when I was the 'Prom King.' "

Shelby sensed that she was hearing an important piece of the puzzle known as Clay Trask. "You haven't enjoyed yourself tonight, have you?" she asked quietly.

He smiled. "I've enjoyed being with you."

"But not with all the others, even though they act so happy to see you."

Clay's smile became strained. "Oh, there are

76

some very nice people here, but basically they're interested in the discount tycoon or the ace tennis player. These images satisfy them. You saw that, didn't you?"

Shelby nodded, but she was slightly embarrassed because, to some degree, she liked Clay's splendid facade, too. "And the one thing not allowed," she added, "is failure."

His eyes flashed back in surprise. "And yet it's my constant worry. The Tramarts, the one enterprise that I didn't *inherit*, is still a risk." He laughed, but it was hollow, ironic. "Sometimes I actually feel guilty when I'm depressed or stressed because I do have so much. So I hide my feelings. I bottle them up and tell no one."

"Tell me."

He gazed at her with an expression of tentative hope that made him vulnerable to her for the first time.

"The only person in this room that I am comfortable with is you." He set his glass down on the ledge and moved closer to her. "You treat me like a man, not a label."

An odd sensation overtook Shelby. She was discovering a real man behind the facade, and that man touched her in a way she'd never felt before. Clay was so like her. Both had fought labels all their lives.

On the other hand, she wasn't sure who the real Clay Trask was. Was he the ruthless businessman, the protective grandson, the confident bachelor, or the lonely scion of Park View? Shelby wanted to solve this puzzle, but she wondered if the confusion was deliberate. Was Clay counting on her fascination with him to blind her to his true personality? With his eyes sending her a sensual invitation, she was ready for a more intimate investigation.

He took her in his arms, and when his lips touched hers, she felt an electricity that transcended her doubts. In a dizzy instant, pure passion exploded within Shelby, her lips sharing a hunger with Clay's.

His mouth was wet and warm, an inviting place to taste and explore. When her tongue matched his curiosity, a low moan escaped from within him.

Shelby felt Clay pull her tighter against him as she wrapped her arms around his neck. Their nearly equal height meant that her breasts rubbed against his chest, and her hips melded against his hips as she felt the increasing hardness between his legs.

He pulled slightly away, and her body immediately missed the exquisite pressure. He gently kissed the hollow between her jaw and ear, as one hand left her waist and began to tease one breast. His long fingers, so adept at rugged pursuits, proved to be equally skilled in sensual matters. The delicate silk of her dress offered little protection from his inquiring touch. He found the raised flesh of her nipple, and Shelby inhaled sharply when his finger circled it and then rubbed with sublime expertise. To increase her pleasure, he leaned down and kissed the tender peak. The smooth slide of silk between his warm lips and her cool skin only heightened the sensation.

His lips moved to the valley between her breasts, where his kisses traced a maddening line to her collarbone. He then found the delicate skin of her neck to torment, with hot nips above and below her pearls. Slowly his mouth returned to hers, bringing another thrill of tongue and taste. One of his hands caressed her breast, rubbing it, teasing it with playful, insistent strokes. A languid pressure began to build between her legs.

Shelby wanted these delicious sensations to go on forever. But this wasn't real, was it? After midnight Clay would vanish, her dress would turn to rags, and she'd be back, alone, in Desiree's pumpkin of a house. But she'd had tonight.

"I finally went to the prom," she murmured.

"What?"

"Nothing. Just . . . thank you for tonight."

"You'll see me again?"

"Clay, tonight was magic, but—"

He ran his finger over the ridge of her collarbone. "Next Tuesday, dinner, Mack's Shack on the river. C'mon, think of the barbecued ribs, think of the huge onion rings—"

"Think of my figure!"

"I am," he said softly.

In the two weeks that followed Clay squired Shelby frequently enough to keep him in her life, but not enough to cause pressure, exactly. He never

79

mentioned her land, except to comment on how rundown the garden was. A little elbow grease and—He caught himself. If Shelby sold him the land, she knew her aunt's garden would be part of a parking lot.

Although he refrained from discussing the land with her, Shelby knew from Bryant that Clay had kept in an active bid. Buzz topped every offer, apparently beside himself to beat Clay, no matter what the cost. Shelby received other offers, some for very good causes but for a lot less money. She was determined not to let money be the only factor, but she was stunned at how quickly she got used to expecting large offers.

Much of her time was spent untangling Desiree's financial affairs. Desiree had avoided the real world, and that included pesky things like keeping receipts and such. It would take time to unravel her Byzantine record-keeping, more time than Shelby had originally anticipated.

Her intention to take a leave of absence caused her editor to choke on his danish. Between gasps and coughs he yelled so loudly that Shelby was sure she didn't need a phone to hear him. She promised go to New York that weekend to discuss it, but her mind was made up. Desiree's estate needed her personal touch.

She announced her trip to Clay during one hair-raising ride in his fire-engine-red Mustang convertible. They were barreling down River Road, the road that, near Louisville, paralleled the twists of the Ohio River.

"Eeeha! You really nailed that curve!"

"Shelby, let go of my arm."

"How fast are you going?"

"Fast enough."

"Would you believe that I'd never been in a convertible before last week?"

"Shelby, I've lost all feeling in my upper arm."

Shelby released him. It was a gloriously sunny day, a perfect day to be out in a convertible with this wickedly good-looking man beside her. Shelby reveled in it. In fact, she was having the time of her life.

Clay was so much fun! Shelby couldn't remember when she'd felt so relaxed and carefree. For the first time she hated leaving Louisville.

"Clay, I'm going away for a few days."

She immediately felt the car slow down. "You are?"

"Yes, I have to arrange for a leave of absence from work."

Shelby saw him nod slightly, almost as if he had expected this. "How long of an absence do you think you'll need?"

"I'm not sure, but at least a month, maybe two."

Clay fell silent. Shelby glanced at him, but he seemed intent on the road. His blond hair blew back from his face, accentuating the sharp lines of his profile.

"I won't lie to you," he finally said. "I have mixed feelings about it. I'm delighted you're staying longer, but . . ."

"It delays my decision on the land. I know."

He shifted gears, and the car resumed its speed. They drove back to Desiree's house in silence. He got out and came around to her side to open her door. She stood up, and he put his arms around her. "I'll miss you," he said.

Shelby missed him, too. And Louisville. Her New York apartment seemed claustrophobic after having an entire house to roam around in. She'd also gotten used to the sound of — no sound at night. Her editor grudgingly agreed to the leave of absence, but only after she promised to really try to find a Kentucky family worth investigating.

If it weren't for Clay, Shelby mused, the Trasks would be worth checking out. Clay always got around her questions about his family with a quip or a kiss. But those kisses pushed questions out of her mind. He was like no one she'd ever met — so apparently open, yet when she thought about what he'd actually revealed, so elusive. Clay had insisted on taking her to the airport and picking her up. Shelby had intended to be gone three days, but her agreement with her boss took less time and was less cordial than she'd hoped. A close co-worker asked her why she was risking the very job she'd worked so hard to get.

Shelby had no reasonable answer. How could she tell her friend that the cynic's heart was now ruling her head? How could she explain that the workaholic sometimes went into the field behind her house and made daisy chains? She hadn't even tackled Desiree's personal effects yet. Mostly she couldn't explain Clay.

She left New York on Saturday, after only two days. She tried to call Clay and tell him her new arrival time, but Mapes informed her that "Mr. Clay is at the club this evening." He didn't know what time he'd be in. Shelby thanked Mapes for his customary helpfulness and decided to take a cab.

Standing in front of Desiree's house, Shelby thought that this was the first time she'd come back to it without a sense of dread. The ancient plumbing and the sagging porch seemed endearing now.

She saw her empty garbage cans on the street and decided to take them around to the back porch. As she repositioned them, she heard movement in the house. Stunned, she realized that the footsteps were getting louder. Whoever was in there was coming closer. She started to run but, in the dark, tripped over a chair on the porch and twisted her foot.

The intruder would be out the back door at any second, and here she was sprawled on the porch. Yelling for help was useless. Her nearest neighbor lived a mile down the road. There was only one thing to do. "I have a .357 Magnum and I'm not afraid to use it!" she screamed.

The shadowy figure came out. She scrambled to get up, her hurt foot slowing the process. It was a man, and there was one last defense against a member of the male species. She positioned her good foot and, just when she could see enough to make out his form, made a valiant kick to his groin.

He was too fast for her. He deflected her foot, throwing her off balance. She would have hit the ground except that he caught her. "I'd rather be shot than that!" came an all-too-familiar voice.

It was Clay Trask.

Chapter Four

Shelby struggled to escape his arms, but Clay wrapped them tight around her, pinning her body to his.

"Let me go!" she demanded, feeling his hot breath on her neck. By twisting and wriggling, she loosened one elbow and jabbed it into his ribs. Her ploy drew a painful gasp from him, allowing her to escape, but her sore foot betrayed her. Clay picked her up as if her long frame was of no consequence.

Shelby had rarely been held this way, and despite the tumult in her mind, she liked it. She also liked the smell of his skin and the pressure of his hard chest against her breasts. Physically, there was nothing about Clay Trask she didn't like. Too bad he'd just broken into her house!

Her knee connected with his stomach. "Ow! Stay still, Shelby," he cried.

"No! Let me go!"

But his grip tightened around her legs and arms, blocking further moves. The struggle had hiked her navy miniskirt almost to her hips. She felt his hands on her bare thighs. "I won't hurt you," he insisted. "Let me explain!"

"What were you doing in my house?"

"I'll tell you everything if you'll just stop fighting me!"

Shelby could barely see his face, but she could feel his heart pounding. He was as stunned as she was. Something in her knew that Clay wouldn't hurt her, even as she wondered why he'd sneaked in like this. The instinct to fight had come from her surprise and twelve years of living in a big city.

"Okay," she said. "I'll spare your procreating ability."

"I humbly thank you. Now, is there a light back here?"

"You mean you don't know?"

"I'd hoped to go *un*detected."

"To the left of the door."

The porch light allowed Shelby to see him clearly. Clay's legendary cool had vanished, but he appeared unrepentant. They stared at each other for a long moment.

"So," Clay finally said, "how was New York?"

She let out an angry breath. "You have exactly fifteen seconds to put me down and start talking."

"Your command is my wish," he said dryly. He took her through the back door and into the kitchen, setting her down on a ladderback chair. She winced as she took off her shoe.

"Can you wiggle your toes?"

"Yes. I think I just twisted my ankle."

"Do you want me to take you to the emergency room?"

Shelby gazed up at his concerned face. Their tussle had mussed his thick blond hair. Several strands fell on his cheek, giving him a rakish look that was wildly attractive—damn it! "Your fifteen seconds are up," she announced. "I realize that breaking and entering is a mere felony, but someone in the Louisville police force might be interested."

Clay nearly smiled. "Ask for Captain Tucker. He's a friend of mine."

"I'm waiting."

Clay pulled another chair around to face Shelby and sat down. He wore black jeans, a black shirt, and black running shoes. Perfect apparel for a robber. What could this old house have that he wanted?

"I'm not exactly sure where to begin," he said, gazing at the multitude of refrigerator magnets, mostly for pharmacies that delivered, on the ancient icebox.

"Try starting at the point where you broke into my house."

Clay looked at her, but his face possessed none of the cockiness that she'd come to identify with him. There was sadness in his eyes, and pain.

"I think I'd have to start earlier than that," he said, "much earlier—perhaps as early as sixty years ago."

"What?"

He looked beyond her. "Yes, that's where the story really begins."

Shelby stopped rubbing her foot. "Clay, you've lost me. What happened sixty years ago?"

"Actually, I'm not sure."

Her exasperated sigh caused him to refocus on her. "I'm sorry. It's just that what I'm about to tell you will seem unbelievable." He inhaled, as if to brace himself. "After your aunt died, a letter was delivered to my grandfather from one of Bryant Fisk's law clerks. It had been part of your aunt's legal papers, and on the sealed envelope was the note 'To be delivered to Ford Trask of Park View after my death.' The letter was a farewell note from your aunt to my grandfather."

"What!"

"Yes. It seems that sixty years ago your aunt and my grandfather had a love affair."

"A love affair." Shelby repeated the phrase, but the words were too astonishing to penetrate her brain.

"And it ended sadly. At least that's the impression I got from the letter."

"You've seen the letter?"

"Yes, my grandfather let me read it."

"Would he let me read it?"

Clay's eyes dropped to the cracked linoleum floor. "I doubt it. It was a private message, and he's only let family look at it. That's why I haven't mentioned it to you."

"Please, you must ask him if I can read it. I . . . Clay . . . I . . . can't believe all of this. Desiree never mentioned your grandfather, or even a lover. In fact, I thought she went to her grave chaste."

"We do crazy things when we're young."

"But not Desiree! At least, not the Desiree I knew." Shelby looked at Clay and saw the answer in his eyes. "I guess I didn't know her as well as I thought I did," she said softly.

"Don't feel alone. My grandfather never said a word, and we're so close. I thought I knew everything about him."

Shelby understood his bewilderment. From her experience as a reporter, she knew that people kept secrets. She just didn't think that secrets existed in *her* family. Who would have thought that Desiree had a "past"? Incredible. But Clay's eyes conveyed more than bewilderment. There was an anxiousness in them, a foreboding.

"Clay, tell me everything you know. And then tell me why you broke into my house."

He shifted uneasily in the chair. "Both questions are connected. I broke into your house because of the letter, or rather, because of the romance."

Shelby felt her cotton top begin to stick to her chest. "An old love affair propelled you into a life of crime?"

He emitted a short, tense laugh, as if he knew his actions seemed absurd. "I *told* you we do crazy things when we're young." Sighing, he said, "Let me explain. Sixty years ago Desiree and my grandfather had a romance. From her letter I gather that the affair was somewhat clandestine, which wasn't so surprising for that era. My grandfather was a farmer at that time, and the Langstaffs were still socially prominent. The classes didn't mix so much then."

Shelby nodded. "I wonder how they met."

"The letter mentioned the state fair."

Shelby sat up. "Not the 1932 Kentucky State Fair, where she won a blue ribbon for her needlepoint!"

Clay smiled. "I think that was the one. Grandpa won a blue ribbon for his pig, Homer. Perhaps the winners met each other. Anyway, the romance was conducted largely through the mail, although according to the letter, there were rendezvous that were pretty . . . passionate."

Shelby was astonished, though pleased. "Good for you, Auntie," she murmured. No matter how briefly, Desiree had found a man to love and Shelby was glad.

"Then the romance ended. Apparently their love couldn't overcome their differences in background."

"Who ended it?"

"The letter doesn't say."

"What does your grandfather say?"

Shelby sensed a new tightness in the set of Clay's shoulders. "My grandfather refuses to talk about it."

"Not at all?"

"Well, it's personal, isn't it? I can't expect him to tell me every intimate detail of his life." The slight catch in Clay's voice and his downcast, troubled eyes told another story. He was hurt that his grandfather hadn't confided in him. "Besides, the letter alone upset him so much. His blood pressure went up. His nurse had to give him oxygen."

"Clay, I'm sorry. But you wouldn't be human if you weren't curious. I'm sure as hell curious!"

He eyed her cautiously. "I know, but I hate to see him so unhappy. Some things are best forgotten."

"I'm certain that Desiree meant to lessen your grandfather's pain, not add to it!"

Clay held up one hand. "Please believe that I agree with you. The letter was loving and . . . forgiving."

"Forgiveness for what?"

"I don't know, and in the final analysis I don't think she cared anymore. And I think she wanted him to know that. It was a farewell letter of great tenderness, written by someone who'd reevaluated her life and found some peace."

Shelby's throat tightened. "After her first heart attack Bryant said that she'd . . . changed. She became happy." Clay couldn't know how happiness had eluded Desiree all her life.

"Yes, she mentioned that her . . . imminent demise had made her rethink the past, their past. She wanted to, in her words, 'finally lift the cloud that has hung over my life for so many years.' That's why she wrote Grandpa the letter."

Desiree's own words pierced Shelby's heart. "So their broken affair was the cloud that had hung over her, haunted her all these years!"

Clay's lean torso tensed with an agitation that confused Shelby. There was more to this letter than he was telling.

"I don't think Bryant knows about the contents of this letter," he said, changing the subject. "No one does except my family, and you." Clay ran his fingers over the top of the kitchen table. With what seemed like reluctance he said, "My grandfather has made one request. Desiree mentioned that she'd saved all his love letters. He would very much like them back."

Shelby felt a prickle of excitement. Ford's love letters existed. They could explain what he refused to. Quickly she looked at Clay's empty hands. The letters also explained why he'd broken into her house. "You couldn't just ask me to find them?"

Now Clay was *really* uncomfortable. "Try to understand how personal this is for my grandfather."

"No less than for my aunt! She spent her entire adult life withdrawn from the world—shell-shocked from some terrible calamity. Your grandfather might have been this calamity! And, in turn, this trauma affected my own life. Do you know what it's like to be raised by someone who's lost the ability to love? You're forever doubting yourself, and anyone else who tries to love you. Clay, how could you have kept this from me!"

Her outburst surprised him, and his eyes contracted a little as if he hadn't expected or meant to cause her pain. His voice, however, held no apology. "The letter was to my grandfather, Shelby, not to you, or even me!"

"But you saw it!"

"Yes, but only because my grandfather had become ill over it. He lets no one look at it now. Perhaps I should have told you up-front and asked for the letters. Breaking and entering really isn't my style, but my grandfather insisted on secrecy."

"Why the secrecy, if this was just a relationship that went sour?" Shelby let out a long, slow breath. "Unless . . . unless . . . there's more. This must be some story. Think of it—lovers from two different worlds, a mysterious breakup, treasured love letters."

Clay's eyes flashed for an instant, but that was all the time it took for Shelby to realize why he would *never* have told her about the letters unless she'd caught him.

"You think I might write about this, don't you?"

"That had never occurred to me."

"You're not a good liar, Clay. That very thought is written all over your face. It's responsible for your nocturnal escapade. By the way, how did you get into my house?"

"I jimmied your front door lock with my gold card."

"Now, that's fitting!"

"I never leave home without it."

His wisecrack couldn't divert her. "I take it 'home' means Park View, the residence of Ford Trask, who might have been *my* great-uncle, except that he committed, in all likelihood, some act for which my aunt had to forgive him sixty years later."

Clay exhaled a short, tense breath and shifted in his chair, as if he were undecided whether to leave or stay.

Shelby realized that she'd touched his most vulnerable spot. She doubted that he would have committed a robbery for a Tramart, but for his grandfather? Yes, he would do that to keep his grandfather's past from being discovered, especially if that past held some embarrassing surprises.

"I don't think about what could have been, Shelby, I think about what *is*," Clay said in a low tone. "Dwelling on the past has no place in my life. I'm concerned with the present, and at present my grandfather is beside himself over a tragic love affair—"

"Tragic? Who said it was tragic?"

Clay abruptly stood up. He paced to the window, looked out at the black night, and then walked back to her. His mood matched the night—dark, mysterious, and very hot. "I meant sad, a sad love affair that's eating him up! I'm very protective of my grandfather, and I have no idea, nor do I even want to contemplate, what the disclosure of this story might do to him."

"You say that you are protective of your grandfather. Perhaps he never said anything about this because he was protecting you and your parents."

"From what?"

"From the whole story, the story that these love letters might reveal. You're not just worried about your grandfather, but about the great Trask name being sullied!"

Clay's eyes turned a pale, cold green. Her accusation did not throw him. She doubted much would, but the thin line of his lips betrayed that she'd at least scored a point, and he didn't like it. "Well, skewering the rich is your forte, isn't it?" he said in a steely voice. "No matter who it hurts or what the cost! Shelby, tell me this isn't going to be some rich family drama that you plan to expose and analyze for two-fifty a copy."

Shelby slowly stood up. Her anger was so deep that when she looked at him eye-to-eye, her hand trembled as she pushed a curly strand of hair out of her flushed face. "So you think this is just a story to me, do you? I'm going to profit from this, am I? I've spent years—*years*—wondering why Aunt Desiree acted the way she did—depressed, distracted, afraid of the outside world. And I wondered if this behavior was the reason she couldn't seem to love me. Or was *I* the reason? Was I too scrappy, too intense, too unladylike? *Something* prevented her from loving me, and for years *I* took the blame! You can't imagine how lonely I was. I didn't seem to belong to Desiree. I didn't seem to belong anywhere!"

Tears welled up in her eyes. She blinked them back, fighting to stay in control. "Now I discover that there may have been a reason for Desiree's odd behavior, a reason that had nothing to do with me. Those letters must be in this house somewhere. I'll find them, Clay, because if they can explain to me, even in the smallest way, why my aunt acted as she did, then I *need* to read them. We could have loved each other so much better with a little understanding. I wanted to. Oh, how I wanted to."

She couldn't stop the tears now, but her pride propelled her out of the room, away from the indifference Clay would feel for *her* problems. Even with her sore foot, she made it to the front parlor before she heard footsteps walking, then running behind her.

"Shelby, I'm sorry." Clay's strong arms gripped hers as she attempted the front stairs.

"No, you're not. You're like all the rich—just interested in your precious name."

In her haste she put too much pressure on her bad foot. She stumbled, and Clay quickly caught her. His hands were more gentle now, comforting, but Shelby hated needing his support.

"You're going to be rich soon, too, you know," he said.

"But not like you! I won't be like *you*, a spoiled rich boy who's had everything handed to him on a silver platter. Your most pressing problem, besides stealing letters that legally belong to me, is whether to play serve and volley or a straight baseline game at the Fairview tennis tournament!"

She'd stung him, as she had intended. He seemed paralyzed for a moment, absorbing her words, and in this stillness his vulnerability showed. The murky light captured the unexpected pain in his eyes, but he didn't seem insulted. In fact, his face showed a weary self-contempt. With his fingers he absently stopped the path of her tears before they dropped from her chin to her blouse. "I'm far from perfect," he said softly. "It won't take much to be better than me."

Shelby couldn't believe she'd said those words. Her anger had never made her so vindictive. Clay eased her down on the stairs. She burst into tears again. The shock of her own words mixed with her pain for Desiree. She could finally cry for her aunt, and the sobs shook her body. Dimly she felt an arm steal around her. She gripped Clay's shirt as if she wanted to pound against it, but his other arm went around her, and instead she found his chest to be a bulwark against her tears, a refuge from all her heartache.

How soothing he felt, as one hand lightly skimmed the back of her head, his fingers nestling into her curls. She even thought she felt his lips gently kiss those curls, and this warmed her. She was suddenly cold, so cold, and Clay's arms provided the only protection from the cluttered loneliness of that house.

Why was he so nice to her? She'd hurt him, but then he'd hurt *her*. She wasn't a reporter first and a human being second. Above all, she was a woman. Shelby thought that Clay had seen this. Obviously he hadn't. This added to her pain, as did the fact that she'd confessed her deepest fear to him. No one else had ever known that she wondered if Desiree had loved her.

She pulled away from him, embarrassed at having exposed her vulnerable side. "Please leave," she said.

"Are you all right?" he asked softly.

The answer was obvious but Shelby understood that he still wanted to comfort her. "Yes. I'm okay.

You can go."

But he didn't move. It was as if he could sense how fragile she was at that moment and wouldn't leave her. "How does your foot feel?"

"It'll be fine."

Disregarding her assurance, Clay gently raised the injured foot. "No real swelling," he said.

Shelby pushed herself up. "I'm sure the pain will be gone by tomorrow." The physical pain, she thought. Emotionally, this evening would be with her for a long time. "Good night, Clay."

Reluctantly he stood and walked to the front door. He looked back once before leaving. Shelby's face was tear-stained, and smudges of mascara ringed her swollen eyes. Her expression, however, was determined. The deliberate way she stood on her sore foot left little doubt that no matter what comfort he'd been able to give her, she did not need him now.

Not that he blamed her. Breaking into Shelby's house had been bad enough, but his worst offense had been his insensitivity. "Good night" he said.

Clay let himself out. He took one deep shuddering breath as he started to walk to where he'd hidden his car. He felt ashamed of the things he'd said to Shelby. She'd come on so tough with her impassioned line about the abuses of the rich that Clay had assumed her first impulse, after finding the letters, would be to expose the wealthy Trasks for whatever Ford Trask might have done to her aunt.

But that hadn't been her first impulse at all. Her initial thought had been about a lonely child's need for love and the desperate quest of that child, now a woman, to know why she'd been deprived. To his astonishment, Shelby had admitted a painful vulnerability. Clay could only imagine what it must have been like being raised by an adult who couldn't love. He'd always had so much affection heaped on him by his family. Sometimes their love and their expectations for him seemed . . . suffocating, but he'd always been sure of their support.

Clay's shame also sprang from another source. Desiree Langstaff's letter had been more than a fond farewell to an old beau. In it she had mentioned details of their affair that Clay had withheld from Shelby, details that he now knew she'd want to know.

Those cryptic references had his family in a tumult. His father had always warned him: *Grandpa is not what he seems.* John Trask claimed that his father had rarely confided in him, or anyone, about where he had come from or how he'd acquired the farm from which all the Trask success sprang. Clay had strongly disagreed, saying that Grandpa talked to him all the time, but now he realized that their conversations had centered around the future, not the past.

However mysteriously his grandfather had treated the past, Ford's misadventures must have exacted a price. Desiree's letter inferred that something terrible had happened sixty years ago, something that had triggered a shattering breakup. Desiree hinted at this "crime," even as she forgave. Clay's father was convinced that the sins of

Ford Trask would haunt them all. For the first time in his life Clay was beginning to believe him.

If only he'd been able to buy Shelby's land outright! Then he could have discovered the letters and learned the truth. But now he doubted that she would sell him the land, much less give the letters to Ford—if she found them. There was a chance Desiree had destroyed them, feeling that with the letter of forgiveness, the past was really the past. After all, Clay had not found them in the places he'd looked. The house was big, however. Until he owned it, he couldn't be certain. Damn Buzz Mathis and his jealousy! Buzz's latest bid had topped Clay's, and the Trasks had less liquid capital.

Clay couldn't blame Shelby if she accepted another offer. What he'd said in the kitchen had been harsh. Her words, however, cut no less deep. Clay had thought she'd seen beneath his veneer to the imperfect but real man. He'd thought she liked him. For a few fleeting weeks he'd even imagined a more passionate relationship, if the moments in her arms had been any clues. Now he realized that he'd been kidding himself. Clay opened his car door and slid into the seat. All he knew was that the sight of her tearstained face, so resolute yet so vulnerable, was almost more than he could bear.

The next morning Shelby woke to the blinding glare of an early summer's day and an even more blinding headache. She turned over on the lumpy sofa and groaned. Feeling achy and messy from having been in the same clothes since yesterday morning, she hauled herself into a sitting position. Last night she'd been too exhausted to climb the winding stairs to her room. Instead, she'd limped to the worn velvet couch and fallen into a troubled sleep.

Dawn, however, brought back every detail of the night before. Shelby even remembered that she'd left her suitcase out by the back door—where she'd run into Clay.

A hot shower finished the job of waking her up as last night's revelations started replaying in her mind. Desiree . . . the letters . . . Shelby still had trouble digesting the fact that her aunt had once had a tragic—that was Clay's word for it—relationship. Shelby felt sick that she had never suspected this, but how could she? Desiree had hidden her heartache from everyone. Shelby was convinced that this heartache was the source of Desiree's behavior. Her aunt's defense against the pain had been a detachment from people, but that detachment had crippled her relationship with Shelby.

Had Ford Trask suffered this much from the ill-fated romance? Shelby felt a rising anger. Grudgingly she admitted that Clay would never have risked burglary if his grandfather hadn't been distraught. What was remarkable was that Desiree could inspire such a reaction after sixty years.

Shelby intended to find Ford's letters. She was certain that they were still in the house. Being a recluse, Desiree would have kept them there, and she'd mentioned in her letter that she still had them. Shelby suddenly felt that to discover the events that had shaped Desiree's personality would also clarify the demons that drove hers. And perhaps it would be a belated act of devotion from a troubled niece.

After two cups of steaming coffee she decided to let Clay help her look for the letters. Guilt figured prominently into this rationale, guilt over the completely underhanded remark she'd made to him. She'd been so hurt by his accusation, so stunned that he'd accuse her of the lowest form of journalism, which struck at her own cherished view of herself, that she'd lashed out in a way that would wound his identity.

She'd succeeded. And yet her fury was now turning inward. For the first time doubts about her professional identity nagged her. Before Desiree's death, before the specter of money was in her future, she knew exactly who she was. A reporter, a critic, who sat on the outside looking in at the rich and powerful.

Now she was joining their ranks. The upheaval confused her, but not as much as Clay Trask messing with her mind. The very man who should have fit her most despised stereotype of the undeserving rich broke the mold of any man she'd ever met.

Clay had apologized for his accusation. He'd stayed with her, despite her vicious words, while she wept. Such tenderness wrapped in so physically exciting an exterior had monopolized her thoughts these past weeks. Shelby knew she owed Clay an apology for her remarks. Was that why she was going to invite him to search for the letters, or did she just want to see him again?

Shelby got dressed and called Park View, only to be told by Mapes that Mr. Clay was playing in the club's tennis tournament today. She didn't have to ask which club. On a warm Sunday the Fairview Country Club was the place to see and be seen.

The Fairview Country Club crowned a hill and was accessed by a winding road. The king-of-the-mountain setting was actually the only ostentatious thing about it. The club founders had considered conspicuous consumption to be nouveau rich so they'd painstakingly created an atmosphere of unflashy, almost dowdy comfort. Solid and sedate, the club proclaimed that its members were so prosperous that they didn't need to shout about it.

As Shelby drove to the main clubhouse, which looked like a large, weathered country inn, she thought that with her new money and old name she'd be a good candidate for membership. *Mmm, no, not my style,* she mused as she noticed dozens of middleaged men in loud Bermuda shorts playing golf on the course to her left. She parked her rented car next to a BMW with a Breck Prep Is Party Central sticker on it.

She got out of her car and stared at it.

"Some things never change."

Shelby wheeled around to see Logan Langstaff. "Hey, cousin," she called out, "didn't you make up that slogan?"

"Yes, and I did my best to uphold it."

Shelby laughed and gave him a hug. Logan, as usual, looked snappy, with beige linen slacks and a buff cotton knit shirt that showed off to perfection his blond hair, blue eyes, and a tan that was fairly advanced for late May.

"Are you playing in the tennis tournament today?"

Logan shuddered. "And work up a sweat? No, thanks! I'll leave that to Clay Trask."

At the mention of his name Shelby thought of the revelations from the night before. Perhaps Logan, as her only living relative, might remember some whispered gossip about Desiree—anything that could shed some light on her aunt's early years. She told him about Desiree's romance with Ford Trask and the letters. Logan seemed astounded.

"You mean Desiree might not have been a virgin?" he exclaimed. "Don't tell me any more, Shelby, my heart might not be able to stand the shock!"

Shelby laughed. "Did your parents ever talk about Desiree's past?"

"No," Logan replied, scratching his head, "they never did. But, geez, those letters could be anywhere in that crazy house. Too bad my folks are dead—they might have been able to help." He snapped his fingers. "But I'm available. I happen to be between projects right now, and I would love to help you find them!"

Shelby thought of the invitation she was about to extend to Clay. "Oh, thank you, Logan, but I think I can manage."

"Are you sure? I have some free time."

"Yes, but thanks."

He seemed disappointed. "By the way, did you sell Desiree's land yet?"

"No, the bids are still coming in."

"Bids." Logan laughed incredulously as he pulled a cigarette case out of his pocket. "Who would have thought that house was worth twenty cents."

"Not me. But life is strange."

Logan invited her into the clubhouse for a drink, but she declined, saying she wanted to watch the tournament. Actually, Shelby had hoped to catch Clay before he started to play, but his match had begun. A small crowd watched from the bleachers set up for the tournament.

As she sat down, the chair umpire called out "Deuce." Shelby looked at the scoreboard. The match appeared close. Clay had taken the first set six games to four. The second set was tied three games apiece between Clay and his opponent, Mapother Dewey III. "Third," as he was called by his intimates, had been a year ahead of Shelby and Clay at Breck Prep, where he'd gained fame for missing the capital of Kentucky on a geography test. Claiming capitals "weren't his bag," Third dozed through his senior year, waking up long enough to play in nearly every varsity sport.

His husky body bulged with muscles so defined

that Shelby wondered if he pumped iron around the clock. His style of play was blunt: hit the ball so hard that your opponent will be overwhelmed by the power.

Unfortunately he was playing Clay. In tennis whites, Clay's body was longer and leaner than Third's. There was a rock-hardness to it, as if his muscles were there to work instead of show. Seeing more now than she ever had before, she marveled at his tapered waist, slim hips, and tight behind. Instead of flaunting his pecs and biceps, Clay dazzled with speed, surprise, and imagination. A spectacularly-smooth player, he covered the court with ease, attacking Third where he least expected.

Clay's dexterity on the court belied his height. Cushioning each move were his thighs, tough, sinewy, and perfectly proportioned.

Looking at Clay, Shelby was having trouble concentrating on the game. The early-afternoon sun had already created a film of sweat on his body, making his shirt stick to his chest. But he continued to deftly deflect Third's most powerful shots, and his backhand slice penetrated corners that had his opponent cursing. And when Clay wanted to hit *hard,* Third could only watch helplessly as the ball flew by.

It seemed his body could do anything, and Shelby wondered if all that controlled force was as dazzling on a more intimate scale. With thighs like that and with such stamina he could probably make love all night. Her curiosity lingered over how he would pace his lovemaking, varying his caresses so that the woman was eager for the next level of intensity. Shelby had tasted his mouth before, and now she hungered for a more intimate scrutiny. Perhaps she could know him better from a physical perspective because he was still an enigma to her on a personal one.

Indeed, his game was like his personality, difficult to guess, surprising but always winning. He was beating Third badly now. Did Clay need to win everything? Shelby couldn't figure him out, so of course that made him twice as interesting. But she would. She promised herself that.

Suddenly Clay saw her. He'd stopped to change rackets and had glanced into the stands. Shelby was momentarily flummoxed. She'd come here to apologize for her nasty crack and invite him to help her search for Ford's letters. Seeing Clay, however, made her wonder just what her reception would be.

He very nearly did a double take. Obviously her presence was the last thing he'd expected. He slowly held his hand up in a small wave. Shelby returned the gesture. He smiled hesitantly. So did she. Then his face broke into a smile so warm and delighted that Shelby flushed to the roots of her already red hair. The pure pleasure of his smile filled her with a kind of daffy happiness. She began to envision sun-dappled afternoons of letter searching, and at night . . . Shelby's fantasy took a more romantic turn. Clay walked back to the court with a decided spring in his step. His next shot was an ace.

The day's heat forced Shelby to seek the refreshment stand for a drink. She was sipping a cola when she heard, "Shelby! Shelby Langstaff! I can't believe it!"

Shelby turned around to see the smiling face of Mary-Pete Marcum. "Mary-Pete!" she cried out as she felt the firm embrace of her old schoolmate. Mary-Pete and Shelby had been the mainstays "and terrors," they'd liked to think, of Breck Prep's field hockey team. Mary-Pete was a big woman, although some of her bulk looked to be about five months along.

"I heard you were still in town," she said. "I'm sorry about your aunt."

"Thank you, Mary-Pete." Shelby stood back. "Say, congratulations are in order. I didn't even know you were married."

"I married Kippy Spaulding. You know, Bunty Epps's cousin?"

"No."

"Sure, she's the niece of Chou-Chou Powers, who's now married to Cuddy Wentworth, who's the brother-in-law of Third Dewey, the fellow out there who's getting slaughtered by the Prom King."

Mary-Pete not only knew everyone in old Louisville society, but she also knew their nicknames. Proof of Shelby's status as an outsider was that she had never had a nickname. Mary-Pete's real name was Marigold Patricia.

"You look kind of tired, Shelby. Why don't we go into the clubhouse and get some tea." Mary-Pete didn't wait for Shelby to answer. She simply propelled her into the clubhouse's rather dowdy tearoom all the while chatting away about Shelby's career.

Shelby was amazed and flattered. "I didn't think people around here read *Courant*."

Mary-Pete snorted as she sat down heavily in a green-and-white upholstered chair. The tearoom featured simple wooden tables, a beige rug, and pale-green wallpaper with pastoral scenes of horses, people riding horses, and horses alone, eating. "Honey, we're not in the backwoods here," she said. "I love your stuff. As I said to Peewee Taylor the other day at the club's charity committee, 'Shelby's writing is just like her hockey playing. She blows away the competition.'"

Mary-Pete's warm smile made it clear that she was giving a compliment. Unfortunately her comment reminded Shelby of Clay's accusation the night before. Her smile came out kind of sour.

"Speaking of the charity committee, our recording secretary is right over there. Heather!" Mary-Pete called out. "Heather McKenzie Scott, you get your aerobicized behind over here!"

Of all the people to run into, Shelby inwardly groaned. The Prom Queen bounced over in a tennis outfit that bore more resemblance to a bikini. She looked fabulous as usual, whereas Shelby wondered if her face was still puffy from all her crying the night before. She also wondered if Heather had come to the club today to watch Clay play in the tournament. Heather bubbled a hello to Mary-Pete, but her greeting to Shelby was more subdued.

"Sit down, girl," Mary-Pete commanded, "and tell me why you've missed three committee meetings."

Heather slid into a seat and in her breathy, low voice said, "Oh, I'm sorry, Mary-Pete, I'm just so busy! In fact, I'm thinking of resigning as recording secretary."

"Sugar, you may not have to bother," Mary-Pete retorted. "Your performance at the last food drive may be grounds for impeachment."

"I brought the canned goods that I had at home," Heather said as she pulled a mirror out of her purse. She checked her lipstick and then her teeth. Seeing a smear of pink, she furiously rubbed it off with her finger.

"Poor families need tuna, beans, and vegetables, not hearts of palm," Mary-Pete said.

"Oh, Mary-Pete," Heather sighed. "You and your . . . causes. Always asking for this, raising money for that. I do as much as I possibly can, but you always want more."

"Yes, she is a selfish bitch, isn't she?" Shelby asked, bristling at the criticism of her good-hearted friend.

Heather glared at her. In the moment of silence that followed, Mary-Pete looked as if she were trying to squelch a laugh. "Tell me," she said, changing the subject, "how was the Roses Ball? I would have gone, but my morning sickness sometimes appears at night."

The question perked Heather right up. "Oh, it was lovely, lovely!"

"I heard you went, Shelby," Mary-Pete said, eyeing her with disbelief. "Didn't you once say, sort of like Scarlett O'Hara, 'As God is my witness, I'll never go to the Roses Ball!' "

"I . . . I don't remember saying that," Shelby stammered. Heather looked amused at her discomfort. Shelby thought that perhaps she *had* made a manifesto like that, but there ought to be a statute of limitations on teenage pronouncements about life.

"Didn't I hear that you went with Clay Trask?"

"Mmm, yes, I did." Shelby really didn't want to talk about Clay. The tennis courts were visible from the tearoom. She made a concerted effort not to glance at his court.

Mary-Pete's eyes danced. Shelby remembered too late that her friend loved gossip. Mary-Pete's interest in other people's affairs sprang from her vast sociability, however, not from any meanness. Shelby knew that if her friend realized how uncomfortable Shelby was with questions about Clay, Mary-Pete would have stopped in an instant. Unfortunately Shelby didn't want her to know *that*.

"And didn't I hear at the garden club from Lolly Ratliff that the two of you were spotted at Mack's Shack and a few other places recently?"

"Umm, not that many places."

Mary-Pete tried to get comfortable in her chair. "He's a handsome devil. Not my type, though. I like 'em skinny and sweet."

Shelby wanted to say that Clay had a surprising sweetness, but she didn't want to dwell on the topic

111

any longer.

"Are you here today to see him play?" Mary-Pete asked, cocking her head in the direction of the courts.

"No, not really." Truthfully she'd come to talk to him, not to see him play.

"Oh, no?" Mary-Pete winked.

"She said *no*."

Shelby looked quickly at Heather, who was not nearly as amused now as she had been before.

"Oh, I stand corrected," Mary-Pete said politely. "I thought Shelby and Clay might be keeping company."

"I've been out with him a couple of times," Shelby admitted, "but it's mostly, well, sometimes business."

"There you see, Mary-Pete," Heather said. "You're always making mountains out of mole-hills." She stood. "I'm late for an appointment. See you later." She left.

Mary-Pete tapped her fork on the linen table-cloth. "Heather would be surprised at the molehills I know about," she said tartly.

Shelby smiled. "You were always an unimpeach-able source for Louisville's social scene.

"I try. That's why it's probably better that you and Clay aren't an item."

"Why's that?" Shelby's uninterested tone belied the jump in her pulse rate.

"Well, Heather confided to Pookie Sanders, who told me that Heather mysteriously said there was a new *blond* in her life. We all thought that she had set her cap for Buzz Mathis, but he doesn't have blond hair—or much hair for that matter. My guess, or rather Pookie's and mine, is that perhaps Heather and Clay's high school romance has recommenced."

Shelby suddenly felt sick. Mary-Pete took her silence as encouragement.

"Clay has always been very discreet about his private life, and Heather may not want Buzz to know yet, at least until she's sure Clay is hooked. She's playing with fire, however. Those two don't like each other, but then nothing makes Heather happier than to be fought over, the more men, the better. Oh, well, once a princess, always a princess."

"Heather was a queen, not a princess," Shelby said quietly.

Mary-Pete pulled her linen napkin out of its silver ring. "What she is, honey, is a twenty-four-carat bitch, who *always* gets what she wants. I thought that Clay would have more sense, but men can be so foolish."

"Not nearly as foolish as women." Shelby finally stole a glance at Clay's court. To her surprise he was gone.

Mary-Pete patted her hand. "I know it's a rumor, but now aren't you glad it's just business between you and Clay?"

"I . . . never thought otherwise."

Chapter Five

Drinking a cup of tea had never seemed to take so long. Shelby extricated herself from Mary-Pete as soon as politeness allowed and hurried to her car.

Facing Clay would have been impossible at that moment. What would she have said? *I know your game, I'm on to you. You're just trying to romance the land and letters out from under me with your wry smile and sexy voice.*

Shelby slammed the door of her rented car. Despite her anger, she wondered when his game had finished and where he was now—not to mention what he was up to. Never in her life had she possessed anything that people would lie or steal to get. Perhaps the rich faced this problem every day, but the experience was new to her, and unpleasant. Becoming a wealthy person was changing her life—not just financially either, but emotionally.

Nevertheless, how could she—cynical chronicler of the rich—have been so taken in by one of their prime members? Shelby honestly examined her feelings and came up with the galling fact that she'd *wanted* to be taken in. She wanted to believe that Clay cared for her because she had come to care for him.

His sardonic wit so matched her own. His lack of pretense, his surprising tenderness, and his passion for his work struck a similar chord in her. And when in his arms Shelby had never felt so physically right.

Something in her wouldn't, or couldn't, believe that all his attention these past weeks had sprung from cold calculation. Her instincts couldn't be so skewed. Clay couldn't have known that she'd show up for his match, and his delight in seeing her not more than an hour ago had been genuine.

Why had she been so quick to believe Mary-Pete? There were *plenty* of blond men in upper-class Louisville willing to get cozy with Heather Scott.

Rumors, however, bred doubt. Mary-Pete was an acknowledged gossip, but Shelby remembered her as being largely accurate. Shelby couldn't shake her insecurities about Clay. Perhaps they were really doubts about herself. Could the Prom King really fall for the brain? Her old self-image mocked her.

By the time she arrived home, this mental tug-of-war had so exhausted her that she didn't sense the intruder sneaking up behind her as she entered the parlor, nor was she alert enough to defend herself against the blow on the back of her head that sent her crashing to the floor.

"Shelby?"

The effort to open her eyes seemed gigantic, impossible.

"Wh-what?" She felt a hand on her forehead.

"What happened?"

It took a second for Shelby's throbbing head to process the question. "I was hit on the head."

She opened her eyes to see Clay Trask bending over her. The afternoon sun coming in from the long windows bounced off his hair, giving him a golden glow. His face bore a worried, stunned expression. Her head cleared sufficiently to ask a pertinent question.

"What are you doing here?"

"I didn't touch a thing. I swear."

When she didn't laugh, he smiled tentatively, and Shelby realized that his coming here was unusual. The last thing she'd told Clay was to leave her home.

"I saw you at the tournament," he began, "and thought you might have come . . . to see me. I looked for you but discovered that you'd left. Mary-Pete told me you looked a little pale, so I came here to see if you were all right."

So Mary-Pete had spoken to him—or had Heather told him that she'd seen Shelby with an old friend? She wanted to ask him about

116

Heather, but questions concerning his love life would have been an embarrassing admission of how much Shelby was interested in him. She tried to get up.

"No! Don't move," Clay said as he braced her back with his arm. His swift gesture kept Shelby from falling again.

"I want to get up," she insisted, although her voice betrayed her weakness.

"I'm calling an ambulance."

"Don't be crazy, I'm not that badly off." Her denial took too much effort for Clay not to notice.

He stuck one hand in front of her face. "How many fingers am I holding up?"

Shelby pushed his hand away. "Two fingers, which is all the bourbon I'll need to take the edge off this minor bump."

Clay's face became testy. "Shelby, I am taking you to the emergency room, where you will have X-rays to determine if this is a minor bump or a concussion. Then you will make out a police report about this intruder."

"What time is it?"

Clay looked confused by the question. "It's two o'clock."

She'd been unconscious for approximately fifteen minutes. Her tired brain chilled her with the thought that this was the second time she'd been surprised in her own home in less than one day. The first intruder had been this handsome Good Samaritan, who'd gone to a lot of trouble to find

117

out where she was. "When did you finish your game?"

"About an hour a—" Clay fell silent. He stared at Shelby in disbelief. Then his eyes shifted downward, and he helped her to her feet, picking up the shoulder bag she'd dropped. "I insist on taking you to the hospital. After that you can accuse me, have me arrested, I don't care."

"Clay, I . . ."

His eyes met hers, and there was anger in those hazel eyes but also a bruised admission that she had a right to wonder. Shelby imagined that no one had ever had a right to feel that way about him, and he was ashamed, even as she knew that he would never have done something like this.

"I would never hit a woman," he said quietly.

Now Shelby felt ashamed.

"You can hate me," he continued. "God knows I gave you cause after the things I said last night. But I would never, *never*—"

"Clay!" she exclaimed, her voice echoing painfully in her head. The effort made her feel lightheaded, and before she knew it, she was in Clay's arms.

"I'm taking you to the hospital," he said roughly. "Don't argue."

"Clay," she whispered. She put her hands on his chest and looked up into his face. Reflected there was an uneasy mixture of concern for her and anger at her insinuation. "I don't hate you," she said.

Those simple words seemed to unsettle him

118

even more. His eyes searched hers for unspoken anger or sarcasm. Finding neither, he seemed uncharacteristically at a loss for what to say. He fell silent, but his eyes conveyed a new tenderness.

Shelby felt completely safe in his arms. The sensation was illogical. After all, he'd broken into her home, held back information about the letters, and called into question her profession.

Still, the feeling of being protected remained. Another feeling persisted whenever Clay held her, but this one was not the warm sensation of being cared for. No, her temperature rose with this emotion, for whenever his mesmerizing body touched hers, she felt a jolt of sexual excitement.

Elemental, electric, *scary*, she'd never experienced such a rush of sensual awareness before. She might be just a reporter to Clay, but she definitely felt like a woman in his arms. Even now, with her head throbbing so badly, she was conscious of the scent of his freshly-showered skin and the fluid meshing of his hips as he guided her out of the parlor.

"Wait, Clay." Something had caught her eye. "Look."

She pointed to a small room off the main parlor. This was Desiree's study, where she'd once read for endless hours and done her "accounts." The door was open, and as they went closer, the full impact of the room's disarray became evident. Desiree's secretary had been rifled. Drawers were open. A bookcase had been pulled away from the wall. Books littered the faded rug along

119

with a few old receipts, tax returns, and several other financial documents that Shelby had painstakingly organized.

Clay's face registered astonishment and a hint of fear. His arms tightened around her.

"I didn't notice anything amiss when I came in," she said. Indeed, the parlor was untouched. If the intruder had been interested in robbery, why were the two pieces of nice silver that Desiree had possessed still on the mantelpiece?

They went into the study. Shelby had to sit down as Clay gathered the scattered documents.

"What do you suppose they were looking for?" he asked. There was an edge to his voice.

"I don't know," she answered, sorting through the papers and putting them back in order. "Everything seems to be here, and Desiree never kept any money in her study—well, perhaps her checkbook. No, she just used this room for reading, handling bills, and any correspondence. . . ." The answer pierced Shelby's fuzzy brain. "The letters. Someone else wants the letters. But why?"

Clay shook his head, his handsome features cast with a new anxiety. "I don't know. I'm going to check the other rooms."

Before she could protest, he quickly went up the stairs, taking the steps two at a time. As he looked, Shelby pondered why anyone besides her and Clay's family should want love letters chronicling an ill-fated romance sixty years before.

"Your aunt's study seems to be the only room the intruder managed to search," Clay said when he came back down the stairs. "You probably surprised him."

"Perhaps he, or she, now has the letters."

"No," Clay said firmly. "The letters are still here."

"How do you know?"

"I searched that room thoroughly. If they'd been in there, *I'd* have found them." He realized the outrageousness of his words and almost laughed. Shelby laughed out loud, her throbbing head jangling. She winced and lightly touched the bump where she'd been hit.

"It's a golf ball, isn't it?" Clay asked.

"Well, at least a pebble," she conceded.

Despite Shelby's protests, Clay took her to the emergency room, where they examined her, took X-rays, and found that she had a mild concussion. She was ordered to stay the night, an unnecessary demand since Shelby fell into a deep sleep.

When she awoke, it was dusk. The room was empty, except for her small overnight bag sitting next to the bed. Had she packed it before leaving her house? She sat up slowly, guarding her head against any sudden movements or jarring. The events of that afternoon came back to her, and she wondered if Clay had left. She rang for the nurse.

In bustled a plump, bespectacled woman who surprised Shelby with a booming voice. "How are we?" she rang out.

Shelby winced and closed her eyes. "We have a nasty headache."

The nurse took Shelby's pulse. "Yes, you will for a while. Do we remember the doctors checking our eyes for inner cranial pressure?"

"No. We don't remember packing a suitcase, either."

The nurse beamed. "Oh, that was your fiancé. Such a charming man, and so handsome!"

With the pounding in her head Shelby wasn't sure she'd heard correctly. "My fiancé?"

The round, ruddy face crinkled in concern. "Are we experiencing memory loss? It's not uncommon. He brought you to the emergency room and sat with you most of the time you were asleep. We do remember the bump on the head, don't we?"

Shelby remembered everything except having acquired a fiancé in the past few hours. Luckily her confusion was short-lived.

"Darling," Clay called out as he walked into the room. "You're up."

The nurse went up to him and in an ill-concealed whisper said, "She doesn't seem to remember you. Be patient." She patted his shoulder sympathetically and left the room.

"Did we get engaged while I was unconscious?" Shelby asked.

Clay smiled and sat down in an orange plastic chair. "I told just a little lie so that they'd let me sit with you."

Shelby couldn't put her finger on it, but something was different about him. "Good grief, Clay, it was just a few hours."

He stared at her. "Shelby, it's Monday."

"What?" She carefully shook her foggy head. "You mean I slept for twenty-four hours?"

"More like twenty-eight," Clay answered, "off and on. The doctors woke you up periodically to check for cranial pressure, but you didn't seem to notice."

Shelby swallowed thickly. So her little bump had turned out to be more serious. She wondered what would have happened if Clay hadn't insisted on bringing her to the hospital. "Am I all right?"

Clay nodded. "You're fine. I just talked to the doctor, and he said that you could go home when you woke up."

"So why do I need an overnight bag?"

Clay had a don't-argue-with-me look. He stood and put his hands in the pockets of his suit jacket. Shelby now realized that he looked different because he was dressed for work. "You are staying with my family tonight." He put up one hand as she started to protest. "You're still not well enough to fend for yourself, and I'm making sure your house is safe before you move back in."

"Of all the nerve!" Shelby exclaimed. "First you break into my house, and now you won't let me live there until you make it burglarproof!"

A ghost of a smile passed over his face. "I suppose this is kind of absurd."

"That's an understatement!"

His smile faded. She saw him jam his hands back into his pockets. "I won't let anyone else hurt you!" he declared.

His vehemence surprised Shelby. She saw in the set of his jaw and the flash of his eyes an intensity that made her look away in embarrassment. What did he really feel for her? According to Mary-Pete, he felt friendly in a merely social way. His passion was saved for Heather. But if his pronouncement just now wasn't filled with passion and anger, then the bump on Shelby's head had affected her vision.

Shelby shivered. Being under Clay's protection seemed comforting and unsettling at the same time. Needing anyone's protection was scary. Who had attacked her? What was in those letters? She vowed to find them.

Clay picked up her overnight bag. "Why don't you get dressed and check out? I'll go get my car."

"You packed my bag?"

He gave his wry, cheeky smile. "I've seen lingerie before."

"I'll bet." Shelby imagined that he'd seen a lot of it, both on and off women. She wondered if he'd seen the black lace nightie that she'd bought last week in a rash moment. Sheer, low-cut, the gown barely came to her knees. The peignoir reflected a sensual side that she rarely showed.

When Clay deposited her overnight bag on her bed, Shelby realized that her hospital gown afforded little more coverage than her nightie—a fact Clay seemed to notice. She sat up a little straighter, but the effort at modesty only pressed the soft cotton against her breasts. Under his gaze her nipples hardened, also impossible to hide. A warm tingle of sexual awareness went through her. It was such a welcome sensation from the strain of the last few days. She felt well enough to go home, but perhaps one night at Park View might be prudent.

She sighed. "Okay, *one* night."

Clay quickly went to get the car. He didn't want to give Shelby any time to change her mind. Her appearance at the tennis tournament the day before had stunned him, making him wonder if she'd forgiven him for his actions on Saturday. It was quite a leap, however, between forgiveness and passion. Clay was an impatient man. He wanted Shelby, the letters and land be damned! But even as he thought this, he knew that the problems unleashed by Desiree Langstaff's letter could not be forgotten. So many people depended on him that he couldn't follow his own inclinations to let the past stay buried.

When he picked Shelby up at the hospital entrance, he saw that she wore the simple slacks and knit top he'd packed. God, she was lovely— those long shapely legs, her delicious lips, the burnished glow of her red hair. Despite her injury, Shelby had a faint, pleased look. She'd found the nightie.

"My parents look forward to meeting you," he said as they headed east.

125

"Your grandfather, too?" Her excitement over the possibility pushed all thoughts of lingerie from her mind.

Clay didn't answer right away. He negotiated a turn as Brownsboro Road became hillier.

"No," he finally replied. "My grandfather doesn't even know you're coming. He's secluded in his suite right now, after a bad spell yesterday. We have a nurse attending him."

Shelby couldn't hide her disappointment. "I'm sorry he's not well. I would have liked to have met him."

He looked at her with compassion. "I'm sorry, too."

His apology was interesting, since the decision had been made not to introduce her without even asking his grandfather. Shelby wondered if Ford had the same boldly-chiseled face as his grandson. Clay had said they were very close. Did Ford share the same sardonic wit? More seriously, had he, in his long life, exhibited the same penchant for risk-taking as his grandson? Shelby was very sorry that she wouldn't have a chance to find out, but with a nurse attending him — or was it guarding him? — no contact seemed possible.

The entrance to Park View loomed ahead. Turning into Park Drive, they drove past the landscape that Clay had so lovingly developed. He parked in the circular driveway. After switching off the engine, his body tensed in a way that made Shelby expectant. Finally he said, "While I'm apologizing, I'd like to say again how much I regret the other night, what I did, what I *said*."

Shelby had been waiting for this opportunity. "Oh, Clay, you don't know how much *I* regret—"

"Miss Langstaff! Miss Langstaff!"

Shelby turned her head to see two figures, one robust and one thin, walking down the front steps, followed by the high-pitched yelp of a ball of white fur. Clay sighed.

"Welcome to Park View! I'm John Trask," sang out a man dressed entirely like a Kentucky colonel, right down to the ice cream suit, goatee, and string tie. "This is my wife, Mary-Alice."

"How are you feeling, dear?" Clay's mother asked. She was the leaner of the two, and sleekly groomed in a peach silk dress with a lovely moonstone necklace. Her eyes were light brown, and her features small and even. In his parents' faces Shelby saw traces of Clay's physical makeup, but he really resembled neither parent.

Shelby and Clay got out of the car. Handshakes were exchanged all around, but the pleasantries were interrupted by the incessant barking of a white poodle.

Clay blanched. "Shelby, this is Cha-Cha." Shelby bent to pet the dog, as Clay continued, "Cha-Cha, don't bite Shelby."

But Cha-Cha hadn't been listening. "Ouch!" Shelby yelped.

"Cha-Cha, bad dog!" chastised Mrs. Trask. She scooped the trembling creature into her arms.

Clay took Shelby's hand, where little teeth marks were just turning red. "She rarely breaks

127

the skin," he said apologetically.

"She doesn't like strangers," came the mournful voice of Mapes. He picked up Shelby's overnight bag. "The east wing, madame?"

"Oh, no, Mapes," Mary-Alice said, "put Miss Langstaff in the south wing. It has a better view." She stroked what looked like Cha-Cha's head. "Getting kicked out of obedience school has traumatized her."

"Well, Mother, you won't let me arrange an exorcism," Clay teased.

"Why don't we go to the south parlor," John interposed politely. His accent betrayed his rural roots, although an effort had been made to camouflage this. In fact, he reminded Shelby of Park View: impressive, expensive, but not quite the genuine article.

Mapes silently led them to a room full of comfortable furniture and lots of fresh flowers. If this was the south parlor, Shelby thought, then how many parlors were there, and how did they find them without a compass? This conspicuous consumption highlighted the irony of the whole Desiree-Ford story. When they first knew each other, one was poor and one was well-off. Then, due to fate or whatever, the situation became reversed.

When she was seated comfortably, Shelby said, "I'm sorry that I won't be able to meet your father, Mr. Trask, but Clay tells me he's ailing."

John Trask shot a quick glance at Clay. Then he eased himself into a leather wing chair. Clay remained standing, but he tempered his guarded stance by casually walking over to a piano and leaning against it. Mary-Alice sat on a love seat with the unlovable Cha-Cha, who despite the gentility of the surroundings, stuck her leg up and began her cleaning regimen.

"My father hasn't been the same since receiving your aunt's letter," John said.

"My aunt wasn't the same after knowing your father, and that was sixty years ago."

"Oh, now," Mary-Alice began, but John waved her off. "Let's be honest, shall we? Sometime in their early youth your aunt and my daddy were romantically involved. It's kind of hard to believe since he was so poor, but Clay tells me that they met at the state fair. Humph. I still think it's strange. Anyway, their relationship fell apart, and she sort of pined away for that shattered romance."

Shelby thought that finally she was talking to someone without a hidden agenda. "Yes, that's it!" she said enthusiastically, "and your father knows the whole story."

"Well, you can forget about finding anything else out from him," John answered, effectively dashing her optimism. "My father is not exactly chatty on the best of occasions. Now, however, he rarely speaks."

"The letters might explain," Mary-Alice put in so rapidly that Shelby wondered if she'd been cued.

"Absolutely," John said, sitting up in his chair.

"Those letters will probably tell us the whole sorry tale. 'Course, nothing could be sorrier than my son's attempt to get them."

Clay shifted slightly in discomfort. "I've apologized, Dad. I was apologizing again when you and Mother came out."

"Well, you are lucky that you're not on your way to Eddyville!" John shot back, referring to the location of one of Kentucky's largest prisons.

Shelby never thought she'd be taking Clay's side. "Mr. Trask, Clay didn't hit me on the head last Sunday. Someone else wants those letters."

"Clay told us and we are shocked," John said.

Shocked, but not surprised, Shelby sensed. A certain crafty gleam in his eyes convinced her that he was more than a genial old gentleman.

"I find it impossible to believe that anyone would want some old love letters," Mary-Alice said. "I mean, I'm surprised that your aunt and my father-in-law can even *remember* their affair after all these years."

Now this was a notion that Shelby had no trouble believing. Lately she'd come to realize that Desiree had shared her own intensity about life. How else could that explain her aunt's obsession with one man for sixty years? "Do you believe in the power of love, Mrs. Trask?" Shelby asked.

Mary-Alice looked startled at the question. She pondered a moment and said, "Yes, I guess I do," but she gazed at Clay when she answered, not her husband.

130

"Hell, forget love," John said, "let's talk about safety. That house is a menace, for more reasons than just the letters. The wiring must be ancient, the plumbing unsound, the walls full of lead paint, not to mention that whatsit, radon, coming out of the shower. That house is a mess, and you'd be well rid of it."

Clay gave his father a warning look that John ignored. "Now I know my son has made you a good offer for your place—several good offers! We need the land, and that's a fact. But I promise that we will not tear down that house until we find those letters!"

Clay sighed. "Dad, Shelby isn't planning on selling right away. She may be in Louisville for a while."

John's white eyebrows nearly went up into his snowy mane. "Is that right? Now, what would a sophisticated young lady like you want with a city whose idea of gourmet eating is barbecued ribs?"

Shelby had to smile. "I'm not sure, really."

He snorted. "Don't get me wrong. Louisville's a great city, a great city. But with our offer, you could go back to New York in style."

He wasn't pressuring her, exactly. John's folksy, blunt patter was disarming but a little less than candid. If he really thought that the relationship between Desiree and Ford was a youthful fling of only historic interest, then why the as-God-is-my-witness pledge to find the letters?

"Mr. Trask," Shelby said, "I'm not planning on

131

going back to New York just yet, and as for my style, well, that might be changing. I've always liked ribs."

He studied her with a tolerant air. "Lord knows I'm in favor of people finding their own style. Hell, if I hadn't, we wouldn't be sitting here right now. We'd still be on that damn farm. I thank Providence every day that Louisville's first mall decided to locate on our land. If not for that fortuitous event, Clay would probably be plowing the lower forty, I'd be slopping some hogs, and Mary-Alice here would be making her own pickles and jam."

"Amen," Mary-Alice murmured, but Clay was not amused. He moved directly into his father's line of sight.

"Farming is an honorable profession," he said. "Scratch any of the Louisville elite and you'll find farmers in the family tree."

"I don't think the Pughs were farmers," Mary-Alice said.

"No, Mother, you're right. They made their initial money from moonshine!"

"My son glorifies what he only vaguely remembers," John said to Shelby. "*I* remember that farm. And believe you me, there was nothing noble about backbreaking work and shabby clothes. Why, we barely had indoor plumbing."

Clay shook his head, but there was no anger in his face. In fact, Shelby saw a slight smile. "I remember the farm, too, Dad. I was a little boy, but I remember. And it wasn't all so bad. We were close then, working together to get the crops in or save a calf. I even remember the smell of summer, which you can't get at Park View because of the air-conditioning."

John looked at his son in utter disbelief. "Humph. Hot weather meant flies and sweat. I hated it."

"I liked it."

"Oh, yeah? Do you want to go back and slop some more hogs or spread some more manure? Give up every advantage that selling that farm brought you? There'd be no Tramarts, that's for damn sure."

Clay's smile vanished. He glanced at Shelby before replying, as if reminding himself that company was present. "I didn't say that. I don't believe in dwelling on the past."

Shelby wondered if that remark was meant for her.

"But I also don't believe in disparaging our roots." A trace of humor reappeared on his face. "There's a part of that farm work ethic that's very much *my* style, but I know you hated it. Spreading manure ruined the crease in your trousers."

John chuckled and pulled at the cuff of his linen suit.

"I do like to dress well. And why not? I can afford it. That's the thing about style, Miss Langstaff. To really show it, you need money. Now we could make you a nice offer on your aunt's home, and then you'd have the money to live wherever you wanted—Louisville, New York, or Timbuktu."

"I make pretty decent money at the magazine."

"I mean real money. Money that does nothing but sit around and make more money."

Clay's father wasn't as smooth as his son. John Trask *wanted* that land.

"Thank you for the offer, Mr. Trask. I will think about what you've said."

He cocked his head as if her noncommittal answer was of little consequence, but his eyes lost their warmth, and they fixed Shelby with a look that was hardly indifferent. "Think about this," he said, rising from his chair. Mary-Alice got up, too. "Finding your style may not mean expanding your horizons, but coming up against your limitations. Now, my style includes good suits, good bourbon, good cigars, and I've got the money to pay for them. I've got a box at the Derby, I shoot a pretty mean game of golf, and I even read a book now and again." He winked at Clay. "But despite all this, I'll always have a trace of the farm clinging to me. I don't really belong with the country club set despite my Christmas card from the mayor. Now Clay here is not from two different worlds. He fits in entirely, but I know the limitations of my style."

Clay's face suddenly stiffened, and he looked at his father with sadness. "Who gives a damn about the country club set!" he growled. "You're John Trask. You built a real estate fortune from the sale of one farm."

John looked at his son, and for the first time Shelby saw the love between them. They were not alike, nor did they always seem to like each other. But Shelby saw the bond—or perhaps the proper word was chains—that Clay's parents had with him. He was their great hope, the fulfillment of their ambitions.

"Don't misunderstand, Miss Langstaff," John continued. "I'm not bitter, hell no! I've come a long way and Clay is going even farther. But I know my style. Now, you left Louisville for a reason and stayed away for many years. Whatever problems you have with New York, it's still probably more your style than our fair city. What you're looking for may not be here." He dipped his head courteously. "Our offer, however, will always be available." He left the room with Mary-Alice and Cha-Cha following.

Shelby sat very still. What a shrewd old goat, she thought. And he could be right. She probably didn't belong in Louisville. New York wasn't the perfect fit, either. Just where did she belong? Suddenly she felt very tired and alone.

A warm hand gently touched her shoulders. She looked up. "Are you all right?" Clay asked quietly. His face was thoughtful and compassionate as if he understood her confusion.

"Sure. My head is just aching."

He sat down next to her. "I want to apologize for bringing up the offer for your home," he said. "Now was not the time, but my father . . . he meant well."

135

"He has me pegged."

"No." Clay shook his head. "He thinks he has me pegged, but he's wrong."

When Shelby had met Clay Trask nearly three weeks before at Bryant's office, she thought she had him all figured out. Now she wasn't so sure. In fact, she might have been unfair. There was a down side to being a golden boy. The overwhelming expectations of others could trap you. Clay looked like a man who made up his own mind, but Shelby could see that every decision had an emotional price.

"If only our parents, or parental figures, saw us as we see ourselves," she said. "Desiree always wanted me to act like a lady, but I was never a pinafore child. I couldn't seem to satisfy her standards for deportment. I remember when we watched the royal wedding of Prince Charles and Lady Diana on television. As Diana was walking up the aisle, Desiree yelled out, 'Stand up straight!' She also thought Diana's bangs were inappropriate with a tiara."

Clay laughed. "I would like to have met her."

"It's funny. After all these years, I feel like I'm just getting to know her." *But it's too late,* Shelby thought. The missed opportunity made her unbearably sad and brought home even more how alone she was.

With that second sense of his Clay put his arm around her and gently squeezed her shoulder. The gesture was meant to reassure, but the nearness of his body provoked that pleasurable aware-

136

ness of his masculine spell. Never had Shelby met a man so comfortable in his own skin, so relaxed in his male identity.

Here in this opulent, impersonal house, however, surrounded by people who loved him but didn't understand him, he seemed as alone as she felt. She longed to bridge his loneliness with a word . . . or a touch. At that moment, however, she couldn't trust her instincts. Reassurance might not mean desire.

She rubbed the spot where the intruder had hit her. "My head hurts too much for anymore self-reflection," she said. "I'd like to lie down now."

Clay nodded. He led her to a guest suite decorated in shades of gray and mauve. "I'll have some dinner sent up," he said, intuitively realizing that she wasn't up to a family gathering.

Shelby collapsed on the huge canopy bed. Looking around, she thought how different this was from her shabby room at Desiree's house. Everything here matched. The pattern on the bedspread was the same as the one on the window curtains. The rug picked up the main color of the drapes, and matched, in a darker shade, the furniture of the sitting area. The room was new, clean, and unimaginative. It looked like the plastic wrapping hadn't been taken off yet.

For all the shiny veneers, Shelby preferred her room at Desiree's house. Oh, sure, the oak bureau had a telephone book under one leg and the wood floor had stains on it from when she'd dropped some peroxide during her hair-dyeing years, but at least the room had personality! Desiree had crocheted the rose bedspread, and her distinctive needlepoint adorned several pillows.

Shelby hadn't appreciated these gestures as a child, but now the effort Desiree had poured into that bedspread brought a tightness to Shelby's throat. As she drifted off to sleep, she thought that a coat of paint wouldn't hurt her room any.

She woke up for the meal that Mapes brought on a tray. He instructed her to set the tray out in the hall after she was finished if she didn't wish to be disturbed. Shelby got the impression that Mapes considered her not, ahem, suitably genteel.

Well, hell, even she wondered if she belonged in all this grandeur, and yet soon she'd have the money to pay for it. The ultimate irony was that the money would free her to live anywhere, but where, *where* was that? Was it in New York, caught up in a relentless rat race? Was it in Louisville, a place where the past painfully intruded on the present?

She didn't know, and the question troubled her more now than when she arrived in Louisville. Clay had made her think about it. He fitted so comfortably here, and despite his family's relentless aspirations for him, he *had* a family. She had no one.

Shelby unpacked her overnight bag. She'd forgotten, until she saw it, that Clay had packed her black lace nightgown.

Why had he done it? The gown was so sensual,

so intimate. Was he daring her to wear it, and if so, how did he intend to find out? Clay the dutiful son was also Clay the athlete, pushing his body to conquer an opponent or take a woman. During the few moments in his arms Shelby had felt Clay hold himself back. She had thought, especially on Saturday night, that the reason was because he considered her a reporter first and a woman second. This nightgown challenged that assumption.

Packing such a private item could have backfired. Shelby might easily have been offended, but Clay was nothing if not bold. She quickly undressed and slipped the cool, sheer garment over her head. The fabric skimmed down her body until the gown was on, the silky material looking like a second skin. She stepped into the matching black lace panties.

The guest room included a full-length mirror. Shelby slowly walked to it. Staring back at her was not a reporter, dedicated only to a good story. Before her was a woman.

The knock on her door startled her. Then she remembered that she was supposed to have put her tray outside. Quickly she grabbed the thin cotton bathrobe that Clay had also packed. It wouldn't do to have Mapes see her in such lingerie.

"I'm sorry," Shelby said as she opened the door.

"Sorry for what?" Clay asked politely.

Surprised, Shelby only managed, "Um, I forgot to put my tray out. I, uh, wasn't very hungry."

Clay took in her wild, curly hair and the cotton robe that clung to her lithe frame. A hint of a darker color bled through the thin fabric. They both knew that the only other nightgown he'd packed had been a long flowered print. Shelby had made her choice. Now *Clay* looked hungry. He looked very hungry.

Chapter Six

Shelby pulled her robe a little tighter, although the gesture offered little protection from his gaze.

Clay picked the tray up and put it outside her door. Now they would definitely not be disturbed.

"I came to see if you were comfortable," he said.

Not anymore, Shelby thought.

Her silence prompted him to say, "I can go if you want. You look tired."

Actually she was feeling more alive than she had in days. Fear, however, mixed uneasily with that excitement. She wanted Clay, but this was a dangerous fantasy, dangerous because she was never sure how Clay really felt about her. Shelby knew she was the kind of woman who, once in a man's arms, committed emotionally as well as physically to him. She wore her heart on her sleeve. Clay was harder to read.

Tonight, however, she definitely read a smoldering sensual awareness in his eyes. Could she turn him away? "No, don't go," she heard herself saying. "Come in."

Clay entered and looked around. The bed obviously wasn't a good place to sit and chat, yet it loomed like an unspoken dare. Adding to the charged atmosphere was the fact that Shelby was wearing the black lace nightie he'd packed. The image of her in it, or out of it, nearly diverted him from his reason for coming. He finally chose a club chair in the room's sitting area. Shelby sat across from him.

She looked more refreshed, but there were still smudges of fatigue—or was it worry?—under her blue eyes. Shelby came on so tough, but in the past two days Clay had discovered a vulnerable side. Her poignant confession Saturday night of her confusion over whether Desiree loved her revealed a desperate need to know more about this enigmatic aunt.

So tonight he decided to risk telling Shelby some of the details of Desiree's letter. The problem was that once he told her some facts, how could he keep that legendary curiosity from discovering more? Clay decided to start on safer ground.

"I want to apologize again for not telling you about the letters. You had a right to know. And breaking into your house was inexcusable."

His words seemed to relax her. She leaned back in the chair, her cotton robe stretching

142

over her supple figure. "Clay, I said things that night that I regret."

He let out a short, bitter sigh. "Whatever you said, I goaded you to it. Then I insulted you further by calling into question your integrity as a journalist."

"That was still no excuse for what I said."

His eyes searched hers. "Wasn't it?"

"No," Shelby insisted. She sat up, her robe parting a little. "When you responded, you were protecting your family. You must have wondered if my reaction to the disclosure of the letters would be vindictive. A juicy story to revenge an understandable desire for privacy."

That's exactly what Clay had thought, and still wondered about.

She smiled in reassurance, the lamplight falling across the angles of her face, accentuating her high cheekbones and creamy skin.

"There will be no story," she said. "That night I called you some pretty contemptible names. My anger, I thought, was over the break-in and your accusation that I put my work over family. The only problem was . . . you were right. I've put my work over family because I never felt I had one. I made my work my achievement, since I found no connection with Desiree. *Now* I do. I'm discovering so much about her, and I must go on until I know her whole story!"

Alarm bells went off in Clay's mind. This was what he was afraid of. The fact that Desiree and Ford's story might not be for publication didn't lessen Clay's fear that once she had some details, Shelby would have to have them all.

Her determination showed in the flush of her delicate skin, the set of her full lips, and the way she'd hit her knee with her hand when she'd said "whole." Such a passionate, head-strong woman! Clay was drawn to this fire in her personality, even as her unquenchable intensity spelled trouble for him—and maybe for her.

"Shelby, this might turn dangerous. Someone else wants those letters. I've had bolt locks, lights, and a trip alarm installed at the entrances of your house, but your windows are so old and warped that, short of replacing them, you can't get them to lock properly."

Her blue eyes widened. "You've certainly done a lot without my permission!"

"You were assaulted! I'm concerned about you living there."

"I'm not!" she exclaimed, squaring her shoulders. "For the first time I'm beginning to feel at home in that house."

Clay gazed at her defiant posture, but he remembered her body lying unconscious on a bare floor not so long ago. The thought of her being hurt again filled him with fury. "Shelby, if you're attacked again . . ."

"I won't be!" She reached over and put her hands reassuringly on his, but the warm contact only increased his desire to hold her and keep her from harm. "How can I be anything but safe with the security system you've given me? I'm surprised you didn't build a moat."

Shelby laughed, her generous lips parting. She refused to see the danger, but then this stubborn recklessness struck a chord with his own unstoppable nature. Clay found himself admiring her, even as he worried about her.

"Does this mean you want to live in Louisville?" he asked.

She ducked her head a little, her smile no longer so confident. "I don't know. I'm trying to figure out where I belong."

The blaze of her red hair contrasted sharply with the white of the bandage placed over her injury to protect it. At that moment the desire to take Shelby in his arms and show her that there was *one* place she belonged was almost overwhelming.

"Then let me help you," he said. "As long as those letters aren't found, you won't have your answers and the attacker might come back. I realize that you have no reason to trust me, but—"

Shelby stood up, still holding his hands. Her eyes were as bright and clear blue as a summer sky. "I want you to help me find the letters, Clay," she said in a breathy rush. "I came to your match on Sunday to ask you that very question, and to apologize."

Surprised, Clay rose quickly. Face to face, he

saw a glow in Shelby's eyes that conveyed more than just an apology. Only someone observing her as closely as Clay could tell that she was trembling a little. Her robe opened a little farther, and he saw the tender, soft skin of her throat where her lace nightie began. She'd offered just what he'd hoped for, and yet it was this hint of another invitation that excited him the most.

"When I saw you at the game, I thought that perhaps you might consider talking to me again. When you *smiled* at me—" he paused "—I began to wonder, to hope, that I might have a second chance."

"A second chance at what?"

"Knowing you." He took one of her hands and turned it over, palm up. Then he bent and kissed the delicate skin of her inner arm, right above her wrist.

This tender gesture, combined with Clay's unexpected declaration, completely unsettled Shelby. He'd asked not for her land, but for time to know her. Considering his many financial worries, wanting to know her promised no immediate return. The intense way he was gazing at her unnerved her more than if he'd said how gorgeous she looked in the lamplight. Florid speech she would have mistrusted. Those two simple words, however, she couldn't ignore.

And so they were far more dangerous.

Her eyes dropped, and the motion drew her

attention to his body, dressed simply now in faded jeans and a workshirt. The jeans tightly outlined the sinewy strength of his legs and hips. She recalled how easily his hips had twisted to meet any tennis shot and how his thighs had taken the punishment for his lunges and thrusts to hit the ball. Shelby had fantasized about his lean frame at that game. She could never have imagined that forty-eight hours later she'd be standing in a bedroom with the reality of her daydream only inches away.

He cupped her chin and tilted it up until their eyes met. A smile teased his lips as he probed her blue eyes. He had not expected her desire, and she was powerless to hide it.

Shelby prayed that he would say something, anything, but the instant his mouth was on hers, she knew that he'd guessed her true wish.

The first kiss was gentle. His lips grazed her's as if to say that he would not rush her. Patiently he explored the outside of her mouth, spending a maddeningly long moment on her lower lip. Leaving that now-sensitized area, he started a trail of soft nips across her jaw until he found the hollow of her throat. While his lips threatened what little control she had, Clay's hands slid into the warmth of her robe.

Shelby released a low sigh as his hands touched the sheer fabric. So fine was the lace that it was as if he were touching bare skin. Her hands reached for his, but once there, they made no attempt to stop his exploration. The warmth of his fingers on her body sent an involuntary shiver up her back. He circled her waist, his hands connecting around her lithe middle. Then they began to travel upward, stopping briefly to cup her breasts, but then leaving as the pressure of his touch became tormenting.

His fingers lightly rubbed her collarbone before, in one quick motion, they lifted the robe off her shoulders, pulled it down past her arms, and dropped it on the carpet.

Shelby felt almost naked before him. Two flimsy pieces of black silk barely hid her. Clay's hands rested on her shoulders, his fingers playing with the spaghetti straps of her gown. "Lovely," he whispered.

Shelby gave up every pretense of rationality as his arms wound around her back. If only his body, pressed tightly against hers, didn't feel so good. If only his lips, now more insistent with every touch, didn't beckon for more, she might have been able to think. When his mouth finally claimed hers, with an urgency that sent her reeling, she succumbed and welcomed his tongue into her mouth.

No longer tentative, her tongue teased his, luring it deeper and deeper. Clay followed, with thrusts from his tongue bringing a soft moan from Shelby. Far from being surprised by her boldness, he seemed to love it. So she pressed harder, explored more eagerly, with an abandon she'd never known.

As he began to caress her back, she felt a tingling in her spine with every touch. When his hands lowered to her derriere, stoking it in tormenting circles, she felt a lush heat grow low within her.

Far from idle, she explored his taut frame, loving the hidden power beneath the soft cloth. As her hands pressed against the faded back of his jeans, his hips rocked forward in a motion that immediately conveyed his desire. Strong, hard, his body wanted hers, and she reveled in the sensation.

He tore his lips away from hers with a small sigh and headed downward, leaving a searing trail of kisses from her neck to her cleavage. His hand slowly lowered one thin strap until it exposed her breast.

"Ahh, Shelby," he said in almost a hoarse prayer. He cupped her breast as if it were a priceless gem, and then he caressed it as if he knew that she wanted to be touched, not worshipped. Clay knew how a woman liked to be touched, and with just the right pressure to drive her crazy with desire. Shelby lost herself in the pure sensation of his fingers teasing her nipple, making the tender bud ache with passion.

She had to know the taste of his skin. With one hand she fairly ripped open his shirt and discovered the warm expanse of his lightly-muscled chest. Her hands roamed around his upper body, enjoying the hard, sharp planes of a man in his prime. Her lips found his right nipple, playing with it until he groaned in pleasure. Then her tongue tasted his smooth, tanned skin, and she inhaled his unique musky scent.

Shelby could feel his heat. It matched her own, and she wondered how far this would go. How far did she want it to go? Clay lifted her, one hand on the outside of her nightie and the other on the inside under her knees. He walked to the bed and gently set her down. With his hand still under her gown he stroked her left leg and thigh, moving upward until he found the lace trim of her panties.

One finger skimmed the top rim of her panties as his mouth invaded hers again, this time with a hungry fervor that left little doubt as to his intentions. Shelby wanted him. It was simple, elemental. She craved him as she had no other man. Why couldn't their making love be just that simple? Why couldn't she just forget the land, the letters, the gossip, and the fact that they were two vastly-different people? If she let him lie down beside her, if she let his hand slip inside her panties, then she no longer would be able to stop.

Despite the incredible pulsing of her whole body, she realized that making love complicated everything. Did she want to become that vulnerable with Clay? He took off his shirt, the lamplight glancing off the ridges of his chest and stomach. He started to lie down, when Shelby put up one hand.

"No, Clay."

He blinked in surprise, his body stiffening. "You . . . don't want to?" he asked.

Shelby slowly sat up. She adjusted her strap. "It's not that I don't want to. It's just that I feel . . . I feel that it's not right, for now."

Clay exhaled slowly, as if painfully trying to calm his aroused body.

Shelby now knew how to penetrate the cool of this man. She had delighted in his unguarded passion—and then had stopped it.

"Don't be angry."

"Oh, no, no," he said softly, running the tips of his fingers over her cheek. "I'm not angry. I know how tangled things are right now. This might . . . no, it *would* confuse them even more."

In truth, Clay was annoyed with himself. His intention, upon coming to the intimacy of her bedroom, had been to divulge aspects of her aunt's letter. When he realized that this proved too risky, he should have left. Instead, he had let the look in her eyes and his own desire lead him to her bed.

Nevertheless, he wasn't ashamed of wanting her. Smiling, he said, "Let's have no regrets, though. I think you're a beautiful woman. Tonight I just wanted to show you how beautiful."

The flowery words sent off small alarms in

Shelby's mind. Compliments always made her wary, but she couldn't deny that she had no regrets. "I'm not sorry, either, Clay. One day, perhaps. . . ." She caught herself. Predicting the future, especially the future of this relationship, seemed risky.

He nodded, that second sense of his reading her mind. He picked up his discarded shirt. "Good night, then," he said.

"Tomorrow, before I leave, we'll come up with a game plan for finding the letters."

"Sounds good," he replied, but Clay thought that Shelby sitting there in that skimpy gown made the present seem so much more riveting than the future.

He left her and walked the long corridor to his suite of rooms. Ahhh, Shelby. How he'd wanted her tonight, with her wild red hair falling past those creamy shoulders and onto that nothing of a nightie. She'd wanted him, too. Clay felt a surge of happiness at the memory of her hands and teasing tongue. True to form, Shelby hadn't apologized for her boldness. She had, however, stopped them before they took the next step in their relationship.

Too much lay between them for things to get more complicated. Clay knew the chief complication involved Desiree's letter. He'd pulled back from telling her more about it, but how could he casually say that her gentle, demure aunt might have been involved in a crime sixty years ago? How could he mention that Desiree had intimated that she was somehow responsible for the Trask fortune?

Clay walked into his suite and kicked off his shoes. Why kid himself? He'd *chosen* not to tell Shelby these details. She was hardly too dainty to hear some unsettling rumors about her aunt. Hell, she was *searching* for the true Desiree.

No, he withheld this information for the sake of his family. Just as Shelby sought the letters out of love, so did he. Nevertheless, she deserved more than she was getting. By not confiding in her, he risked losing the respect of the one person he was increasingly coming to cherish. Clay felt most himself with Shelby, fun-loving, informal, sardonic. In her honest wit he'd found a kindred spirit.

Perhaps one day, after Grandpa's letters were found. . . . Clay stopped himself from dreaming further. The letters might change everything between them. Whatever they revealed would certainly make an impact on Shelby's feelings for him.

He sighed. At least, Shelby had asked him to help her find the letters. He hoped they would discover them before the intruder reappeared. Who was this mysterious person, he wondered, and what did he or she know about the letters?

As Sherlock Holmes would say, the game was afoot. Clay usually enjoyed competing. He was used to winning. For the first time, however, he was in a race he *had* to win—and not just for his family. Shelby's stubborn insistence on remaining in her home worried him. The letters had to be found before the intruder came back.

Shelby teetered dangerously on the ladder. One more spot and then she'd quit. Clay was coming and she had a surprise for him. Shelby put the roller back into the tray. She stepped down and examined her work. Not bad, she judged. In fact, she'd done a hell of a job, for an amateur.

The idea of painting her bedroom had come during her stay at Park View a few weeks ago. When she'd first arrived in Louisville, Shelby hadn't minded sleeping in a dingy room. Her visit promised to be short, so the depressing walls hadn't bothered her. Now, however, she was in her sixth week, and counting. Despite threats from her editor, and more polite queries from Bryant, she had no immediate plans to leave Louisville. The letters hadn't been found. Thus painting her bedroom had become a more practical consideration.

She looked at the high ceiling and the charming trim around the windows. There was so much character in this house! Every room had its own personality. Unfortunately there were a lot of rooms covering three floors. Shelby was making sure that she examined every square foot.

Where were those letters? The more they looked, the more frustrated she got. Clay had begun to think that Desiree had destroyed the letters, despite what she'd said in her farewell to Ford. Well, Clay would certainly change his tune when she showed him the piece of an envelope she'd found this morning. The faded scrap had Ford's signature on it! Still, she'd uncovered no letters near it, and there weren't too many rooms left to search. After they'd been thoroughly combed, Shelby would have to make some decisions.

The Trasks still wanted her house. Her editor demanded her return. So much that she'd worked for now hung in a risky balance. Yet she procrastinated.

Shelby told herself that the letters prevented her from making a decision. When her pulse quickened at the sound of Clay's car, however, she admitted that he presented an equally-powerful magnet.

From her upstairs window Shelby watched him. She loved the seamless meshing of his hips and long legs. His wavy hair shone in the bright June sunlight. Shelby remembered its thick, lush texture from that electric night at Park View. She never regretted not making love. The timing had been wrong, but she couldn't stop thinking about it.

She heard a door slam. "Damn it, Shelby the

door was unlocked!"

She hurried down the long staircase. "I just unlocked it for a moment to get the mail."

"How can you forget?" Hands on hips, he looked up at her in exasperation. The jade of his cotton polo shirt brought out the green in his eyes. The tight jeans brought out the shape of his behind. Normally his eyes greeted her with warmth and a lingering appreciation. Now, however, his gaze spelled a lecture. She'd hold on to her surprise until his speech about security was over.

"Didn't that cop you made the report to impress upon you to keep your doors locked at all times? And why isn't the trip alarm on?" Shelby chimed in with him when he said, "You know I can't be with you twenty-four hours a day," although the thought was tantalizing.

During the past weeks of their search Clay hadn't tried to kiss her. His restraint was sensible, but the effort only heightened the simmering feelings between them.

"I have to repeat myself because you don't seem to be able to understand one simple fact. The intruder may come back!"

Shelby squirmed a little under his justifiable annoyance. She wasn't as unconcerned about the intruder as she appeared. "I haven't been broken into since, have I? And I tripped the alarm on myself twice!"

Clay walked over to the alarm box. "This is

very simple to operate. You put in your code, press this button, and then you have thirty seconds to leave the house."

"Aha! Simple, you say! Every monitored exit has to be closed if the alarm isn't to go off. If I go out the front door, and the back door is one millimeter ajar, then the alarm starts ringing, and it's loud!"

Clay ignored her criticism, as she knew he would. She felt his attention to her security was a way he could show his feelings for her, since he didn't allow himself to touch her.

"Is the kitchen door closed?" he asked brusquely.

"Yes, why?"

"What is your code?"

"One, two, three, four, five, six."

Clay looked at her. "I thought you were a creative artist."

Shelby shoved him out of the way. She punched in her code. A green light flashed, she pulled a lever, and then the light turned red.

"Now the perimeter is secure," Clay said.

"Thank you, captain. Shall I break out the assault rifles and unleash the Dobermans? They haven't had their daily ration of raw meat, and they're itching to find some."

He couldn't stop a smile. "I may seem excessive, but it's only to counteract your carelessness."

Shelby punched his arm. "You gave me an

alarm system with so many red sensor beams that I feel like a prisoner!"

He shook his head. "You're *protected,* although the windows still bother me. The sensor beams basically cover entrances. These windows are so old and warped—"

"What? You haven't found a system for those?" She snapped her fingers. "I have an idea! Why don't we forget about all those complicated buttons and levers and just put pebbles on the windowsills? That way, if an intruder comes in, I'll hear the pebbles roll to the floor."

He gave her a sideways glance as he cased the long windows in the front parlor. "Why do women quake at anything mechanical?"

Ooh, Clay had touched on a typical male lament. What's more, he knew it. In the past few weeks Shelby had found that Clay not only wasn't intimidated by her quick mind, he enjoyed it. So occasionally he dropped a comment guaranteed to produce a pithy Langstaff retort. His lips were already curled in a near smile, and his eyes danced with anticipation. Shelby couldn't disappoint him, especially since he was so wrong.

"I bet you're one of those men who pride themselves on how quickly they can set up a VCR." She plopped into an old settee.

He sat gingerly on the dusty windowsill. "The last VCR I set up took fifteen minutes."

"Yes, but can you program it?" He started to

respond, but she cut him off. "You're probably one of those guys who insists on repairing his own car, and who cosmically knows that a ping means the radiator and a wheeze means the brakes."

Clay leaned confidently against the half-opened window. "What's wrong with a little mechanical know-how?"

"Nothing, but women have figured out that trained professionals can do it better."

"Oh, yeah?" Clay folded his arms across his chest. The intense summer sun outlined the latent power in his frame. He looked like a cat that had decided to play rather than pounce.

"Now, now, don't get your testosterone all in a lather. I know your tools are just as long as the next guy's."

Clay laughed softly. "I thought size didn't count."

"You're trying to change the subject. I have one more comment. I bet you're one of those guys who is absolutely positive that only he can read a road map."

Clay slipped off the sill. "Now you've hit on one of my true talents and, I think, an innate talent in all men."

"Never been lost?"

"Never."

"Never not found what you wanted to find?"

"That ability is part of the Y chromosome."

"Then where are the letters?"

So unexpected was her question that he momentarily was at a loss. Shelby laughed out loud. God, she loved sparring with Clay! It was always such fun. Lately, however, she thought their verbal jousting served a different purpose, as a kind of emotional substitute for foreplay. As long as they kept the banter light, the submerged, more dangerous feelings between them couldn't surface.

Clay recovered his voice quickly. "Shelby, we haven't found the letters because they might not still exist. Desiree might have destroyed them."

She had been waiting for this moment. "Oh, they exist, Clay! Look what I found!"

Shelby pulled the scrap of envelope from her pocket and handed it to him. She watched carefully as he gazed at it, and was disappointed when he calmly gave it back to her.

"Where did you find it?" His voice seemed to carefully avoid any inflection.

"Under Desiree's bed. It was stuck between two floorboards."

He looked at her sharply. "Were the floorboards loose in that area? Did any come up?"

"Well, no, but that's your grandfather's signature, on the return address isn't it?"

"Yes," he replied tersely, but the admission hurt. His slightly-recessed pale eyes seemed to withdraw even more.

"Then it's from one of the love letters! Why do you suppose it's postmarked Indiana?"

Clay took the piece of envelope and examined it. "I don't know, but, Shelby, all this means is that the letters *existed*. We knew that. You and I have gone over Desiree's room. We missed a scrap of paper stuck between two floorboards, but we didn't miss packs of letters!"

"The letters exist. I can feel it! Desiree said in her letter to your grandfather that she still had them. Look at this place. She never threw anything out."

"We can't look between every floorboard in this house!" He put his hand on her shoulder, but she shrugged it off.

"Well, maybe you can't, but I can. I think you just don't want to find them."

Her accusation brought fire to Clay's eyes. "You're half right," he snapped. "I would rather let the past stay buried, but if it's going to come back and torment my family, then *I* want to find them."

Shelby eyed him curiously. "Why should they torment your family?"

Clay could have bitten his tongue. Shelby still had no idea that the letters contained more than a tragic love story. She thought that his interest sprang from Ford Trask's desire to have his old letters back. Clay couldn't tell her that his grandfather had holed himself up in his room, rarely speaking to anyone. His silence terrified Clay.

"I didn't mean torment," he backtracked, "I

161

meant —"

The telephone rang. Shelby started a little and then looked at Clay sheepishly. She walked to the phone and answered it.

"Hello?" She was silent for a moment. "Hello? Is anyone there?" She slowly hung up the phone.

"Who was that?"

"A wrong number, I think." She seemed lost in thought and then snapped out of it. Squaring her shoulders, she suggested, "Let's tackle the attic."

Groaning, he climbed the stairs behind her. Shelby's new discovery troubled him, but as he followed her, his thoughts strayed to the trim figure in front of him. Shelby's faded cutoffs molded nicely to the tight roundness of her derriere, and left her long legs bare. The heather-blue T-shirt accentuated her small waist. Clay saw the subtle movement of her breasts against the cotton top. He remembered, not so long ago, the feel of her bare breast and touching her skin with his lips.

Clay had wanted all of Shelby that night. The minute her robe had fallen on the floor, he'd had but one thought — to give her pleasure. He wanted to take that determined, serious face and make it glow with satisfaction. Had Shelby not called a halt to their encounter, Clay had planned to slowly, languidly kiss and caress her body until they were one, her long legs wrapped around him. A fantasy half-achieved only makes the dreamer more hungry for it.

As Shelby and Clay reached the second floor, Clay smelled the paint. He detoured to the newly-whitened bedroom.

"Like it?" Shelby asked, obviously proud of her paint job. "It's amazing what women can do."

Clay spoke the appropriate words of praise, but his brain locked on to the fact that Shelby had made an improvement on the house. Why go to the bother unless you planned to stay in it for a while? Shelby refused to make any decision about her land until the letters were found. Now with the discovery of this piece of envelope, she was more convinced than ever that they existed.

Although Clay couldn't show it, that scrap of paper had unnerved him. Seeing his grandfather's signature on an actual envelope postmarked in 1933 made the letters *real* in a way he hadn't felt before. How long would Shelby search for them?

Her indecision was costing his family money. Although construction of the new Tramart was in limbo, architects, planners, and builders were on retainer. Clay's father had wondered why Clay couldn't just put on the old charm and "woo" the land from Shelby. Clay had replied that that approach had gone out with Clark Gable. Besides, he wanted Shelby to choose *him*.

163

Standing in her spiffed-up room, however, he wondered if he wanted her to leave Louisville at all. He teased her that he marked time now as BS and AS—"before Shelby" and "after Shelby." Joking aside, when he was away from her, he missed her. No woman had ever gotten under his skin so completely.

"Planning to do the whole house?" he asked. His tone must not have been as casual as he'd thought.

"Not yet," she replied coolly. Her hands flipped her wild red hair off her shoulders in a gesture both nonchalant and defiant. Shelby would do as she pleased. No pesky intruder and no half-million-dollar offer were going to budge her out of this house before she was good and ready. By God, he liked her nerve. He also wanted to wring her neck. Clay mused, however, that once he had his hands on her soft skin, he'd probably forget why he was angry.

They walked up to the third floor in silence. Just as they were about to mount the attic stairs, the phone rang again. Shelby turned around and raced to the second-floor where there was an extension. Surprised, Clay was right behind her. He arrived to hear her say, "Hello? Hello?" and then slam the phone down.

"They hung up," she fumed. Her face was flushed.

"Are you expecting an important call? Perhaps there's a jack on the third floor."

164

"What? Oh, um, no."

"No, what?"

"No, I'm not expecting a call," she said and then turned back toward the stairs.

Totally confused, Clay followed her.

Upon seeing the attic, Clay decided that Shelby would be eligible for Medicare by the time they looked through all the *stuff*. Did the Langstaffs throw nothing away? There were trunks, rockers, paintings, books, and furniture, all even older than the relics downstairs and twice as dusty. The Langstaffs must have assumed that every item they'd ever bought was an objet d'art. Figurines of dancing milkmaids clustered next to old china dolls and brass sculptures. In one corner was a mounted elk's head. Clay tripped over a saddle and caught his shirt on a coatrack holding a fox stole with the animal's head as a clasp, and sneezed.

"Shelby, a person could get black lung being in here too long."

Even Shelby seemed stunned at the clutter. "I'll open a window." Her efforts backfired. Clay finally had to come over and wrench the rusty window from its frame. But the summer breeze just stirred up the dust.

Coughing, she said, "Well, that's better!"

The shaft of light only made the remembrances of things past seem more strange and mysterious. The older the item, the grander the style, as if the family's spirit had dimmed over the years. At one time, however, the Langstaffs had been important in the community. That era was almost enshrined in the attic.

"Kind of spooky," Shelby said in a rare understatement. "I avoided the attic while growing up."

"Hard to see why—it's so cheerful."

Shelby chuckled. She was relieved that Clay hadn't questioned her about the phone calls. Tackling a trunk, she opened it and then gasped in pleasure. "Clay, look! Ohhh. . . ." Inside were meticulously-wrapped garments of another age. Folded on top was a blouse of white linen with wide leg-o'-mutton sleeves and a turned-down lace collar under which was a satin ribbon that passed around the neck and tied into a bow at the throat. Faded, slightly yellowed, and fragile, the blouse recalled the era of the hourglass figure and tea gowns. Shelby pulled out a felt hat with a wide brim ornamented with a stuffed bird, its wings high in the air. A suit of black velvet came next, its short jacket fitting close to the waist, and its long bell-shaped skirt edged in braid and jet beads. High boots of soft black leather, fitted with a row of buttons, completed the outfit.

Clay walked over to Shelby as she gently extricated all the clothes in the trunk. He knelt to examine her discoveries. Each item was exquisite. Despite the passage of time, the handmade garments were in remarkable shape. Shelby marveled at the variety of colors, decorations, and fabrics. "The waists are so small," she said. "How did women fit into them?"

"With this," Clay said, unwrapping a corset. "What time period would you estimate these clothes are from?"

"My guess would be the late nineteenth or early twentieth century," Shelby replied. "This house was built in the 1890s by my great-grandfather, Bowden Langstaff, who was Desiree's father. His father turned a salt lick into a small fortune," she said proudly. "Desiree told me that this was one of the fanciest houses of its day."

Clay held up a parasol. "Yes, when the Langstaffs were the power elite of this city."

"Yes, we were."

"You seem awfully proud of your ancestors."

"What do you mean?" Shelby asked.

"I mean that you are the leading *opponent* of ancestor worship in the press today. You portray yourself as a rebel, but your roots are very definitely in the class you so disparage. A class, I might add, that you will soon join."

Shelby started to put the pieces of apparel back into their wrappers. "Respecting the past is not wallowing in it. I don't confuse a dead relative's achievements with my own, as the rich invariably do, nor do I expect that having money will change my viewpoint."

In the uncertain light Shelby saw Clay chuckle and shake his head. "You're not the naïve type,

Shelby."

"I'm not naïve," she fumed. "Having money won't make me feel like I'm better than anybody else!"

His smile turned rueful. "No, but you'll be treated differently just the same."

She tried to rewrap a satin evening bag. "Besides, I may not . . . sell the house."

Clay suddenly took her by the shoulders. "I didn't think you were a coward," he said almost harshly.

"A coward!"

"Yes, refusing to deal with this remarkable good fortune means you aren't completely sure how you'll react when you have money. You might not be as hungry for the big stories as you are now. Your professional edge might be gone."

Shelby hated that he could see her so clearly. "You're just worried that I won't sell the house to you!"

His jaw clenched in anger. "That's not true!"

"I don't belong in that kind of life!" She looked at the dresses. "I . . . I wouldn't have belonged in these clothes."

Clay let out a slow breath, as if he'd just realized something important. "Now that's where you're wrong." He released her and picked up an evening dress of pale-green silk. "You do belong in an aristocracy of taste and merit. Having money won't exclude you from it, as you're

168

afraid it might. Having money will let you *choose* where you belong."

Clay had again zeroed in on her private fears. "No," Shelby said softly. "I'll be just as confused as ever." She sighed. "Desiree's legacy has upended my life. I now have more questions than answers."

Clay said gently, "The solution can't be to hide behind these walls like Desiree did."

Shelby's blue eyes flashed. "You always get back to the land, don't you?"

He returned the gown to its wrapper. "Look, I won't pretend that I don't want the land, but I'd rather you sell it to Buzz Mathis than refuse to deal with what this windfall can give you."

"Oh, I intend to deal with it!"

He smiled. "That's my Shelby, a fighter to the end."

How did Clay do it? She'd just begun to feel sorry for herself when a few challenging words from him had her raring to take on the world again.

She held up a pair of bloomers. "I still don't think I'm Gibson Girl material."

"You most certainly are!" Clay exclaimed. "I can just see you leading a suffragette march or being the first woman to wear a bathing suit in public. That era produced strong women. You'd have fit right in."

Shelby warmed to the compliment. "I couldn't have fit in this," she said, pointing to the green dress. Secretly, however, the stunning frock reached through the decades to grab her imagination. Shelby prided herself on not being a slave to fashion. She seldom thought about clothes.

This gown, however, transcended fashion. A draped silk overskirt was fringed with lace, and a wide satin sash emphasized the small waist. The silk sleeves were leg-o'-mutton, full to just above the elbow, then close-fitting lace to the wrist. The high collar completed the dress's hourglass look: tight at the neck, ballooning at the bosom and sleeve, cinching in at the waist, and then gently extending again at the hips until the skirt's bell shape brought the gown in and then out again at the ankles. The dress was ultra-feminine and refined, two adjectives rarely used to describe Shelby. "Probably too small," she muttered.

Clay bent closer, as if he wasn't sure he'd heard correctly. His lips curled slightly. In a swift move he reached for the gown and stood up. The dress unfolded to its full length.

"Now I see where you got your height," he mused. "Great-grandmother Langstaff must have towered over the women of her day. The men, too." Casually he added, "Why don't you try it on?"

Shelby nearly sputtered. "What? Here? In all this dust?"

Clay tried to look guileless, but his cheeky

smile gave him away. "We could leave the attic. I, for one, would be overjoyed."

"No," she said, still eyeing the satin sash, "we have too much searching to do. Besides, I'm not sure I could get into it."

"I'll help you."

His offer brought a smile to her face. Rising, she brushed dust off her knees "I can dress myself," she said, taking the gown from him. "If you'll just turn around."

"Of course. I'll look at this stamp collection over here. Perhaps Desiree hid the letters between the stamps of Madagascar and Mongolia."

Shelby fingered the fragile lace. She felt afraid to test the ancient seams, but the dress kept calling her to try it on. Quickly she shed her T-shirt and shorts and dropped the yards of silk and lace over her head. With growing astonishment, she felt the gown make it past her shoulders, waist, and hips. Great-grandmother Langstaff hadn't been quite as tall as Shelby — the dress didn't reach the floor. Now came the hard part.

"Clay, will you button me up the back?"

He turned around and slowly walked back to her. Shelby saw immediately that he was entranced. Silently he looked at her with a growing smile as if what he beheld was twice as wonderful as he'd expected. His hands reached up, and Shelby thought he was going to touch

171

her face, but he gathered her long hair and wound it on the top of her head.

"Sometimes the past is worth remembering," he said quietly.

"I don't look silly?"

He didn't answer. He just slowly let her hair down, sliding his fingers through the fiery curls. His hands rested briefly on her shoulders before they traveled to the small of her back and began the long process of buttoning her dress. All those buttons, and his warm fingers seemed to glance off her bare back with each fastening. Shelby held her breath when he came to her waist, but the dress strained only a little. She lifted her hair so that he could finish the tight lace collar.

"You need to see yourself," he said. Without waiting for a reply he took her hand and led her out of the attic.

The gloomy third floor seemed bright after the attic. Clay opened up one room after another until he found one with a full-length mirror. "I want you to see how lovely you look," he said, bringing her before the mirror.

Clay wanted her to see how unique she looked, and that her striking originality could be beautiful. *He* was certainly mesmerized by it. The pale green of the gown contrasted beautifully with her red hair and made her blue eyes sparkle like sun on spring water. The dress deserved Shelby's commanding height to show off all its glory. And its perfectly-molded silhouette proclaimed a love and profound respect for the feminine body.

Such a lavish dress, and Clay thought that something of its unabashed extravagance matched Shelby's wild spirit. Neither the gown nor the lady was afraid to be different. Surely Shelby could see that the full impact of this dress was due to her wearing it, and not the gown itself. He saw it.

I am pretty, Shelby thought as she gazed at herself. For the first time she realized that her body had the power to please—or was she just seeing herself through Clay's eyes? He'd always made her feel beautiful, but she'd mistrusted that sensation, assuming that an ulterior motive guided his actions. Mary-Pete's rumor still lingered in her mind. With each passing day, however, the gossip became less and less believable.

Perhaps she just wanted to deny the rumor because of moments like these when he saw something in her that she hadn't noticed before. His attention was so personal, his perceptions so strong that Shelby felt a special connection to him. Granted, he hadn't kissed her since that torrid night at Park View. Yet the way he regarded her now went beyond friendship. Clay stood behind her as she faced the mirror. *Look, look how pretty you are,* his gaze seemed to be saying.

Shelby could see it for herself. She understood now the unique appeal of her body, and she was proud. Whatever happened between Clay and her, she would always be grateful to him for helping her see this.

He put his arms around her. "You are beautiful," he whispered.

"Yes."

He kissed the back of her head and nuzzled his face in her hair. Shelby turned to face him, and in an instant her arms were around his neck, and her lips were pressed against his. The feelings that had been restrained since that night at Park View now broke free.

With mutual impatience their mouths opened to allow the exquisite exploration of tongue and touch. Empowered by her newfound confidence, Shelby let her hands wander over his shoulders and back, feeling the rock-hard play of his muscles. Clay pulled her tight in a hot, suggestive embrace. His tongue made a mad dance in her mouth, teasing her, inflaming her. He dared her to be as wanton as *she* wanted to be. Shelby responded, feeling an acceptance and ease that she'd never experienced before. She was completely herself, and the knowledge brought a mad thought: perhaps the place she belonged was with Clay.

The idea was preposterous, impossible, but his lips seared hers with a force that confused her.

The phone rang. Dimly Shelby heard it, and the old prickle went up her spine. With difficulty she pulled away from Clay. "I . . . I have to answer the phone."

"What?" He looked dazed.

She had no time to answer. As quickly as she could move in that dress, she ran down the stairs to the second-floor phone. Unfortunately the caller hung up before she got there.

Clay appeared a second behind her. "What is it, Shelby?"

"Nothing," she insisted, but her hand was shaking.

"Don't tell me that! You run to the phone like a crazy person. What's going on?"

Shelby started to answer, but the phone rang again. Clay's hand grabbed the receiver before she could get it.

"Hello? Hello!" he demanded. His brow crinkled in confusion. He put down the instrument. "I heard heavy breathing, and they hung up."

Shelby nodded. "Yes. That's the pattern."

"The pattern? How many times has this happened?"

Shelby couldn't look at him. "I don't know. A few . . . several."

"Several?" Clay was astonished. "When did these start?"

"After I was hit on the head. I got a few and thought they were wrong numbers. Lately, however, they've been coming more frequently. I think . . . I think the caller was my assailant. I think he wants to know when I'm not in because—" Shelby returned Clay's gaze with shaky defiance "—because he wants to come back and find the letters. But he's in for a surprise because I've decided that I'm not leaving this house until I find those letters!"

Chapter Seven

"Shelby, you're becoming a recluse!" Clay said. He wiped his perspiring forehead with a linen handkerchief.

"I'm not leaving until I find those letters. Everyone will just have to deal with that."

Two weeks had passed since the disclosure of Shelby's odd phone calls. During that time Clay had tried every ruse he could think of to pry her from the house. She wouldn't budge, determined more than ever to find the letters. She had her food and toiletries delivered. She did her laundry in the ancient washer near the kitchen and hung up her clothes on the backyard line — within earshot of the phone. As long as the calls kept coming, she felt sure that the letters existed. But as long as that damn phone kept ringing, Clay worried for her safety.

Shelby wouldn't leave, and nothing anybody tried worked. Pleas from Bryant, threats from her boss at *Courant*, luncheon invitations from her cousin, Logan, and Clay's constant harping made not the slightest dent in her resolve. She was convinced that understanding the riddle of Desiree would help her make decisions concerning her own life.

Ironically the mysterious caller had also made Clay think that the letters still existed. So he was worried on two fronts.

"I'm beginning to see a pattern," she told him. Out of Desiree's old secretary she pulled a graph with the times of the calls plotted on the days of the week they were placed. "Look, the calls increase on the weekends, so I deduce that the caller must work. I also think that the caller could be a woman. All that heavy breathing made the caller cough the other day, and I *thought* that the cough seemed somewhat high-pitched."

Clay put the handkerchief over his eyes and groaned. "You're analyzing coughs now? Shelby, listen to yourself."

"I sound fine," she said briskly. "I had another extension put in on the third floor. All that running from the attic to the second floor was too much."

"You didn't find the letters there, did you?"

She glared at him. "No."

"Then why—"

"We have to start over. Search the house again. Obviously we overlooked something."

Clay waved the handkerchief as if it were a white flag. "I give up." He started to walk to the front door.

178

"You won't help me?"

Clay turned around. Shelby's anxious face belied her bravado. How could he leave? When he wasn't with her, he worried about her. She was all he thought of these days. Her refusal to leave the house meant that if he wanted to see her, he had to come here. But that was fine by him. The search for the letters had become not just his painful duty as a grandson, but a pleasure. Being with Shelby was the highlight of his day.

Shelby swore that she didn't need protection from this mystery caller. As long as she stayed in the house, the caller, of whatever sex, wouldn't come. Despite this certainty, her face had dropped when Clay started to leave. Was she secretly frightened but too hardheaded to confess it, or was she admitting that she wanted his company?

"C'mon," she said, those blue eyes wrapping an invisible net around him. "I need you."

Did she really? He remembered that magic moment two weeks ago when she'd bewitched him in that antique dress. For a few wild minutes, she'd needed him, wanted him, with eager lips and roving hands. Then the phone had rung, and she'd dashed off, obsessed again with the letters.

He couldn't forget those incredible minutes. Clay didn't know if Shelby needed him, but as long as the possibility existed, he knew he'd come back, and back, to her. He hoped her need for him wasn't merely as a search partner or even a protector. He hoped the need sprang from their enjoyment of each other.

"Okay, what cobweb do you want me to look under? I never saw a house with so many crazy rooms."

Shelby's spirits immediately perked up. The thought of Clay abandoning the search had upset her more than she'd realized. As set as she was with finding the letters, her mind kept returning to Clay and what he'd come to mean in her life. For the first time Shelby had begun to depend on someone other than herself. In fact, how much she'd begun to depend on Clay scared her.

Shelby liked to rely on no one but herself. Growing up with the distracted Desiree had made her self-reliant. As an avowed outsider, she mistrusted anyone ensconced in the privileged class. Money meant power, and power corrupted. Was Clay the exception, or was she just dazzled by his attentions?

Moreover, would money corrupt *her?* Large sums were waiting to be taken, yet her fear paralyzed her. She used Desiree's letters as an excuse not only to avoid the money issue, but also her feelings for Clay. Her mind didn't always function logically when she was around him.

"We're not looking through rooms today," Shelby said. "I have a different idea."

"I'm all for that."

Clay looked as if he'd dressed for another bout with the attic. His jeans and work shirt were so faded and old that his tantalizing frame was outlined in soft pale blue.

Late at night Shelby thought of those strong arms and unyielding chest. Having experienced the taste of his mouth and feel of his hands, she fantasized about a complete consummation. The search brought them together frequently in the privacy of this old house. Clay's presence lifted the difficult task to the level of play. Ironically, however, her obsession to find the letters put added strain between them.

Because of the phone calls, Clay wanted her to leave the house. He accused her of putting her need to find the letters above personal safety. So Shelby couldn't let on that the phone calls did unnerve her. The specter of the intruder reappearing loomed as a price for her obsession.

"I thought we'd look through old photo albums," she said.

"We did that."

"I found some really ancient ones in the cellar."

Clay rubbed his jaw. "This project is sounding better by the minute."

Shelby laughed. "Don't worry, I lugged them to the parlor." She pointed to the moldy leather-bound books sitting on a coffee table. "After that we'll have lunch."

Clay tried to look enthusiastic. "Another Langstaff creation?"

"Mushroom omelets and a green salad."

He walked over to the albums and sat down on the sofa. "Don't forget to sauté the mushrooms this time."

"Are you supposed to?"

His face expressed a mixture of disbelief and dread. "I'll make the omelets," he said firmly.

Shelby smiled. "If you insist." She loved it when a plan came together.

They settled into the lumpy sofa and started to peruse the books. Shelby gave Clay a running commentary on some of the more colorful members of her family tree.

"That's Great-uncle Beaumont, better known as Monty. He owned racehorses in his day. Desiree told me that he got into some trouble once at a track in California for allegedly doping a rival horse with a laxative. The charges could never be proven, and Monty swore he was innocent, but he avoided California for the rest of his life.

"Oh, and that's Grandmother Ward, also known as Bunny. She was from my mother's side, the Shelbys, but Desiree knew her well. She thought Prohibition was ridiculous and used to pretend she was pregnant and smuggle brandy in her "stomach" off the *Queen Mary*.

"And then there's my cousin, Edwards Shelby, also known as—"

"Don't tell me! Ted, Eddie, Ed, Ward . . ."

"Shelb."

Clay exhaled a short laugh as he ran his fingers through his wavy hair. "All these relatives!"

Shelby paused. "Yes, and now it's just Logan and me."

She felt a sudden pang of sadness. A half-gasp, half-sob escaped from her lips.

Clay remained silent, sensing that she needed a moment to recover. Finally he suggested, "Why don't we see what your aunt looked like as a young girl." She nodded, inhaling deeply to calm herself before facing more memories.

They sifted through the albums, which fortunately were dated, until they got to the time in which Desiree and Ford had been sweethearts. No letters were wedged between the pages, but Shelby found photos of Desiree.

"There she is. Wasn't she pretty?"

Clay looked at the photo thoughtfully. Desiree's heart-shaped face was more delicate than Shelby's, but they both possessed full, beautifully-cut lips. "Yes, she was," he said. He flipped a page. "Hey, what do we have here?"

He pulled out an eight-by-ten photograph of people in various uniforms lined up on either side of a stern looking man. Shelby colored. "Um, that's a picture of . . . the help."

"And quite a *large* group they were, too," Clay observed. "Who's that standing in the middle in all his baronial splendor?"

"My great-grandfather, Bowden Langstaff."

"Don't tell me, they called him Bow-wow."

"According to Desiree, he was too proper to ever receive such a nickname." Shelby hesitated. "I always got the feeling Desiree was afraid of her father. My grandfather, Bowden Junior, didn't like him much, either, she told me, and left home as soon as was humanly possible. As the daughter, however, Desiree was supposed to stay until such time as she got married. That was the custom. Bowden Senior died from a head injury when she was a young woman."

Clay glanced at her. "Head injuries seem to run in your family."

Shelby plucked the picture out of his hands. "This was a long time ago. Even as my great-grandfather was posing for this picture, the Langstaffs had lost much of their money due to the stock market crash. I doubt that half the staff remained two years after this photo, and I — "

She paused. A face in the picture had caught her eye — a young man dressed in footman's attire. He seemed familiar, but Shelby wondered how that could be. And yet something about the face and those beady eyes was familiar. She flipped the picture over and read the notations on the back.

She stood up. "I can't believe it!"

Clay scrambled to get up. "What is it?"

Shelby pointed a trembling finger at the smirking man in the picture. "Who is that? Take away the folds of his skin and put some hair on his head, and tell me who do you know who has those eyes and that rubbery lower lip?"

Clay squinted at the faded photograph. Then his face became still. He looked at her. "No."

She showed him the back of the picture with all the names printed on it. "Yes."

He shook his head. "It can't be Mapes."

"It is!" she exclaimed, pulling a picture of Desiree out of the album. "Quite a coincidence, don't you think, that he should have worked for my family, and now he works for yours?"

She stuffed the two pictures under her arm and made a beeline for the front door. Clay gazed at her from across the room. *"You're* going out?"

She picked up her car keys from a table near the door. "I'm going to risk it. My heavy-breather called just a few minutes before you got here, so he thinks I'm in."

"But why—"

"Don't you see, Clay? I have to ask Mapes a few questions face to face! Are you coming? I want to lock up."

"Shelby, no!" Clay raced to her side.

"Why not? Who hired Mapes, anyway?"

"My grandfather, but he—"

Shelby's eyes widened. "Your grandfather? Did he know Mapes from the days of his affair with my aunt?"

Clay seemed stunned.

"You didn't know about this, did you?" she asked.

"Of course not!"

But Shelby wasn't convinced. There seemed to be a war of emotions going on behind those hazel eyes, try as he might to hide it. "Then why are you fighting me on this?" she asked. "Your grandfather said he wanted his letters back. You have an obligation to find out as much as you can about them—and what do you know? A vital source works in your very house!"

185

Her fevered stare told Clay that to protest any more was to convince her that he was holding something back. The fact that he *was* made the situation more dangerous.

Ironically, the piece of information he *hadn't* withheld was Mapes's former history with the Langstaffs. That's because he hadn't known it. Was it so strange that his grandfather would hire a former servant of the Langstaffs? Shelby admitted that they had been let go. People have to work somewhere. But why had Grandpa insisted that Mapes work at Park View? Clay's father had told him that not only had Ford hired Mapes, he'd staunchly kept John Trask from retiring him.

Clay followed Shelby's car to Park View after they made sure her house was locked. With some bemusement he even watched her check the pebbles that she'd put on the first-floor windowsills to alert her to any intruder who might come through that way.

Even at the best of times Shelby was an unpolished driver. She lurched into Park View's circular driveway. The sound of gears grinding told him how excited she was.

He barely managed to catch her before she rang the bell. Her spectacular eyes had darkened to sapphire, and she was breathing deeply.

"How do you plan to handle this?" he asked.

Shelby nearly laughed. "I'm a reporter. I ask questions for a living."

Clay put his hand over the doorbell. "Usually the subject isn't so personal."

186

She pressed her hand so hard on his that the bell chimed. "What are you afraid of?" she asked.

"You, with a story between your teeth."

Before Shelby could respond, the door swung open. Mapes squinted into the bright daylight. "Yes? Oh, Mr. Clay and Miss . . . Langstaff."

"Hello, Mapes," she said in a friendly tone. "Could I talk to you?"

His eyes blinked in confusion. "Talk to me? Of course, what can I do for you?"

"We mean privately, Mapes," Clay added.

The old butler tilted his head back a little in surprise but lost none of his composure. "Why?" he asked.

"Not on the front steps," Clay said. He steered Shelby and a reluctant Mapes through the foyer and into the same pretty room she'd been in before. Clay didn't even stop to acknowledge the hello from his father, who was strolling through the hallway. John Trask noticed the omission, too, Shelby observed, and his brow furrowed in confusion.

After the door was closed, Mapes protested that Mrs. Trask was expecting guests for lunch and he had to oversee it.

"You can slap some burgers on the grill later," Shelby said cheerfully as they sat down on a sofa, Mapes in the middle. She handed him the ancient staff photograph. "Mapes, it has come to my attention that you used to work for my family." She pointed to his youthful face in the

187

photo. "Would you mind answering some questions about that time?"

Mapes examined the picture. After turning it over and reading the back, he looked at Clay. "My past work history is no concern of hers."

Clay said, "Ms Langstaff is interested in some nonwork-related events. They involve her late aunt and my grandfather."

Mapes stared at Clay, who seemed surprised at the butler's reticence. "*I* would appreciate hearing what you can recall," Clay said.

Mapes handed the photo back to Shelby. "I can't remember that far back. My memory isn't what it used to be."

"No recollections?" Shelby said. She showed him a picture of Desiree. "No memory of this woman?"

She put the picture practically under his nose. Mapes had no choice but to look at it. He swallowed, and Shelby thought she detected a nervous tremor in his hands, but that might have been old age.

"Not really, no."

"Desiree Langstaff. She was the daughter of the man you worked for."

"I worked there only briefly."

"How briefly?"

"Um, two years."

Shelby whistled. "That's a long time."

"Not when you've lived as many years as I have. As I said, I can't remember."

She nodded in sympathy. "If it will help, I can

dig up your work record. My family kept everything."

For the first time she sensed real fear. He shifted his large bulk on the couch. "The Trasks have my work history, if you'd like to see it."

"We do?" Clay asked. "I've never seen it. I don't even know what position you had before you came to us, or the name of the agency who placed you."

"It's gone out of business."

"What was its name?"

"I can't remember."

"You can't remember much, Mapes," Clay said, his voice as cold as dry ice, "but in my years of living in this house, you've seemed remarkably alert."

Mapes returned Clay's wintry glare. "Your grandfather has always been satisfied."

This reply brought Clay to the edge of the sofa, where he angled himself so that he was facing Mapes. "And Grandpa's the only one who matters, right? I always thought your devotion to him was touching. Now it seems like you're stonewalling about a time in the past that involved him."

Mapes didn't answer. By now Clay seemed very annoyed. He looked as if he wanted to grab Mapes by his starched shirt and shake him. Instead, he took a deep breath and said, "Mapes, through the years I've come to realize that anything that goes on in this house you know about. So you're well aware that I've been looking for

189

my grandfather's letters for two months. And yet you have deliberately withheld the fact that you *worked* for the Langstaff family and most certainly *knew* Desiree Langstaff at the time she and my grandfather were involved. Why would you do this?"

Mapes pulled at his cuffs.

"Why, Mapes?" Clay persisted.

"Ask your grandfather."

Clay's face paled. "What do you mean by that?"

The butler started to push himself up from the couch but thought better of it when Clay put a restraining hand on one of his shoulders. "I asked you a question," Clay said. "Just how far back do you and my grandfather go?"

"That's for him to say."

"He's not talking."

"Neither am I."

"Oh yes, you will, Mapes. Shelby and I can dig up your work record, and with my contacts and her reporting ability I just bet we could put together a pretty accurate biography of your life."

Tiny beads of sweat had formed on Mapes's long forehead. He started to breathe heavily, the low raspy breath of a longtime smoker. But Clay's gaze was relentless. Mapes wouldn't get out of that room without confessing. Shelby puzzled over the change in Clay. When they had arrived at Park View, she'd been the one eager to grill the old butler. Now Clay was the more insistent.

"I'll save you the trouble," Mapes finally said. "In my youth I had an indiscretion that unfortunately involved the law."

"What was the charge?"

The old butler had a coughing attack. He took out a handkerchief and touched his lips and head. "Robbery."

Shelby gasped. "What kind of robbery? Houses? Banks?"

Mapes seemed offended. "Only the best houses, I assure you."

His absurd pride almost made her laugh. "Oh, I believe you, Mapes," she said. "We know *one* fine old house that you're intimately acquainted with, and it hasn't changed at all since you worked there."

Clay inhaled sharply.

Mapes turned an unpleasant purple. "I don't know what you're talking about."

"I'm sure you do. "You're the one who broke into my house!"

"I did not!" he feebly protested.

Shelby nearly jumped off the couch. "You attacked me!"

"I did not!" Mapes got up. Shelby could see little blue veins on his sweaty head. He was extremely upset, but oddly enough, not at her. "Mr. Clay, why are you doing this?"

Clay stood as well, an angry, incredulous look on his face. "I'm trying to help my grandfather!"

"So am I!"

"By attacking Shelby?"

"I never attacked her!"

"Do you deny breaking into her house?"

"Absolutely."

"Never made odd phone calls to her full of heavy breathing?"

Mapes's posture became ramrod straight. "I may be a thief, uh, have *been* a thief in my youth, but I'm not a ruffian. You accuse me of assaulting Miss Langstaff, robbing her house, and being a pervert in general. But why would I do this?"

"To get the letters," Shelby cried, "or drive me from my home."

In a deadly tone Clay asked, "You'd do anything for my grandfather, wouldn't you, Mapes?"

"No more than you," the old gent retorted.

Clay nodded as if that statement were true. He calmly folded his arms across his chest, but Shelby could see that he was barely, just barely keeping his temper. "Well, I committed a crime for my grandfather," he said quietly. "Have you?"

Either he'd hit on the truth or Mapes finally lost it. The butler shook a bony, trembling finger at Clay and shouted, "May I remind you that the only person *caught* so far breaking into Miss Langstaff's house is you! And if you hadn't been such an amateur at it, no one would ever have known about the letters. You didn't help your grandfather. *You* put him in jeopardy!"

Clay grabbed Mapes's lapels. "I'm tired of riddles! What are you and Grandpa hiding from me?"

"Nothing that shouldn't remain silent."

Clay nearly lifted the old butler up by his livery. Shelby touched Clay's arm. He released Mapes, who pulled at his collar for more breathing room.

Shelby was completely confused. "Mapes," she said before Clay could speak again, "you're implying that somehow I'm out to hurt Ford Trask. I'm not. I'm merely trying to find some harmless old love letters."

His eyes were like dark granite. "Harmless?" He uttered a cold, mocking laugh. "Since when has love ever been harmless?" He quickly opened the door to the hall and exited.

Clay started after him, but Shelby grabbed his arm. "What did he mean by that?"

Clay's face was flushed. "Shelby, let me go!"

"Wait! What did he mean?"

Her last words were to thin air. Clay had released her hand and run from the room. She followed, but to her surprise he dashed toward the back of the mansion, not to the front door where Mapes usually manned his post.

She lost him in the maze of stately rooms, made all the more confusing by the fact that the Trasks decorated in one style—pre-Civil War Southern with a dash of rococo. The house was steeped in gilt, or was it guilt? Why was Ford Trask so afraid of her finding the letters? What did Mapes mean when he said they could put Ford in jeopardy?

Shelby could understand wanting something so

private, but sending your grandson and butler to commit burglary bespoke a more frenzied need. She had no doubt that Mapes had broken into her house to find the letters. She even thought she detected in his raspy breath a similarity to the heavy breathing of her menacing phone caller. Shelby was less sure that he'd assaulted her. Mapes, with his massive, lumbering body, would not have been able to sneak up behind her as her intruder had. But if he hadn't hit her, who had?

Shelby didn't want to consider the other possibility. Clay had been at the club when she'd been hit—or had he? His game had ended before she left. Shelby didn't seriously think Clay capable of violence, and yet . . . he'd nearly hit Buzz Mathis at the Roses Ball and Mapes might have been in jeopardy himself if she hadn't been in the room. The enigma that was Clay Trask continued to perplex her. How far would he go to protect his family? Shelby broke out into a sweat despite the air conditioning.

Mapes's participation in pursuing the letters had obviously been a surprise to Clay. One hand didn't know what the other hand was doing, a fact that enraged Clay but didn't faze Mapes. Shelby suspected that the old butler had a history with Ford Trask, a history that she felt certain included her aunt.

The bottom line was that there was more to Ford's letters to Desiree than a shattered love affair. This begged the question of how much of the story Clay knew. He'd accused Mapes and his

194

grandfather of holding out on him. Shelby was beginning to put nothing past Ford Trask. She even suspected that a man who needed oxygen could make a decent raspy phone call. Clay's anger, however, seemed to be not that he didn't know anything, but that he didn't know *everything*.

Shelby vowed to find out the truth. She walked out onto the back terrace. The steaming July sunshine matched her emotions. Just when she'd started to trust Clay, she'd found another piece of the puzzle that he'd withheld from her. She looked around. Where had he gone? In the distance she saw the swimming pool and tennis court. Then her eye caught the greenhouse. She knew immediately that Clay hadn't been looking for Mapes, but his grandfather.

As she neared the structure, she saw two figures through the windows — Clay and his grandfather! Quickly she ducked to the side of a tree and angled herself so that she could see them clearly but yet they couldn't see her. For a split second she considered storming into the greenhouse and finally confronting the man who held all the secrets. But she doubted that such a move would force the Trask patriarch to bare all. No, she decided that for the moment more information would be gleaned by watching the meeting between grandson and grandfather.

In Ford Trask's face she saw Clay's true heritage. Both had the same sharp lines and rugged simplicity of men who weren't afraid to get their hands dirty.

Clay knelt in front of his grandfather, who sat in a wheelchair. The old man shook his head and seemed to be talking rapidly, his hands jabbing the air.

Clay appeared to be pleading with his grandfather. He caught hold of Ford's hands and brought them to his chest, making what seemed to be a declaration. His face was etched with worry and strain. He spoke as if every word hurt him.

Suddenly Clay's expression turned to fear. Ford's body began to jerk in small spasms. Clay yelled to someone, and a nurse ran into the greenhouse. Quickly an oxygen mask was pulled from a tank attached to the back of the chair, and Clay fastened it onto his grandfather. Shelby held her breath as the old man clutched the mask, his eyes closed.

Slowly Ford's hands let go of the mask and dropped into his lap. His body relaxed, sagging a little. Shelby couldn't even believe what she was seeing. Desiree had never meant her farewell letter to be lethal. Clay said that she forgave Ford. The past was past.

Wasn't it?

Shelby stifled a sob, her eyes locked onto the motionless patriarch. She wondered if the Ford-Desiree story had finally ended.

Then Clay smiled slightly. He rubbed Ford's arm with his hand as the patriarch opened his eyes. Ford seemed dazed, but after a minute became more alert. The mask was removed. Ford's nurse checked his pulse, gave him a pill, and began talking to Clay. They were obviously talking about Ford, who emphatically shook his head several times. The nurse left.

Shelby felt herself breathe again. She found that she'd been clutching a low branch of the tree she'd been hiding behind and released it slowly.

Clay's face regained its composure, but Shelby saw his hand fumble reattaching the mask to the oxygen cylinder. Ford looked at his grandson beseechingly. Clay seemed torn and, at first, didn't make eye contact. He pulled a comb out of his pocket and put Ford's thick white hair back into place. Then he used his handkerchief to wipe the glow of perspiration from the old man's face. He readjusted Ford's cardigan and retied his grandfather's bow tie. The tie had a wild, snazzy pattern that clashed with the more sedate cardigan. In a gallant gesture Clay took his handkerchief and ran it back and forth over Ford's shoes.

Clay finally gazed into his grandfather's face, then gently kissed Ford's brow. At the touch of his lips the old man clutched the strong arms of his grandson. They held on to each other for a long moment until Clay broke away and quickly left the greenhouse.

He walked fast, head down, his hands jammed into his pockets. Shelby followed a distance behind. Crowding him right now seemed insensitive, but she still needed to talk to him. His restless steps took him around the huge house and through a small glade of poplars and elms. Her lack of familiarity with the grounds caused her to lose Clay behind some willows. Hot, irritated, and more confused than ever, she trudged in the direction of the house.

"Why are you following me?"

Clay's sudden appearance made Shelby start. Not only had he detected her, but he'd doubled back and surprised her. His tanned face only made his pale eyes seem more distant, and bleak. "You ran from the room, Clay. I was worried."

"About me?"

"Yes."

"Is that all?"

His abruptness rattled her. He held himself stiffly, as if any physical contact would break down his resolve.

"No, I'm still confused by our conversation with Mapes."

"Not to mention my conversation with my grandfather. I picked up that you were following me not far from the greenhouse. A piece of advice: if you're going to tail someone, wear something to camouflage your red hair. I saw it through some tree branches."

His tone was damning. "I didn't hear your conversation in the greenhouse," she said evenly.

Relief registered briefly in his eyes, but then they resumed a cold, almost numb stare. "Too bad."

Shelby was getting angry. "I *did* see it through the windows."

Clay showed no surprise. "Ever the intrepid reporter. It must have been like a bad silent movie."

"More sad than bad. Why were you so upset?"

His gaze chilled. "We were discussing *Bambi*."

"Clay, what's the matter with you?"

"Nothing!" he snapped. The small explosion threatened to break his composure, but he held on. "I have to go now, Shelby," he said almost formally. They were near the circular driveway. "We can look for the letters tomorrow."

So odd was his behavior that Shelby didn't know whether to shake him or put her arms around him. "Perhaps we could discuss them today," she said. "I have a million questions."

"Of course you do. The problem is that you think I have all the answers."

"I know you have some of them! I know you've been withholding information from me!"

For a moment his facade cracked, and Shelby saw such acute pain that her heart trembled for him. "It's an epidemic," he said. Then the mask reappeared.

"What does that mean, Clay? What is your grandfather hiding?"

"I'm afraid I have an appointment now." He walked to her car and opened the door. "I'll call you."

She had to shake him out of this strange detachment. Every ounce of energy he possessed seemed to be focused on staying calm, controlled, and silent about his grandfather. Whether the effort gave him this haunted look or the information he'd just learned in the greenhouse, she couldn't tell. All Shelby knew was that she couldn't leave without hearing some answers.

She walked up to him and slammed her car door shut. "You won't call me. We won't 'do' lunch. I want to know *right now* what those letters are really about."

"I don't know."

"You do! You've known all along!"

She'd hit a nerve. Clay grabbed her by both shoulders. "What do you expect those letters to do for you, Shelby? Will reading about a time long ago explain your insecurities or the huge chip on your shoulder? You're obsessed with the past, and I don't just mean Desiree, but with all the snubs you received at Breck Prep. Move on, Shelby! Take the money for the land and get on with your life! *Forget the letters.*"

His grip was like a vise. "I can't! They could help me."

"Did they help your aunt? She lived in the shadow of those letters her whole life. My grandfather hasn't been the same since he knew they existed. Those letters hurt, Shelby, they don't heal, and if we don't let the past lie, they'll come back to hurt us . . . if there is an us."

She searched his tormented eyes. "How do you know all this?"

Abruptly he released her, turning away toward the house. Shelby blocked his path. "I want the truth," she insisted.

200

He blinked as if the concept was new to him. "The truth?" His laugh was short and bitter. "The truth isn't always the clear-cut beacon of light you'd like to think it is. Your life is a holy mission to expose the truth."

"And your life is a holy mission to evade, camouflage, and protect! White lie here, shade the truth there, until you can't call your soul your own!"

Clay's shirt was blotched with perspiration. It clung to his chest, showing the heightened breathing of an astounded man. "My soul is just fine, thank you," he said with some difficulty, "but it's nice to know that when I misplace it, you'll be there to remind me."

Shelby knew she had gone too far. "Clay. . . ." She reached out to him, but he backed away. Turning to his convertible, he quickly slid in and started the engine.

"Clay, wait!"

He began to back up. Shelby couldn't let him get away. Running beside his car, she wrenched open the passenger door and jumped in. She miscalculated the distance, however, and not all of her made it into the Mustang.

"Shelby!" Clay lunged to grab her before she tumbled out of the car. She felt a hand grasp the back of her jeans and pull her into the Mustang's soft interior. The open door swung back, nearly closing on her foot.

"You fool!" Clay raged. "You could have been hurt." He stopped the car. Drawing in short breaths, he let go of her jeans. For a brief moment his face reflected a profound relief that she was all right — and then the mask reappeared. "Get out, Shelby."

"I'm sorry for what I said."

He revved the engine. "I need to be alone."

"I'm afraid for you to be alone."

"I'll go get Cha-Cha."

"Damn it, Clay, let me apologize!" She touched his cheek with her hand. The mere contact was like a burn on his skin. He gasped and the car shot forward, pushing Shelby back into her side of the car.

Barreling out of Park Lane, Clay turned in the direction of the river. Picturesque country lanes whizzed by as the Mustang went faster and faster. Shelby had enjoyed Clay's daredevil driving once. Now he seemed to take chances recklessly. What had happened in the greenhouse to provoke this?

"Clay, slow down," she shouted, fumbling for her seat belt, but he just accelerated. The beautifully-crafted car was only too happy to oblige. Fewer and fewer houses appeared. Shelby smelled burning rubber as he turned onto River Road. She wondered where they were going and if they would get there. Sweat trickled down her neck.

Clay made a sharp turn off the main highway. Dust flew as the car adjusted to a dirt lane. The swirl of dust and gravel got into her eyes, stinging them and blurring her vision. The world seemed to be in fast-forward, chaotic and terrifying. Clay remained like a machine, pushing to the maximum another machine.

He made another sharp turn, but this time the dirt and gravel didn't hold the car like asphalt and the car skidded in circles. Shelby screamed until the Mustang came to an abrupt stop. When her eyes cleared, she realized they were parked in front of a log cabin.

Throwing off her seat belt, she sputtered, "Why didn't you just let me die at Park View?"

Clay sat very still with his eyes closed. Far from scaring him, the wild ride seemed to have worked out some of his demons. "You wanted to come."

"I want to live."

A hint of a smile passed over his face. He opened his eyes. "This is my house."

Shelby looked at the unpretentious dwelling. "I thought Park View. — "

"Is where I live, yes. This is where I call my soul my own."

Chapter Eight

Clay silently let Shelby in, and she glanced around. The cabin was the essence of simplicity and craftsmanship. Not exactly rustic — it had electricity and modern plumbing — but the atmosphere embraced an uncluttered serenity. Two bedrooms opened off the living-dining area. The smaller one functioned as an office, with a computer system and fax machine. The large bedroom, however, featured a brass bed covered in a quilt of reds, golds, and greens. Built-in bookshelves lined the living room walls. Comfortable furniture in muted prints surrounded a stone fireplace.

An understated home for an unpretentious man, except that the computer system and fax machine gave Clay away. He yearned for simplicity, Shelby thought, but couldn't completely escape from the world. Conflicting currents ran through him.

His jeans and work shirt matched the easy ambience, but when he looked around the living room, there was a touch of defiance on his face, as well as affection. "I love this place," he said.

"It shows."

"My parents have never seen it. When I told my father I was building a cabin, he just stared at me. Finally he said that there was some furniture in the basement of Park View that might go really well in a cabin. I checked and the pieces turned out to be the ones we used to have in our old farmhouse. The hutch in the dining room and the brass bed came from there."

"A link with the past?"

Clay caught her eye. "Yes," he said firmly. "Although I don't believe in living in the past, I think it's false to pretend that you don't have one. My parents want to forget our past. That's why they've never come here."

Shelby had been waiting for the right moment to bring up the letters again. "Clay, my future will be shaped by the past. What I do with Desiree's land, what I do with my *life* is bound up with the past, and that means the letters."

He sighed and moved restlessly to the stone mantel. Clay didn't seem angry at her so much as he seemed troubled by a situation he'd lost control over. And Clay was a man who expected to be in control.

"I don't understand how finding them can hurt us," Shelby continued, sitting on a small sofa, "or why your grandfather would be in jeopardy if we did. He asked that we find them, didn't he?"

Clay ran a finger over the mantel, and came up with a smear of dust. He frowned. "This place needs a good cleaning."

"Didn't he?"

205

"Yes!" The word rang out like the crack of a whip.

"Then why do you want me to forget them?"

Clay put his fingers to his temples and rubbed them. "The mistakes that two people made sixty years ago can hardly help us today."

Shelby sat closer to the edge of the sofa. "You said at Park View that the letters could hurt us, if there was an *us*. I'm confused as to how an affair in the past could impact on our, uh, friendship in the present."

He looked directly at her now. With anxiety in his voice he asked, "Is that all we are, just friends?"

He'd put her on the spot. Why was she the one to have to admit how much she needed him! If she confessed her growing love, would Clay run from her intensity, or, worse, would he secretly rejoice that he'd gotten her to fall for him? A woman in love will give her man anything. "I don't know," she said softly, "are we?"

Without hesitating, he said, "*I* don't think so. At least, I hope our relationship is more than just superficial or . . . some brief summer romance. I want more." His broad shoulders relaxed a little. This was something he was sure of.

Shelby was unprepared for Clay's candor. His eyes showed none of the evasiveness they'd contained all day. Did he really care? Shelby had never admitted that she needed someone or belonged to another human being. The step terrified her, even as his declaration produced a joy she'd never experienced.

She stood rather unsteadily. "If you feel that way," she said, going to him, "then we can face what those letters contain together."

Now she'd put him on the spot. Clay was far more comfortable admitting that he cared for Shelby than admitting that the letters frightened him. She, who attacked the world so directly, would never understand the lies and evasions that had surrounded the letters from the first moment the Trasks had become aware of their existence in Desiree's farewell message to Ford.

Clay knew he had to protect his family, but he began to wonder at what cost. Shelby meant more to him than any woman he'd ever met. Fundamentally they connected. Two loners, driven to dispel the labels that society had ascribed to them, had found acceptance only in each other. He needed her, but he couldn't let his family down, either. Especially not now, when he was convinced that the letters would hurt them. Clay knew what he had to do.

He took her hands in his. Shelby's blue eyes, so open now with hope and eagerness, gazed at him. Her strong face seemed fragile. "Shelby, those letters don't belong to us. They belong to my grandfather. If we find them, let's just give them to him and move on with our lives."

She blinked, surprised at his response. Her eyes, which had been so warm and happy a few seconds ago, now seemed wary. "No, the letters belong to me, too, at least technically. I told you all along that I wanted to read them so that I could finally understand Desiree."

As gently as he could, he said, "What if you don't like what you find?"

Her face flooded with color. "What is it that you're not telling me? What did your grandfather say in the greenhouse?"

Clay couldn't confide his deepest fear, but he could tell her a remark made by his grandfather. "Grandpa said that anyone finding the letters should have love in their hearts because, after reading them, they would see two very human, flawed people. He hoped they would forgive."

She stared unseeing at the mantel. "Forgive what?"

"I don't know."

Her face turned a darker red. "You do know! You've known all along."

"That's not true!"

She dropped his hands, as if suddenly they'd burned her. "Can't you for once just tell the truth!"

"I *am* telling you the truth! My grandfather said those very words."

Shelby let out a short, bitter laugh. "Rather convenient words, too, wouldn't you say? You know that I had a rocky relationship with Desiree. I have trouble forgiving her for the way I was raised. Now you lay on me that I shouldn't read the letters unless I already have forgiveness in my heart!"

Clay couldn't let her harsh words go unchallenged. "You think I'm not worried about what the letters could tell me about my grandfather?" he asked. "Of course I'm anxious, but you want more from these letters than the story of a failed romance. You want them to explain why Desiree

208

couldn't love you. You want a clear-cut reason so that, unequivocally, you will know for the rest of your life that it wasn't *you* she didn't love. You want the letters to validate yourself as a human being, to be a quick fix for shaky self-esteem, and they won't be able to do that!"

All the color drained from Shelby's face. She felt her body go numb as if an unexpected shock had knocked out all feeling. Without thinking, she stepped back but caught her foot on a small stool. Stumbling, she reached out, but the man who shot out his strong arm to her was the last person she could ever accept help from again.

Because Clay had seen through her. He now knew that the real Shelby was a scared insecure woman whose pretense of being a sophisticated, tough cookie was a facade. Never had she been so furious with anyone for seeing her so clearly.

"Don't!" she cried as he tried to help. Grabbing the arm of the sofa, she recovered her balance. Then she bolted for the front door. Seconds before she reached it, the door slammed shut and the solid frame of Clay Trask stood in her way.

"Shelby," Clay whispered. "I'm sorry."

Her body trembled. She felt she couldn't breathe, and yet deep down she knew that her rage wasn't at Clay, but directed toward his perceptive words. Clay had been blunt, but oddly enough, the truth produced a strange sense of freedom in Shelby. No longer would she have to wonder and worry over a relationship with Clay.

For how could he love her when he knew how fragile and insecure she was?

"It seems you can read me like a book." Her voice sounded brittle, dry, and dead.

With his body tensed against the door, Clay sighed raggedly and shook his head. He started to reach out to her but stopped short of contact. "You've pretty much got *my* number," he said, "but I thought, with each other, the truth wouldn't stop us from . . ."

"From what?"

His chest rose in one steadying breath. "Caring for each other."

Shelby emitted a short, disbelieving laugh. "Look, Clay, the game is over."

"Game?"

"Sure, the I-care-for-you-despite-your-flaws game."

His hazel eyes locked onto hers with a fierce insistence. "It's no game, Shelby. I do care."

She waved away his declaration, even though his words were what she most wanted to hear. "I'll sell you the land. Isn't that what you want? Once the letters are found, I'm . . . not sure I want to stick around."

He scanned her face in confusion. "This isn't about the land."

"Isn't it?" She could no longer meet his gaze. Swallowing thickly, she said, "Sometimes I feel like I'm in a triangle, with the land as your true love and me as a temporary mistress, fun for a while, useful even, but much too imperfect for real love."

"I'm not romancing the land out from under you!" he said, echoing Buzz Mathis's accusation at the Roses Ball.

But Buzz had known the score, Shelby thought. Clay belonged with Louisville royalty. His consort should be from among the fold, like Heather Scott.

She looked into that handsome face and knew why the truth hurt so badly. "Can't you, for once, be honest with me?"

His frustration boiled over. He took her by the waist, wrapping his hands around her slim middle, and pulled her to him. "How can I convince you?"

Shelby couldn't bear the closeness to his body, the look of yearning in his face. Didn't he know that he could stop this performance? The land was his. He needn't keep breaking her heart. She reached to push his hands away and accidentally knocked a small antique lamp off a table near the door. Its colored glass shattered into dozens of pieces.

"Oh, no," she cried.

Clay didn't even glance at it. "It was a piece of furniture," he said. "Your land is just a plot of earth. These 'things' don't mean as much to me as people. Do you want to know what means a lot to me?"

She shook her head violently. "Don't say it."

"You on a sunny day."

"Oh, please!" She twisted to break his hold, but his warm hands, so gentle yet so firm, would not let her go. In his eyes she saw that he could not let her go. No other sensation topped being held in his arms. Why did the pleasure have to be mixed with so much pain?

"I want to leave!"

"When I'm finished." His face was filled with the determination of a man who needed to set the record straight, no matter what the cost. Shelby could feel the quickening of his body, the faster breathing, the heightened heartbeat. "You think I don't always tell the absolute truth," he said. "You're right. I don't."

Shelby's eyes widened.

"I'm not a perfect person! I'm not nearly as good a human being as you. Don't shake your head. It's true! You never compromise. If something is right, or the truth, then you tell it like it is. Your life is simple. You've made it simple by deciding what you stand for and never deviating from it. Do you know how much I admire that? No, you probably don't, since that's not what this is all about."

He loosened his hold, but now Shelby was riveted. "Oh, no?" she asked.

"No," he declared, shaking his head. Several strands of his wavy mane fell over his forehead. He looked like some wild Viking out of a Norse legend, but he didn't seem to be about to tell her a fairy tale. No, his liquid eyes burned into hers in a way that made every nerve in her body tingle. "This is about something more fundamental. You know you're a good writer, a good person. The validation you want is as a woman, and I don't think Desiree's letters will cover that subject. So let me."

Clay's face showed a conviction, an intensity that startled her. Her heart pounded in anticipation.

"You are . . . beautiful. Yes, you are! Perhaps

212

it's not a traditional beauty, but it's something more rare. Your beauty is an extension of your vitality, your humor, your soul. Oh, don't get me wrong. I love your red hair, and your legs go on for days, but . . . but what makes a man sit up and take notice is the force of your personality coming through your pretty face. The beauty you so admire is transitory. The beauty I see each time I'm with you is timeless, and will only become richer with time."

If she had written the words, Shelby could not have come up with a more moving declaration. She was momentarily silenced by his eloquence, overwhelmed by his fervent tone. "I . . . I want to believe you," she finally said haltingly, "more than anything."

He dropped his hands to his sides. He wouldn't keep her there by force. But now she couldn't leave.

"Fair warning, Shelby. I'm not perfect. I never was—not in high school, not now. You never compromise, but then you're accountable only to yourself. I'm not, and what's more, I don't want to be! I want to let people into my life. I want you in my life."

He touched her arms again, but his hands were gentle now, tentative. "So you've been warned. You know my flaws. But I'm asking you—and if you believe anything, believe this—I'm asking you to let me in. We belong together."

He said the one word that terrified her. "People don't belong to people!" she cried, instinctively moving away from him toward the interior of the room.

213

Clay followed, his eyes insistent. "But that's the only thing that makes sense in this world! Buildings crumble, paper fades, but what happens between a man and a woman endures. I feel alive with you. You can't convince me that you don't feel special with me."

His face was now inches from hers. "I don't," she lied.

His arms stole around her back, gently, inexorably drawing their bodies together. He rubbed his cheek against hers and then kissed the tender spot where her neck met her jaw. "Yes," he whispered, running his tongue over the outside of her ear. He found the soft lobe and lightly sucked it.

"You want my land," she said faintly.

"I'll tell you what I want."

His mouth captured hers in a kiss that marked his claim on her. The kiss was rough, unsubtle, as if he were demanding that she admit her need for him. Shelby responded with an abandoned invasion of his mouth, her tongue stroking the soft, wet interior. More than simple desire, her kiss was also a confession of a risky vulnerability. She did need him, she did want him. As if tongue and touch could convey her feelings, she kept her lips melded to his while her hands wantonly stroked his back and behind.

Sensing the change within her, Clay's hands began to explore the willowy contour of her body. Every sensitive curve was touched, as if he were afraid he might be parted from her slender frame without experiencing every inch. The heat from his roving hands penetrated her damp cotton T-shirt and worn, faded cutoffs. The air was hot, so hot, and their bodies needed relief.

His fingers skimmed the waistband of her shorts. It would take but seconds for all her clothes to be shed. As Clay rubbed one breast, enticing the soft mound to almost sinful pleasure, a tormenting heat began to build in her very center. Shelby wanted Clay inside her, to be one with him, to belong.

He understood her so well. She'd never belonged, not at school, not with Desiree. Now the man of her dreams was offering her warmth and love. And she'd been cold such a long, long time.

Could she take the risk? Her mind said no. Joining any group, even if the group was one person, had always scared her. What if the rules weren't her rules? What if they didn't like her? As an outsider she would never have to compromise or be rejected. She would also be alone. Could she take the risk of letting Clay Trask into her heart? A tiny voice, growing joyfully within, whispered yes.

She would believe that Clay cared. Her body trembled with the satisfaction of that decision and the pure excitement of his touch. His hands stroked her derriere, pulling her hips against the tight front of his jeans. She rhythmically responded to the thrust of his pelvis, the sensation stoking the fire in her body.

Even as she fantasized about the big brass bed, she couldn't help remembering that Clay had warned her. He wasn't perfect. Others' needs sometimes came before his own. The question was whether her needs meant more to him than his family's. She still didn't know what had happened in the greenhouse. Clay still remained a mystery to her.

But all that blurred by the thrill of his touch. Shelby became disconnected from the cabin, from Louisville, from the planet. She didn't immediately hear the sound of the door being flung open and a booming baritone shouting, "Clay! What the hell do you mean leaving Park View when—"

John Trask halted at the sight of them. They stopped kissing, but their bodies were entwined in a way that could only suggest future intimacy.

John's rich store of words temporarily failed him. "Oh! Uh, I beg your pardon," was all he could muster. He pulled a handkerchief out of the pocket of his golfing outfit and wiped his flushed forehead.

"Why, Dad," Clay said calmly. "This is a first."

Shelby politely disentangled herself from him.

John dabbed at his goatee. "Uh, yes, I needed to talk to you, and your grandfather said you might be here."

"And I am. Welcome. You remember Shelby?"

"How do, Miss Shelby," he said. "Whooee, it's hot in here! Son, don't you have an air conditioner?"

"There's a unit in the bedroom," Clay said. "Would you like a tour?"

John snorted. "No, thanks. All this looks mighty familiar." John walked up to his son and bent his head, whispering, "Look, I would have called you, but you always turn that damn phone machine on. I need you back at the house. Paw-

paw's not well. You know I can't handle him."

Clay nodded. Turning to Shelby, he said, "We should go back. You know my grandfather had that spell in the greenhouse."

John's head snapped up in amazement. Clay put his hand on his father's shoulders. "She knows, Dad. She saw it from outside the greenhouse."

This explanation did little to dispel the look of alarm that flickered across John Trask's face. But he recovered his affable composure enough to say, "My father has a heart condition."

"I'm sorry," Shelby said.

Clay gave her a sidelong glance of apology, but somehow the glow of the afternoon had faded.

Before John got into his Cadillac, he said, "You are coming to the Tramart company picnic next week, aren't you? We'd be pleased to have you."

Clay had not mentioned it. He looked vaguely irked but said, "You are invited, Shelby. We ask our friends as well as the employees. I didn't bring it up since you'd refused to leave your house."

Shelby conceded that this was a fair assumption, but he'd tried every other ruse to pry her out of Desiree's house. Why not a company picnic?

She became curious. "I think I can make it."

John smiled. "Be prepared for some good eating. We're going to have barbecue, a good half-side of beef, mind you, roasted over a spit with Mary-Alice's own special barbecue sauce, and ribs, hamburgers, hot dogs—"

Shelby and Clay laughed. "I'll pick you up next Saturday morning at eleven," he said to her.

They got into the car and snapped on their seat

217

belts. Clay started the engine. "Try not to fly this time," she cautioned.

"I'm behind the slowest driver in Kentucky."

Shelby smiled. As she sat back in the bucket seat, she thought that just a few minutes before, *she'd* been flying high and wide on a jet stream of passion.

Saturday morning dawned hot and sunny. Luckily a thunderstorm the day before had cleared the air of a punishing humidity. The ground had dried, the sky was blue—a perfect day for a picnic.

Shelby viewed the upcoming Tramart picnic with interest. So far that summer she'd only heard about Clay as a leader of men. She hadn't actually seen him with his employees. Shelby judged people by how well they treated those less powerful than themselves. She found that the most charming magnate could be the most ruthless robber baron. Today would fill in another piece of the puzzle that was Clay Trask.

This picnic, however, wouldn't suddenly make him an open book. A part of Clay still eluded her, but Shelby was powerless now to pull away from him. Ever since last week when she had finally believed that he cared, she'd floated in a daydream. The letters, still unfound, mattered less. Her world centered on the present.

The odd phone calls had persisted, but not with the same regularity. Shelby assumed that Mapes must be on a tighter leash, and she wondered if Clay had had anything to do with it, or whether his grandfather had issued an order to the old butler.

As positive as she was that Mapes had been her intruder, Shelby still felt a risk in leaving the house. She hadn't left it since the Saturday before when she'd rushed out to talk to the Langstaff's former employee. Since there was no evidence that someone had broken in during that time—not one pebble had fallen from a sill—she decided to go to the picnic with Clay. Shelby had a hunch today would be special. The feeling had been brewing all week.

Clay had come to the house twice to help her search, and more of his sweetness showed with each visit. He brought a hand-picked bouquet of summer flowers from Park View the first time. During the second visit he had a gourmet meal cooked in her home by the chef of one of Louisville's finest restaurants.

Despite these romantic gestures, Clay seemed almost shy around her. Shelby sensed that he'd rarely been as honest or open as he had that day in the cabin. Confessing vulnerabilities was risky business for a man like Clay. Now he seemed to be waiting for Shelby to make the next move. The picnic, she decided, would be the catalyst. Some secluded spot would do, with tall oaks offering privacy and shade. She'd fan the fire that had been smoldering since that day at the cabin.

For this event she chose a white eyelet sundress, which set off her light tan and red hair. The dress also promised a welcome coolness in this hottest month of the year. At the stroke of eleven Clay's Mustang pulled up in front of the house. Shelby was so happy to see him that she rushed out of the house, tripping the alarm.

"I hate this thing!" she yelled over the earsplitting alarm. She reset it after Clay came laughing through the doorway. The smooth way his body moved always caught her eye. At the sight of her sundress he whistled and twirled her around. He wore tan slacks and a light-blue polo shirt with a button pinned to it that said Tramart Employees Make Better Lovers.

Indicating the slogan, she asked coyly, "What about the owner?"

"That's a given."

"We shall see," she retorted.

Clay's eyes widened in surprise. Then he smiled wickedly. Shelby very nearly suggested skipping the picnic.

"Won't some people take offense at the button?" she asked after they locked up her house and headed east in his car.

"Not this crowd," Clay assured her. "Be prepared for a good time."

Shelby assumed that the picnic would be at some park. To her surprise, Clay drove to Park View. As he pulled into Park Lane, she saw in the distance a Ferris wheel looming over lots of red-and-white striped tents.

"Clay, what did you do?"

He grinned with boyish excitement. "Every picnic has to have a theme. This year I decided on an amusement park. I found a traveling fair and rented their rides and booths, plus I came up with some booths of my own that I put together."

"This is besides the barbecue?"

"Oh, that's my father's province. He insists that every man, woman, and child leave our picnic barely able to waddle."

John Trask was a man of his word. Besides the variety of red meat and pork, he offered barbecued chicken, grilled sausages, potato salad, french fries, onion rings, tossed salad, fruit salad, ice cream, cake, cookies, pies, several kinds of candy, homemade lemonade, soft drinks—and tofu burgers. "My idea," Clay said.

By noon the picnic was in full swing. Shelby wandered with Clay through the gaily-festooned stalls and tents, watching people win stuffed animals, scream with delight on the rides, and eat themselves into a stupor. Clay kept promising her that a "big event" would happen at one o'clock.

Shelby estimated the crowd to be at least several hundred people, and Clay seemed to know most of them. Many approached him to say hello. Charlene, from the housewares department of the South Louisville store, showed him her new baby and thanked him for the generous maternity leave. Bud, from automotive, assured Clay that his Tramart Employees Make Better Lovers button was accurate. Mrs. Bud, well into her sixth month of pregnancy, confirmed it.

"I told you these were fun people," he said as he ate some salad. Shelby had guiltily passed over the tofu burgers and settled on a barbecued pork sandwich with french fries, pecan pie, and a tall lemonade.

"A fi-i-ine picnic!" roared John Trask as he sat down at their table. His florid face beamed with satisfaction. After calling out "hidy" to various people, he turned his attentions to his son. "Everyone *loves* the barbecued beef and pork," he teased, "despite all those hormones or whatever that you say is in it."

Clay smiled. "Dad, you put on a mean picnic."

"Enjoying yourself, Miss Langstaff?"

"I've gained three pounds and I haven't finished my pie yet."

"Good! Good!" John boomed. "A few extra pounds never hurt anyone."

He tapped his frosty glass on the wooden table. Shelby suspected that it contained something stronger than lemonade.

"Uh, son, what's this surprise I'm hearing about?"

Clay wiped his mouth with a paper napkin. "You'll see."

"Is this going to besmirch the family name?"

"I'll do my best."

John snorted. "Well, the fair is your idea." He got up. "You will excuse me, Miss Langstaff. I must see to our guests."

After John left, Shelby said, "I want to ride the Ferris wheel."

Clay glanced at his watch. "I'm afraid we can't just yet. It's one o'clock, time for the big event."

She hastily finished her pie. "I'm as curious as your father. You've been alluding to it all morning."

He took her hand, and they got up from the table. "I think you'll love it." They walked to a central booth, which was covered by a huge tarp. Several men joined Clay. He walked up a staircase at the side of the booth. Someone handed him a microphone, and he issued the following challenge, "Fellow Tramart employees! Are you ready to do something for charity and fulfill your secret dream at the same time? Then step right up!"

The tarp was pulled off, revealing a glass-enclosed tank of water, with a small platform over the water. Attached to the platform was a lever with a large red disc fastened to the end of it. A sign on the tank said Dunk Your Boss for Charity. A roar erupted from the crowd. People abandoned other booths to see what was going on.

"What we have here," Clay continued, "is a dare. We—that is the managers of all the Tramart stores—dare you to hit that big red disc next to the tank with a baseball, which will plunge your boss into the tank. For every try, Tramart will donate ten dollars to charity, and for every hit, we'll quadruple it!"

People applauded and whistled. Clay waited for the crowd to settle before speaking again. "I guess you're wondering who'll go first," he said. "As president, I feel I should set an example. C'mon, who'll try and dunk *me?*"

He tossed the microphone to another man and climbed onto the platform over the tank to the cheers and hoots of the Tramart populace. Shelby couldn't believe he was doing this, but the crowd loved it. No, they loved *him.* He didn't set himself above them, yet their affection also contained respect.

With some persuasion the crowd was encouraged to back up to the agreed-upon distance. "Let the game begin!" Clay shouted, and a few brave souls lined up. The first man, a lanky fellow, missed all three of his shots. People groaned at each miss.

A second man stepped up. "Barney, you can do it!" Clay encouraged him, but Barney's aim barely got the ball near the mark. "I can't sit here all day," Clay complained, "I have raises to give out."

Everyone laughed, but the next two contestants proved just as inept, whereupon a rather hefty woman came to the throwing line. "Okay, now we're getting serious," Clay said. "Hattie, do your duty."

Hattie flexed her shoulders, assumed the position of a major league pitcher, and zinged a fast ball straight into the circle, which touched off the lever connected to the platform. The platform trembled for one instant and then collapsed, dropping Clay into the tank.

A deafening cheer greeted his watery descent. Clay quickly rose to the surface and climbed the ladder at the side of the tank. As he stepped out, he started to laugh his deep, infectious laugh which made everyone join in. Once on solid ground dozens of people shook his hand. The platform was reset, and the manager of the East Louisville store cheerfully dared his employees to dunk him.

"My hero," Shelby said, kissing Clay lightly on the lips. The cool, wet sensation on her dry mouth tantalized, as did Clay's body, so completely outlined by his wet clothes. Shelby wanted to escape to the little stream where she'd once seen him planting

224

a tree. There he would shed his wet clothes, and she would quickly remove her sundress and lingerie. Under a willow his cool body would meld with her hot one, the difference in temperature adding exquisite friction between their skin.

She couldn't get him alone, however. So many people came up to him as they walked to the main house.

"Come in while I change," he said softly. "My parents are entertaining some friends. The food will be more pretentious, but the punch will definitely have some punch."

Shelby demurred. "Thanks, but I think I'd rather go on some rides. I'll meet you at the Ferris wheel after you change."

Mapes's fleshy face glared at her as he opened the front door for Clay. Just as quickly he closed it, producing a gust of cool air.

"They should have sent *you* to obedience school, not Cha-Cha!" she exclaimed. As she walked over to the amusement area, she glanced back at the house. At a second-floor window Shelby thought she spotted someone sitting in a chair, looking out at the festivities below. She guessed that the solitary figure was Clay's grandfather. Why didn't he come to the picnic? It seemed strange that the creator of the Trask fortune, and thus all the fun today, wouldn't partake of it.

The merry-go-round brought back good childhood memories for Shelby. Children screamed in delight as the horses went up and down.

After eating some cotton candy, she ambled to the Ferris wheel. Clay wasn't there, but she figured

225

he'd been waylaid by friends and employees. Shelby waited for a few minutes, and when he still didn't show up, she decided to walk toward the house.

She caught sight of him just outside the house. As expected, he was surrounded by people. Smiling at the tumult, Shelby started to walk over when she stopped cold. The butterscotch streaks in one well-wisher's hair seemed awfully familiar. Clay said something, and the woman threw her head back in laughter.

It was Heather Scott.

Chapter Nine

Shelby felt cold, even though the temperature hovered in the mid-eighties. What was Heather doing here? Who had invited her? Shelby remembered that it was John Trask, not Clay, who had first told her about the picnic. Heather was very social. Perhaps Mary-Alice Trask had extended an invitation to her. Shelby hoped so.

She had put to rest Mary-Pete's rumor about Heather and Clay. Since that day at the cabin, when Clay had declared his feelings for her, Shelby had chosen to believe he cared, that she was special to him. So why was her mouth dry all of a sudden?

She leaned against a giant poplar, grateful for its shade and privacy, as she watched Clay talk to the crowd around him. Heather seemed to be getting no special treatment. Clay spoke to everyone, giving each person a few personal words. Shelby imagined that every employee walked away feeling some special bond with him. He had that effect on people. He'd had that effect on her.

Shelby usually played it safe with her feelings. These she kept hidden against pain and betrayal. Then the windfall from Desiree had forced her to examine her life. The results had been this glorious summer when her heart had ruled her head. She'd finally risked intimacy with Clay. Surely her heart couldn't be wrong.

Mary-Alice Trask joined the crowd and whispered something in Clay's ear. He shook his head and pointed toward the Ferris wheel where Shelby was to have met him. Mary-Alice and Heather exchanged a warm embrace, and then Heather and Clay left — in different directions. No kisses were exchanged, just cordial farewells.

Shelby sighed. Why was she jumping to conclusions strictly from Heather's mere presence? Even if Mary-Alice hadn't invited Heather, Clay could have invited her as an old friend — especially if that's all she was. Shelby realized that her problem had less to do with trust in Clay than with trust in herself. She had to break her reporter's penchant for suspicion and cynicism. At moments like these a terrible urge filled her to escape back into the safety of her career, where being a lone outsider made sense.

But that would be taking a step back for her as a person. With a man like Clay there would always be women like Heather. Shelby would have to face them all with confidence in herself and in Clay's feelings for her.

Suddenly a voice coming from behind her shattered her reverie. "Shelby? Hey, Shelby!"

Someone waved a hand in front of her face. "Logan?"

Her cousin bowed slightly. "At your service." Decked out in khaki linen, he was the picture of wrinkled elegance. "You seemed to be off in a daze. Perhaps dreaming of the square dance contest that's about to start?"

Shelby smiled. "That did sound interesting. Are you go — Hey! wait a minute, Logan . . . what are you doing here?" Logan Langstaff at a Trask picnic?

He grinned. "I was hoping to dunk Clay, but that woman beat me to it. Actually, my date was invited. Why are you here?"

"I came with Clay."

Surprise registered on his deeply-tanned face. He ran a hand through his blond hair. "So it's not just business between you two."

"Well . . . some business, some pleasure." Shelby still felt tentative about declaring more. "Are we being gossiped about?"

He shrugged. "Clay's a big deal in this burg, and you're something of a celebrity. So . . . there is truth to the rumor?"

Shelby was tired of rumors! "Perhaps."

Logan lit a cigarette. "I guess it would *have* to take love to pry you from that house."

He winked as he said this, but Shelby detected a slight wounded tone. He'd called her several times over the last few weeks to invite her to lunch or a day at the track. She'd turned him down, saying she *had* to find the letters. His invitations had been

229

sweet and well-meaning. Their last conversation had occurred yesterday when Shelby admitted that the letters still eluded her. Now Logan saw that she apparently could leave the house without having found them, and for a man who wasn't even family.

"I'm sorry if I haven't been more social."

"Ah, no problem," he said, blowing a puff of smoke into the air.

"As for love, well, you know how cautious I am." Actually, she was thinking of how to politely leave Logan and run to meet Clay at the Ferris wheel.

"That's good, Shelby, because Clay—"

"I really have to be going," she interrupted.

"Oh, don't go," Logan said, dropping his cigarette on the grass and grinding it out. "I want you to meet somebody."

"Logan, I—"

"Somebody special to me, Shelby. Clay can wait a few minutes." He turned and motioned to a woman standing near a popcorn cart. Heather Scott waved back and joined them.

Shelby was astonished. She cast a disbelieving eye when Heather walked up to Logan and put her arm around him. But Shelby's mouth dropped open when she saw Logan lean down and kiss Heather!

"You'll catch flies that way," Logan said gently.

After snapping her mouth shut, Shelby managed to say, "Oh . . . I'm just surprised."

"A lot of people will be," Logan said. Then,

with the first totally-genuine, non-cynical smile she'd ever seen on his face, he turned to Heather and said, "I was telling Shelby about us."

Heather looked like a fair flower of the South in a lacy garden party dress. "Now, sugar," she said, lightly tapping his hand with her lace fan, "we said we weren't going to announce anything just yet. This has all happened so fast."

"I can't help it."

"Well, try, honey, try." Her slight criticism was muted by the dazzling smile she gave him. It seemed sincere. Shelby's mouth nearly dropped open again. Could Logan be the "blond" in Heather's life?

"Um, how long have you two been going out?" Shelby asked.

"Since the Roses Ball," Logan answered. "We sort of discovered each other there."

Buzz Mathis had been Heather's date at the ball, but he wasn't nearly as handsome or charming as Logan. Buzz did have a lot of money, a quality that Heather used to rate highly. Then again, Buzz had treated her like a possession at the ball, something to lord over Clay. Logan obviously adored her. Perhaps Heather had discovered that she needed affection more than money. If so, Shelby had underestimated her.

"Yes, we met," Heather said, "and the rest is history!" She laughed and gave Logan a quick kiss. He held on to her lips and kissed her so deeply that Shelby suspected their tonsils were tingling. She didn't know how much of Heather was genuine, but Logan certainly was in love.

"Oh, cousin, I'm so happy for you," Shelby exclaimed, after he'd come up for air. Logan released Heather and gave Shelby a quick hug. She refrained from giving Heather an embrace. Instead, she quickly kissed the air near Heather's face. Heather responded with another air kiss, and the two of them looked like insincere socialites, which at least Heather was. Shelby genuinely delighted in the news.

"So what are your plans?" she asked.

Heather hesitated, then catching Logan's eye, she threw up her hands and laughingly said, "Our situation is somewhat fluid right now, but we hope to be engaged by Christmas."

Engaged? Shelby's spirits soared. Heather didn't joke about marriage. Logan *was* the blond in her life! Mary-Pete's rumor had been accurate—just with the wrong blond!

"What are *your* plans, Shelby?" he asked. "Have you decided who you'll sell your land to?"

"Mmm, not one hundred percent," she replied. "The Trasks made a handsome offer, which I'm seriously considering."

There was an awkward silence. Obviously Logan had told Heather about the value of the land and Clay's interest in it. Heather's reaction was intriguing. The former Prom Queen pursed her lips in annoyance. She let out a short, agitated breath as she glanced at Logan, who struggled to appear unconcerned. He did care, however. His rivalry with Clay showed in the pensive way

232

he tapped a cigarette out of the pack and lit it.

Shelby could understand why he didn't want her to sell Langstaff property to Clay Trask. Logan still resented Clay for building the first Tramart on the land Logan was forced to sell because his warehouse business went under. Heather, however, had no negative history with Clay. She must love Logan, Shelby decided, to take his side against Clay.

"Well, it's your land," Logan said. "You can do what you want with it. Tell me, when do you expect to make a decision?"

"Soon."

"Soon? How soon?"

"I don't know." Shelby was anxious now to join Clay. "Look, I'm very happy for you both, but I must be going."

"Are you leaving the picnic?" Heather asked.

The idea was appealing. Shelby had intended all day to find a private place with Clay, away from rumors and prying eyes. "I think so," she replied.

Logan kissed her cheek. "Goodbye, then. But, Shelby . . ."

"Yes?"

He paused, and she saw the rare emotion of worry crease his brow. "Take it slow," he pleaded, "and I don't just mean deciding about the land."

She knew he meant well, but his suggestion irked her. "I'm a big girl, Logan. I can take care of myself with Clay Trask."

Logan shrugged in defeat, and Shelby thought that this would be the end of the discussion. To her astonishment, Heather touched her arm.

"Listen to Logan," Heather said. "We've all been dazzled by Clay at one time or another."

Irritated now, Shelby replied, "If you dislike him so much, Heather, why are you here?"

"I don't dislike him as much as I understand him," Heather replied calmly. "It doesn't pay to get on the wrong side of Clay, and there *are* two sides."

"Just remember that you can call me," Logan insisted, "day or night. Don't do anything rash."

"You worry too much," Shelby said, beginning to step away. "I came to Louisville with no expectations. How can I be disappointed?"

Logan waved, his cigarette leaving gray trails. "Be careful, honey."

"I will, I will!" She said these words to empty space, for she had already turned around.

With more unfettered happiness than she'd ever experienced, she fairly ran to Clay.

The sudden smile on his face warmed her more than the intense summer sun. She could hide in that smile and never be lonely or unhappy again.

"Where have you been?" he asked. "I was beginning to worry."

"Why is everyone worried about me?"

"Who else is worried?"

"Oh, no one, really," Shelby said, not wishing to bring up the lovebirds. "Sometimes I think concern is just another word for sour grapes."

Clay took her hand. "You've lost me."

Shelby couldn't help herself. She flung her arms around Clay in front of all the passersby. "No, I think I've finally found you. And I'm not ever letting you go."

For an instant he didn't seem to understand, or maybe he just didn't believe the new light in her eyes. Then his expression changed, as her loving face convinced him.

Embracing Shelby, he squeezed her so hard that he partially lifted her off the ground. The elation that his face reflected found full measure in her heart. If a moment of pure joy could be crystallized and kept for all time, this would be that moment for Shelby.

She belonged with Clay. Shelby saw this clearly now, with no insecurities to cloud her judgment. Clay accepted her completely, with no regrets that she wasn't wealthier or prettier or more ladylike. The essential Shelby suited him just fine. They were a match for drive, wit, guts—and passion. On this elemental level Shelby most connected with Clay. He enjoyed her strength, her boldness.

He was such a loving man. All day Shelby had witnessed his affection and commitment to each Tramart employee. He wasn't some robber baron who set himself apart from his workers. Her prejudice against the rich had blinded her to his goodness. The only complaint about his style had come from Logan, who nursed his own grudge against Clay. No, the man gave of himself, and Shelby now experienced the thrill of being his sole focus.

"Let's get out of here," she whispered.

He glanced around. People were watching. One took a picture. He slowly released her.

"I don't have to stay," he said, as if convincing himself. "My father is here, and the picnic will go on into the late afternoon. We can come back."

"What makes you think you'll have the energy?"

His eyes danced with anticipation. "So this is to be an experiment?"

"Of endurance, yes."

He sighed dramatically. "Oh, the pressure!" He grabbed her again and lifted her off the ground.

"Save your strength," she said, laughing.

"Where would you like to go?"

"How about the cabin?"

"You read my mind."

During the drive to the cabin Shelby thought about the step she was about to take. She wanted Clay, but making love to him would expose her last vulnerability. For as direct as she was, that moment before Clay became one with her would be the ultimate risk. She'd never thought of sex as sport. There always had to be more between her and a man. But with Clay the stakes were higher. Once her clothes were shed and she lay naked beside him, all her emotions would lie naked, as well. And what woman, at that moment, doesn't wonder if it's all for real?

Clay drove that fine line between topping the speed limit and getting a ticket. He looked at Shelby. She possessed a quiet radiance. Only the slight pensive set of her lips made him worry that she was having second thoughts. He had none.

No, Clay banished thinking for the afternoon.

He refused to worry about the picnic or the Tra-marts, and he definitely blocked musings over his family. Those fears would destroy the happy feeling that coursed through his body. And wasn't he entitled to one afternoon where his needs, and Shelby's, came first?

The cabin was shuttered and locked tight. "I'll turn the air conditioner on," he said as he opened the front door. Stepping in, however, convinced him that the cabin needed a few minutes to cool down. And he was hot enough.

"Would you like to take a shower?" he asked, quickly turning on the unit.

Shelby would have liked nothing better, but she felt suddenly awkward. "Um, would you like to take one first?"

"No, no, you go first. I'd like to tidy up," he said, starting to make his bed. Shelby wondered why he bothered, but she smiled as he hastily picked up books, socks, a T-shirt, running shoes, and an empty bag of pretzels from his floor.

"Maid's day off?" she inquired.

He dumped everything into a closet and closed the door. "I'm the maid."

Her hand shook a little when she accepted a thick towel. Closing his strong fingers over hers, he said, "What is it?"

"I feel like it's the first time."

Her confession brought an unexpected response from Clay. His eyes, which had radiated an electric desire for her all the way from Park View, now showed a sudden shyness. "In a way it is for me, too," he said. "This is the first time I feel that a woman is going to bed with just me."

Shelby felt a dizzying spiral of pleasure go through her. "I won't be long," she promised.

The bathroom was a good size, with a small table where she put her purse, sundress, bra, and panties. With some difficulty Shelby pinned her hair up with a couple of hairpins she remembered she had in her purse. After turning on the shower, she tested the temperature and got in.

How good the thundering spray felt! She quickly soaped herself washing a very hot day from her body. An old love song came to mind, and, as was her penchant, she began humming it. Caught up in such a good mood, she began singing the lyrics. She didn't hear the door open, but she most certainly heard an off-key chorus of her love song.

"Clay!" she cried, clutching the shower curtain around her and peeking out. "What are you doing?"

"A medley. You *were* asking for a duet, weren't you?" Shrouded somewhat by the billowing steam, Shelby still knew that Clay was naked.

She couldn't take her eyes off his body. His tanned skin promised a smoothness she couldn't wait to touch. She pulled the curtain to one side, sending a spray of water onto the bathroom rug.

His eyes kissed every curve of her lithe body. The glistening water accentuated the valley between her breasts and the round full mounds with dewy peaks. He let out a sigh, of gratitude and appreciation.

238

And then he was in the shower, his vital presence crowding the narrow bath. The first touch of his naked body against hers shocked Shelby with its immediate intensity.

Water streamed over his taut frame, highlighting the light ripple of muscle in his chest, arms, and abdomen. "I want to see all of you," he whispered.

Confused, Shelby wondered how she could be more exposed. He reached behind her head and pulled out the pins, setting free the tumble of her long curly red hair.

Shelby's lips parted in a smile. Taking full advantage, Clay's mouth covered hers with a kiss that left no doubt as to his urgency. Using deep, voluptuous strokes, his tongue urged her to let go, give in to this wet celebration of taste and touch.

Helpless against this invasion, Shelby melded her body against his hard torso. The erotic power of his kiss stunned her. She matched his questing tongue with a lusty probing of her own. His hands roamed over her, lingering on the slick curves and valleys of her back and derriere. When one hand teased her inner thigh, a low moan escaped her.

He pulled back, leaving her panting against the tile wall. "I don't want to rush," he said in a voice barely audible above the pulsating water.

He picked up a bar of soap and lathered up his hands. Then slowly, with maddening gentleness, he proceeded to massage the scented suds over her body.

Starting with her shoulders, he used circular motions to slide his hands past her throat and down to the upturned swellings of her breasts. With infinite tenderness he massaged the sensitive orbs, cupping them and admiring their fullness with his fingers. The friction against her nipples sent sublime tingles through every pore.

"Oh, Clay," she murmured, her eyes half-closed.

He laughed softly, obviously pleased at her reaction. His own body showed signs of arousal, and Shelby marveled at the thought of his manhood filling her totally, completely.

Wherever his hands caressed, they left a trail of fire that couldn't be extinguished by the spray of water. Moving downward, Clay's hands skimmed over her stomach before stopping at the juncture of her thighs. Unbidden, Shelby parted her legs, and Clay probed the entrance to her silken core.

Shelby nearly cried out. The unbelievable pleasure caused by the skill of his hand made her dizzy. Clay steadied her to keep her upright. "Too much?" he whispered in her ear.

"No, no," she managed, "but let me wash you, and then let's get to bed. If I don't have you in me soon, I'll go crazy."

"You drive me crazy," he said in a throaty growl.

Quickly Shelby lathered her hands and began the most intimate touching she'd ever done. Clay wanted her. The invitation was evident. As she encased his manhood in her fingers, stoking it, he gasped in a kind of ecstasy. She was pushing him to the edge. She knew it but couldn't stop.

With a low curse he crushed her to him again. Their fevered passion threatened to be consummated in the steamy pulse of the shower.

But Shelby needed more than a swirling wet world for this special union. She wanted to see his naked splendor in full daylight. She longed to sink into a mattress under the driving rhythm of his body.

"Not here," was all she had to say. Clay turned off the soothing water and wrapped her in the thick towel. He found one for himself, but his haste still left glistening spots on his marvelous form. Almost as in a dream she let him lead her to his bed.

The room now registered a comfortable coolness, but after the shower the air conditioning seemed chilly. Sensing her discomfort, Clay eliminated the problem. He discarded her towel and placed his own warm body on hers as she reclined on the bed.

This was the moment she'd fantasized about, but unlike dreams she wouldn't wake up from this one. Clay was real. His delight in her body was real. She couldn't imagine anything more right. With nary a thought she bid her safe, career-obsessed world farewell. A miracle, a physical miracle was occurring that nevertheless touched the emotional core of her being. Feeling the unbearably sweet friction of his body on hers, and as his caresses became firmer and more insistent, Shelby abandoned all doubt and fear.

He kissed her again and again, leaving her mouth to tantalize the velvety skin of her inner thigh, so near the pulsing core of her body. He moved to her stomach, rubbing his cheek against the supple skin before his questing mouth ascended to her breasts. Nuzzling between the soft mounds, he rubbed against each curve, tasting her, inhaling the scent of her charged body. Then his mouth lifted to focus on her nipple. With a gentle suckling, then a maddening tease of his tongue, they became almost painfully erect peaks.

Shelby melted under his consummate artistry, and she matched him touch for touch with a brazenness she'd never known. Nothing was held back in their naked heat. They sought and savored the hidden secrets of each other's body. Within her feminine depths Shelby felt an exquisite pressure demanding release.

His fingers tested her wet center.

"Oh God, Clay!" she gasped, nearly writhing in desire. "Wait, I've got to—"

"Shhh," he said, shifting his body. One hand drew protection from the night table. This simple action impressed Shelby. For once a man had taken the responsibility. She felt safe with Clay. She belonged to him.

When he entered her, the sheer physical sensation tore a cry from her lips. Clay murmured her name over and over as his thrusts created a mutual rhythm of fire. Their bodies were one, and in her soul Shelby knew that this moment had fused their hearts, too. At least, she felt the bond. No longer was she on the outside looking in for love.

This discovery, combined with Clay's driving hardness, threatened to overwhelm her. She felt the spasms begin as Clay finally gave in to his own need for release. The climax brought cries from both of them.

Her life had now changed, forever.

In the moments after Shelby lay satiated under Clay's body. She could feel his still-ragged breathing as they both relaxed from their sexual intensity.

She smiled in a drowsy reverie. Goodbye, uptight cynic, she thought. Farewell, captive of the past. The future promised to wipe out all former hurts.

Clay gently removed himself and went to the bathroom. At once Shelby missed his body. She wrapped the quilt around her for some artificial warmth, but it wasn't the same. There would never be any heat like the fire generated by Clay's magnificent body.

She heard him leave the bath, but he didn't immediately return to the bedroom. Pouting, Shelby called to him.

"Keep your pants off," he laughingly called back. When he finally returned, he was carrying a bottle of imported champagne and two tulip glasses.

"What every cabin needs," she quipped as he sat on the bed with the bottle. He was still naked but obviously very comfortable in that state. He popped the cork and poured two glasses of the bubbly. Giving her one and holding up the other, he said, "To us."

"To us," she repeated, believing those words with all her heart. She sipped the champagne. "Mmm, there is something to be said for money."

He slid beside her, and she spread the quilt over their bodies. Sitting against the brass frame, he put one arm around her. "You're beginning to see the virtue in filthy lucre?" he teased.

"I'm beginning to see that money means choices — opportunities even."

Clay set his champagne on the night table and turned to face her. "This is new."

"Yes," she said, "but the admission is overdue. I've been so prejudiced all my life against what money does to people. I assumed that no one could really handle it and remain a human being." She gave a wry grin. "I was quite firm in my conviction."

"Really? I hadn't noticed."

She chuckled. "But then I met you, and my ideas took a spin. Were you the exception to the rule, or was the rule faulty from the beginning?" Her voice grew serious. "I resisted my feelings for you. I wanted you to be a fake, to be an uncaring robber baron beneath all the charm. But I was wrong."

His face had grown still. "What do you see now?"

"I see a man who cares, really cares for people. I see someone who works harder than any of his employees, and they know it. All afternoon people spontaneously came up to you to say hi. They thanked you for the health plan, the flexible hours, the working conditions. I finally realized that money can have positive effects, if it's in the right hands."

"Do you think my hands are?" Clay asked

the question quietly, as if he'd grappled with it.

"Oh yes!" Shelby exclaimed. "You want to make a profit, sure, but your focus is on others. Your employees, your family—"

"I'm a saint," he said, reaching for his champagne glass.

"I think we dispensed with that notion a few minutes ago."

He smiled, but Shelby sensed that her words hadn't made the impression she'd intended. "Clay, I'm trying to say that I was wrong about you. I've been wrong about a lot of things."

He shook his head. "No, you've awakened me to some hard truths."

She rubbed his chest with her hand. "What, that you're not perfect? Hey, I'll forgive you if you'll forgive me."

Clay fixed her with a gaze that was at once hopeful and disbelieving. "Do you mean that?"

His reaction puzzled her. "Of course. What could be so terrible that I couldn't forgive?"

Clay started to speak, then stopped. Shelby couldn't read what was behind his green-eyed stare, and for a chilling second she thought the old, elusive Clay was back. He pulled the quilt up. "Oh, I don't know," he said, still with no emotion in his voice. "People can disappoint you, even the ones you love." He glanced away. "Especially the ones you love."

Shelby nuzzled his neck, anxious to lighten the oddly-charged atmosphere. "Hey, I'm supposed to be the pessimist in this team, remember? No relationship is problem-free, but I think we're on a roll here."

He laughed as she tickled him out of this strange bad mood. Shelby felt buoyant, and she wanted Clay carefree. He could stop worrying about others for one day. A long, slow kiss got him back into the proper frame of mind.

"Are you happy?" she murmured as she licked one of his nipples.

His breath caught, but he managed a husky "yes."

"And you're never going to let me go."

"Never!" he exclaimed as he shifted his position so that their bodies pressed against each other.

Shelby thought they were going to make love again.

"I want you to stay," he said.

Shelby blinked. "Of course, darling, I'll stay the night, too. Oh, can I use gushy terms of endearment?"

He smiled widely. "You can call me whatever you like except Prom King. But, Shelby, I didn't mean one night. I meant I want you to stay in Louisville permanently."

She leaned unsteadily on one elbow. "Do you really want me to?"

His expression made her more lightheaded than the champagne. *"Yes,"* he declared. "I just don't know if I have the right to ask you to stay. So much has happened this summer, and another summer just like it sixty years ago. Both of us carry a lot of baggage—you could even say scars—from the con-

246

sequences. If you stayed in Louisville, there would be so many reminders, not to mention the impact such a move would have on your career."

That was Clay, thinking of someone else besides himself. "Just suppose one of those reminders didn't exist, Clay," she began, "would the question be easier to ask?"

He sat up. "What do you mean?"

The answer had been forming in Shelby's mind all day. "I mean that once I realized that the money from Desiree's land could actually *liberate* me, rather than corrupt me, I thought of all kinds of writing projects that I'd always longed to do. I just never had the money to support myself while I tackled them. Longer pieces on social problems and fiction. These can be done anywhere."

His face softened, but he wasn't sold. Shelby knew that her next words would truly convince him. "I think my final liberation took place about two hours ago. That's when an incident at the fair showed me how much I'd not only lived in the past, but also clung to old fears and paranoia."

He looked concerned. "What incident?"

"Oh, not anything to worry about. It was just a situation where I'd let my old fears run wild, only to find out that I'd been wrong. The point is that I now know that I must move on. Let the past go. And I'd like to move on, with you."

He now believed her, every word. His face registered joy mixed with an almost painful tenderness. "Oh, Shelby," he said as he buried his face into her cascade of curls. She closed her eyes to the silky sensation, feeling the pleasure of his happiness and relief.

"I've come to love Desiree's house," she said, laying her head against the juncture of his neck and shoulder, "but I have too many sad memories there. Perhaps it should make way for the future."

"Our future," he promised. Tilting her head up, he kissed her again. The kiss bore little resemblance to the fiery ones of their lovemaking. This kiss spoke of thanksgiving, of emotions less explosive than desire, but deeper, found only in the human heart.

They made love again. This time Clay moved under Shelby, and she rode him, totally giving, totally uninhibited, in perfect rhythm.

The picnic was just over by the time they returned to Park View. Clay took her home and gently kissed her good night. Rather proper, Shelby thought with amusement, until she realized that her lips were slightly bruised by the scores of kisses that afternoon.

Clay had wanted her to spend the night at the cabin. At first she'd wanted it, too but then she decided that it would be too much of a risk to be away from her house all night. Thankfully the house appeared quiet and untouched, but even if it hadn't been, Shelby would not have regretted her decision to go to the picnic. As she canvassed room after room, she knew that it was finally time to come to terms with the past. It was time to pack

Desiree's belongings, and her own, for the eventual closing up of the house.

Now that she'd made the decision to sell, Shelby wanted it to happen quickly. Clay had insisted on topping the highest bid, which happened to have come from Buzz Mathis. She had acquiesced, since he refused to take no for an answer.

Standing in the gloom of Desiree's room, Shelby wondered where to begin. The room had been thoroughly searched, but what to keep had never been dealt with. She decided on the clothes closet first. The closet was very deep, with rows of clothes on either side. It was actually deep enough to walk several feet into but surprisingly unlit. Not surprisingly, Desiree had thrown nothing away. Shelby thought with pride that some of these garments were classically beautiful. She just hadn't noticed as a child because they were out of date. One, a black wool dress in the forties' style, she put aside to keep, then folded the others into bags.

Shoes were next. Taking a paper bag, she got down on her knees and gathered all of Desiree's pumps, boots, and orthopedic oxfords, finding the last ones in the furthest reaches of the closet. Using the floor and back wall for support, she hoisted herself into a standing position again. But something felt strange. Her hand detected a thin groove in the ancient wallpaper that lined Desiree's closet.

Shelby traced the groove with her fingers, and to her astonishment it outlined the shape of a door. Despite the light in the room, the closet was so deep that the back wall was virtually unlit. Shelby couldn't feel a doorknob, but she could just get her fingers in the groove. She pulled once, but the wall didn't budge. With greater effort she tried several positions along the groove, breaking two fingernails in failed attempts. Rapping her knuckles against the wall, however, convinced her that the part outlined by the groove was different than the rest.

Her fingers became sweaty with anticipation as she kept trying to pry the mysterious door open. Then suddenly she must have hit on the right combination because the wall creaked for an instant and gave way.

Stunned, Shelby stood in front of a black void. Before she could bring herself to step in, she went downstairs and got a flashlight. She put the beam on high and aimed it into the opening.

It was a room. Shelby flashed the light around and picked up a fixture with a long cord hanging from the ceiling. She pulled it and turned on a light.

The instant the room was illuminated, Shelby knew where the letters were. The small antechamber was a shrine to a specific time long ago. There was an early-thirties feel to the room, in the furniture, rugs and lamps. An empty diet soda in the wastebasket, however, told Shelby that the room had been used in recent years. Still, the occupant of this room wanted time to stop at a certain era when she'd been happy.

The existence of the room puzzled Shelby until she remembered that Desiree had often mentioned the myriad rooms, some oddly placed in the house. During Prohibition, one had been sealed off and used to store liquor. Perhaps this had been the room.

Whatever its origin, the room had one function now. It served as a place of remembrance for one man.

His picture was in a frame beside an easy chair. Shelby nearly gasped when she saw it. A mirror image of Clay stared back at her, a tad more gaunt, with slicked hair parted in the middle, but it was Clay's face, all right. Shelby knew this to be Ford Trask. With trembling fingers she opened the small bureau near the chair.

In neatly-tied bundles she found the letters.

Chapter Ten

Shelby stood immobilized. The day's euphoria had changed to an ominous fear. Part of her wanted to close the drawer, shut the secret door. She had been so happy, and a voice within her warned that the letters would change that.

She couldn't ignore them, however. Desiree's true self permeated the chamber and cried out for release. Shelby had thought of the letters in terms of what they could tell her about herself. This had been a selfish motive. Now she realized that for Desiree, and Desiree alone, she had to read them. Her aunt deserved a final hearing.

But not in this room, Shelby thought. She quickly picked up the neatly-tied bundles, turned off the light, and reentered the bedroom. She should have known after she found the scrap of envelope under Desiree's bed that the letters were nearby. But why this passion for secrecy? What was in these letters? The secret door snapped shut.

Back in her room, Shelby untied the packs of

letters and found them in chronological order. A story should always start at the beginning, so she picked up the envelope with the earliest date written on the bottom lefthand side in Desiree's handwriting, September 12, 1932. Though every letter was addressed to Desiree, few bore stamps.

The reason became apparent after the first four or five letters. Desiree and Ford had been star-crossed lovers.

They had met at the Kentucky State Fair in August 1932. With simple but heartfelt words, Ford had written,

You were so pretty. I didn't know if I had the nerve to go up to speak to you. I pretended to look at all the needlepoint in the exhibit, admiring it and such, but really I was looking at you. Your pretty blue eyes, your pretty hair, your pretty smile. I listened to you talk to people, with your voice so refined, and wondered at my gumption to even want to speak to you. But then you looked at me, and I knew I could.

Shelby remembered her conversation with Clay when he'd divulged the existence of the letters. He'd mentioned the state fair as the first meeting place for Desiree and Ford. Desiree had won a blue ribbon that year for her needlepoint, and Ford had taken home a first prize for his pig, Homer. Sixty years later Shelby had overheard people at the picnic talking about this year's state fair, only a few weeks away.

She sighed and struggled to make out Ford's faded handwriting. In adjectives both flowery and touching he described how wonderful their first "outing" was and asked if Desiree would like to "keep company" with him. Shelby swallowed. Desiree had kept his very first letter. A courtship seemed to have started, a sweet, tender connection between two people so different in background yet so right for each other.

Ford wrote that with Desiree he'd begun to have dreams and plans. She made him feel like a gentleman. In turn, he said it made him happy that he was someone she could talk to since she was so lonely in that great big house.

All went well until Desiree's father, Bowden Langstaff, became aware that this tenant farmer was seeing his daughter. From what Shelby could figure out, Desiree had planned their meetings away from her home and relied heavily on the mail for communication. As a poor farmer, perhaps Ford didn't have a phone. It was inevitable, however, that as their relationship grew, Ford would meet her family.

Bowden was furious, not only at the secrecy of the romance, but also at the very *idea* of it. Ford apologized for his "ungentlemanlike" conduct, but her father spoke to him with words

I'd be hard pressed to pass by. Calling me

riffraff! I never meant to shove him, my darling, but he acted so mean. I can't believe that a lady like you has such a bully for a father.

Bowden forbade his daughter to see Ford, and the description of Ford's acrimonious argument with Desiree's father became the first letter without a stamp and postmark. Shelby puzzled over this, until she read further in the letter.

Forbidding them to meet, Desiree's strict Victorian father took the extra measure of checking her mail. A go-between was needed to pass letters and help set up secret rendezvous. The young couple was more determined than ever to be together. How wonderful, Ford wrote, that Desiree found one servant she could trust to pass the letters. Of course, she slipped him some money every time he made a delivery, but the footman was taking a risk.

"A right feller" was how Ford described Mapes, the go-between. Shelby nearly gasped. The Mapes-Ford connection had finally been revealed! She felt an ominous prickle. Sixty years after this letter was written, the two men were still connected. A coincidence? Shelby read on.

The letters for weeks and months after spoke of Ford's continued and growing love for Desiree. Mixed with his paeans to her perfection, however, were his urgings for her to stand up to her father. The man was her "jailer," he wrote. Ford wanted to take her away from that "house of hate," but he didn't know how. He had plans to eventually buy the farm where he worked as a tenant, but that would take years.

Shelby's opinion of Ford Trask changed as she read. Ford had always seemed the most puzzling player in this drama. Why had he wanted these letters so much that he'd either encouraged or demanded that Clay and Mapes go after them illegally? Why had he been so devious? The Ford Trask in the letters, however, was a touchingly-direct, open man. His devotion to Desiree permeated every letter—as did his growing desperation.

He wanted to marry Desiree. Making her his bride would render him

the happiest man alive. Last night, when I held you in my arms, I knew I could never let you go.

That particular night had sealed their commitment to one another, for as Shelby read with some wonder, Desiree had given herself to Ford. Even in his blunt, unschooled style of writing, Ford's reflections on this interlude were positively lyrical.

I had no right to ask for what you gave to me. I know a woman wouldn't give up that which she cherishes so much unless true love is in her heart. Your gift humbles me, and

256

my love grows ever more faithful with each passing minute.

In a lighter vein, he wrote,

People would say as to how I *have* to marry you now and make an honest woman of you. I would say to them that you are already the most truthful and sweet girl that ever lived. And I would move heaven and earth to make you mine, even though I feel that I'm married to you now in my heart.

Tears came to Shelby's eyes. This love seemed indestructible. What had gone wrong? Her clock now read past midnight, but she couldn't rest until all the letters had been read.

The situation got stickier. Despite their best efforts, Ford worried that Desiree's father still suspected the attachment. Conflicting with his anxieties over this was Ford's desire to go public with their love. Desiree counseled patience. Ford had nearly come to blows with her father the first time they'd met. And Ford admitted that he was in no financial position to marry her yet.

When Bowden Langstaff surprised Desiree with a gift of a European tour, Ford was sure her father had found out about them. Several months in England, France, and Italy were presented to Desiree as a twenty-first birthday present. Ford panicked. Even if they eloped, he couldn't support her now as a tenant farmer, nor was that the life she deserved. What were they to do?

To Shelby's astonishment it was gentle, sheltered Desiree who came up with a plan. Desiree owned some land east of the city in conjunction with her father. Being twenty-one, she could sign the deed over to whomever she wished, but she needed her father's countersignature for the transfer to be valid.

Desiree concocted a plan to *forge* her father's signature on the transfer. With both "proper" signatures and as an adult, she could dispose of the land as she saw fit. The transfer was done, and Ford took possession of the land.

Shelby sat up in bed. Desiree's final gift to Ford Trask was the very land that started the Trask fortune thirty years later. Sweat broke out on her forehead. The secrets were tumbling right and left now.

With good fertile land to support them, Desiree and Ford made plans to elope. On the day they were to run away, however, disaster struck. Shelby read of this day in letters that began to have stamps and postmarks from other cities. Ford wrote,

It was an accident, my darling. You know that. Your courage that day will sustain me in our time apart. But we will be together again. I swear to Almighty God that we

258

will! I just don't know how it all got so out of hand.

What got out of hand was the accidental death of Desiree's father. Mapes "sold us out," Ford wrote, alerting Bowden Langstaff of their elopement plans. Desiree's father forbade her to leave their home. When she didn't show up at the courthouse, Ford became frantic. He decided to go to her house to get her, and to

finally talk it out with your father, and put my honorable intentions on the table.

A catastrophic decision, as it turned out. In the privacy of his sitting room Bowden and Desiree's mother refused to listen to their pleas. When Desiree insisted that she would marry Ford with or without her father's permission, he struck her.

This action pushed Ford over the edge. He wrote,

I couldn't let him treat you that way! My blood boiled at such behavior. I had to defend your honor. I had to!

The fight that ensued caused the death of Bowden Langstaff. The sound of the scuffle brought in Mapes, who must have been "listening through a keyhole," Ford wrote. Mapes tried to stop the fighting, but from what Shelby could figure out, Desiree's father went out of control, attacking Mapes and Ford with a poker from the study's fireplace. In the melee that followed, Ford threw a wild punch propelling Bowden into a marble table, where he hit his head and died instantly.

How horrible, Shelby thought, for Desiree to see her father accidentally killed by her lover, and yet it was Desiree who again came through in a crisis. Ford praised her with

> You were so quick to see that no one would have believed that it was an accident, especially since my first fight with your father was seen by the other servants. I will never forget how you thought of my troubles when you were suffering so with your own.

Desiree must have had to think quickly. She told her hysterical mother that two choices existed. The first was to call in the police, explain the incident involving her lover, her father, and a servant and hope that the police—not to mention the neighbors—would see it as an accident. Or they could say that Bowden Langstaff accidentally fell, hit his head, and died.

Desiree's mother accepted the second scenario. All parties agreed to the coverup. Ford fled Kentucky for a while. A small funeral was held. Mapes left the Langstaff employ soon after, apparently filled with remorse and a lingering fear of being implicated someday in Bowden's death. Ford wrote,

So Mapes was sorry about the whole thing. I guess he'll have to live the rest of his life knowing that he told on us, and what it caused.

After the funeral Desiree sat back and waited. "I'm coming back for you," Ford promised again and again in the weeks after the accident. Absenting himself from Kentucky had been Desiree's idea—"only till things simmer down, though," Ford warned, because

My life has no meaning without you. I'm sorrier than I can say that you've cried over me. I never meant to hurt him. I just couldn't stand his hurting you.

His letters showed postmarks from different cities in various states. Ford wrote that he took jobs where he could find them. The last letter was postmarked Indiana. It was dated October 14, 1933. The letter ended with a little poem:

I love you more than the stars in the sky, and the fish in the sea. Before you know it, you'll be seeing me.

But she never did. Desiree Langstaff never saw Ford Trask again. She must have waited for years, Shelby thought, in torturous anxiety, wondering what had happened to him. Perhaps she'd even tried to find him, but his last letters showed a man on the move.

And then she must have realized that he wasn't coming back. She pined away, the shattered love slowly killing her enjoyment of life. Guilt must have seeped into her soul, as well, guilt and remorse over the forgery and coverup. Ford's disappearance made a mockery of her sacrifice. All was for naught. This crushing fact must have hastened her retreat from the world—a retreat to a time when she'd been happy. The secret room bore testimony to this, and to her love for Ford despite what he'd done.

By the time Shelby had come to live with her aunt, only a wounded, fragile shell remained of the vibrant girl of long ago. How devastated Desiree must have been when the Trasks began to get in the news with their real estate killings. She must have realized that Ford had come back to Kentucky, but not to her. On top of that, the land she'd given him had made a fortune for him and his family!

Where was your rage, Auntie? Shelby wondered. Tears streamed down her face at the thought of her aunt's silent suffering. Desiree always said that ladies bore their burdens stoically, but Shelby was no lady. She was livid. How *dare*

Ford Trask do this to Desiree? Why hadn't he returned to her? What possible excuse could justify such cruelty?

Shelby cried out in anger and frustration. Dawn was a few hours away. She would try to rest until morning because she'd need all her strength to face the Trasks and demand an explanation.

Demand it she would, however. Desiree may have shriveled up inside with grief, but Shelby was very nearly exploding with righteous indignation.

And yet Desiree had found it within her to forgive Ford at the end of her life. Bryant Fisk had mentioned how happy she'd been her last days. Perhaps she realized that to forgive Ford was to forgive herself for once being young, desperate, and in love.

Shelby punched her pillow. Well, maybe Desiree could forgive Ford Trask, but she could never—Her breath caught. That afternoon she'd promised to forgive Clay anything he did, and he'd been disbelieving. He must have known that something existed that she couldn't forgive—or would have great difficulty doing so. Had he known about the contents of the letters all along?

Her stomach contracted in a painful spasm. A mere few hours ago she'd banished doubt, and now suspicion invaded her heart again.

The letters revealed more than a tragic love affair. Confessed very clearly in their faded pages was collusion by Desiree and Ford in a crime—two if you counted covering up a homicide, accidental though it was. No wonder Ford was desperate to get the letters, but surely Clay saw the deeper danger.

If Bowden Langstaff's signature had been forged, that made the original transfer invalid. And if the transfer was invalid, who really owned the land that the Trask fortune sprang from? The original owner? Since Desiree was dead, all rights would go to her sole heir—Shelby.

Three aspirins did little to stop her throbbing temples. Had Clay known this all along?

She struggled against rushing to judge. The possibility that the letters contained evidence of a forged deed posed incredible problems for the Trasks. Whatever Clay had withheld from her, he'd done it for his family.

Shelby thought of her new intimacy with Clay. A connection had been made that she couldn't dismiss. At least, to break it would now break her heart. For she'd always known that cynics were, deep down, the biggest romantics. And when they finally fell in love, they fell hard.

Shelby tried to sleep, but her slumber was fitful with unnerving dreams of mazes and dark alleys. She phoned Clay as early as she dared to say she'd like to come over and talk to his family about an important matter. Clay seemed surprised, and asked if this was about the land. She said yes. Couldn't the sale be handled by the two of them, he asked? She said no.

His confusion matched hers. *You'll find out soon enough,* she thought, hanging up. Two seconds later the phone rang. Picking it up, Shelby said, "Look, Clay, I'll explain it all to you when I see you!"

"Uh, Shelby . . ."

"Oh, Logan, I'm sorry. I thought you were—"

"Clay Trask, yes, I gathered that. You seem kind of tense, honey. You okay?"

His concern touched her. Logan had acted like a true friend this summer, calling her up to see how she was doing, offering to help her find the letters, understanding when she wouldn't go out. He'd offered the same sympathetic ear that he had when they'd been kids. Shelby needed someone like that now. Despite his opinion of Clay, he wouldn't say "I told you so."

She told him the whole story. The letters, the land, Desiree and Ford, she nearly cried as she spoke. Logan was soothing. When she finished, he gave her one piece of advice. "Don't tell Clay that you have the letters yet. Call Bryant and find out what your legal rights are first. You can bet Clay will have the finest legal representation if this should ever go to court. You don't want to say anything at Park View that could hurt you."

Shelby promised to think it over, but she only said that to get him off the phone. Despite his sound advice, she couldn't wait one more minute.

Jumping into her rental, she ground gears all the way to Park View. As she drove down Park Lane, she saw the cleanup detail for the picnic the day before. *Seems like a million years ago,* Shelby thought.

Clay was standing on the front steps as she pulled up. Seeing his powerful body and remembering the ecstasy of less than twenty-four hours ago made her weak with worry and confusion.

His brow furrowed as he bent to kiss her lips but got her cheek. "What's the matter? What's in that bag?"

"Can we go inside?" she asked.

He looked so cool in his white slacks and white linen shirt. The summer sun had given him a rich tan that accentuated the gold in his hair. A golden boy. Yes, Clay had always been one— rich, confident, and lucky. Right now, however, the worry etched on his face belied that image. Perhaps his luck had finally run out. "Shelby, my family is quite puzzled over your call. Can't you tell me?"

My family. Did he ultimately think of no one else? She decided to tell him straight. "I found the letters. They're in the bag."

A stunned breath escaped from his lips, but he said nothing. His skin paled as he looked at her and then glanced to the stone steps.

"Where?" he finally managed.

"In a secret room off her bedroom."

Clay nodded, still dazed.

"You have nothing to say?" she asked.

He quickly made eye contact. "I thought you were going to tell me."

"You mean you don't know what the letters say?" Her eyes were glued to his face. Any evasion would be spotted.

His gaze never left hers. "No, I don't. I just suspected . . ."

"That it was bad?"

He closed his eyes. "How bad is it?"

Despite her confusion, she felt terrible when she said, "Desiree and Ford were involved in a fraud and a homicide."

"Oh, God!" He leaned against one of the massive pillars. The sinewy strength of his body couldn't compete with the emotional beating he was taking. Perhaps Shelby had misjudged his part in this affair. He looked as upset over the revelation as she'd been.

"You know," he said in a hoarse whisper, "Desiree mentioned a 'crime' in her letter to Grandpa. I just couldn't believe it."

"What!"

"Miss Shelby! What brings you to our home so early? Did you have fun at the picnic?"

John Trask stood nervously at the front door. His cheerful courtesy couldn't hide his worried expression as he glanced at his son.

"Yes, Mr. Trask, I enjoyed the picnic very much."

"Good, good!" he bellowed too heartily. "Clay

tells us that you and he are keeping company now. Mary-Alice and I couldn't be more pleased."

Clay's glance told her that he believed this, too. For him, nothing had changed since yesterday. Pain knifed through Shelby's body.

"And Clay tells us," John continued babbling, "that you've finally decided to sell us your property. Now we—"

"There may be a hitch in the proceedings," she interrupted in a voice heavy with fatigue.

This stopped him cold. A sweat broke out on his florid face, and Shelby felt compassion for this man. She did not feel so kindly toward his son, who stared at her now with sadness.

"She found the letters, Dad."

"Oh, Lord," John moaned. "What did Paw-Paw do?"

Clay went up to his father and put his arm around the man's shoulders. "Dad, let me handle this." He guided John into the foyer.

"Miss Shelby, please, my father is old, old . . ." John called out. His voice trailed off, and Clay returned to the steps. His eyes were heavy.

"Can we talk?" he asked softly.

"I want to," Shelby replied. Ford Trask had hurt *her* family, but then the sins of the father shouldn't be put on the sons, or grandsons.

Clay escorted her to the same parlor where she'd been before. Mapes was nowhere in sight.

As soon as the door was shut, he said, "Can I see the letters?"

Shelby held the bag close to her chest. "What did you mean when you said that Desiree mentioned a 'crime' in her letter to your grandfather?"

Clay sighed and leaned on the back of a leather wing chair. There was a hint of relief in his sigh, Shelby thought. She sensed that Clay wasn't completely unhappy having to finally come clean with her. No matter how justified, these secrets were a burden.

"In her letter to Grandpa," he said, "she mentioned their, and I quote, 'crimes, of the heart and otherwise.' She wrote that my grandfather had betrayed her love, and that without him she never would have committed the acts that had haunted her all these years. But then she said she'd realized that each of us is responsible for what we make of our lives. We cannot blame others or the past for why we're unfulfilled. She forgave my grandfather for what he did. She forgave *herself*."

The words shook Shelby in a way she hadn't anticipated. How different would her relationship be now with Clay if he had told her up-front about a possible crime? Would she have trusted him less? Would she have become his lover, knowing that his grandfather had somehow betrayed Desiree? The answer eluded her. All she knew was that withholding this vital information was affecting her trust for him now. "You should have told me this!" she cried.

"I did."

"No," Shelby said. "You just told me the forgiveness part. You never said anything about a possible crime having been committed."

"Her words were so vague! I had no way of knowing if the 'acts' she regretted were illegal. 'Crimes of the heart' aren't necessarily real crimes."

"They ought to be!" she said, glancing at the letters. "What your grandfather did to my aunt was despicable! You suspected more than an emotional crime, however. That's why you broke into my house to get the letters!"

His posture stiffened a little, but his voice held not a note of apology. "You'd have done the same thing to protect your aunt."

"That's where you're wrong! I would have told you as much as I knew. We'd have searched for the whole story together. Secrets and lies destroyed my aunt. How could continuing that pattern help her?" Shelby sat down heavily on a sofa. Her agitated state combined with little sleep left her drained.

Not Clay, however. He angrily stood back from the chair. "I don't believe that for a second! You wouldn't have divulged the whole contents of that letter if you'd thought it could destroy your family! If everything they'd worked for was predicated on a . . ."

He couldn't say it, but she could. "A crime?" He looked away.

Shelby's worst nightmare was coming true. "I think you knew what was in those letters from the beginning," she said miserably.

"No! I only suspected."

Shelby tossed the bag to him. Surprised, he nevertheless caught it with that special agility of his that she had admired on the tennis court and in bed. He sat down and looked inside. "Well, here's your proof," she said. "Read them and weep." Her voice cracked slightly. "I did."

Clay began to read. To make it quicker, Shelby pointed out the more important letters. As he read, she watched his face turn from sadness to a kind of dread. Her thoughts were in a tangle. She wasn't clear about how much Clay had lied to her. When he finished, she saw him swallow hard, as if his mouth had gone dry.

"I . . . I must talk to Grandpa," he said.

Shelby saw in his stunned face that reading the letters had been just as wrenching for him as for her. "Of course," she agreed softly, feeling her anger subside a little in compassion. "I found the letters he wanted. He would assume we've read them. Now he has to talk to us."

She waited for Clay to agree. He didn't, nor did he look at her. He kept opening and then refolding the last letter. His prolonged silence unnerved Shelby. He was hiding something from her again. She just knew it.

271

"Grandpa never asked me to get the letters," he finally said.

Shelby didn't think she'd heard properly. "What?"

"I said . . . my grandfather never asked me to get the letters."

She definitely understood him the second time and was now completely confused. "But . . . but he sent not only you, but also Mapes to get them."

Clay shook his head. "He didn't send me. I decided to go because I *suspected* that the letters might reveal some wrongdoing. He did send Mapes, yes. But I didn't learn about that until I talked to my grandfather in the greenhouse."

The enormity of what she was hearing made Shelby feel ill. "From the beginning you told me that your grandfather wanted his love letters back."

Clay sighed, his eyes shiny and bleak. "He wanted just the opposite. He only sent Mapes to find them because he was afraid I would. Now I know why. He was terrified the letters would change my love for him."

Trembling, Shelby stood up. "This . . . this has certainly shaken my love for you."

In a shot Clay was beside her, his arms enveloping her. Shelby would have shaken them off, but they were helping her to remain standing. "Please don't say that!" he said. "I'm sorry I wasn't up-front from the beginning. It was wrong of me not to tell you everything, but can't you see why I had to hide things? The survival of my family was at stake!"

"It's always your family!" she said, realizing for the first time that her true rival for Clay had never been Heather Scott.

"That's not true," he insisted, "but when we met, I didn't know I'd fall in love with you! That first day, in Bryant's office, I really didn't know you."

"So you assumed I'd skewer your family just like I'd done to all the other rich people I write about!" Her anger gave her the strength to break away.

"No, Shelby, you have to listen to me!" he pleaded, still holding one arm. "I've never been proud of what I had to do, but put yourself in my shoes! My grandfather became ill, my father desperate over those letters. For years my father tried to warn me that the other shoe was going to drop as far as Grandpa was concerned, but I didn't listen. *I* hadn't struggled up from a farm. *I* hadn't had to compromise my soul. Everything has been given to me. Now it was my turn to give back. Don't you see?"

His eyes begged her to believe him. Despite her anguish, Shelby saw the almost palpable pain etched across his face. He'd never meant to hurt her, she knew that. But people made choices in life, and his choices seemed to revolve around relationships he already had, not the one relationship that could have been part of his future.

"Clay," she said, "I'll tell you what I see. I see a man so obsessed with saving his family that he compromised his *heart*. I think I could forgive the lies about the letters, but if you lied to me about something so important, how can I *trust* you now?"

His fingers pressed into her flesh. "You have to trust my feelings for you. I never lied about that! I love you."

"No," she said weakly.

"It's the truth! I love you!"

The three words scalded her heart. "Oh, how can you say that!" she cried, shaking free his hand. She retrieved the letters and started stuffing them back into the bag.

Clay positioned himself so that she'd have to face him. In a voice roughened by emotion he said, "I guess I have no right to ask you to believe me when I've lied to you before. But my lies all had to do with the *past* — the letters, Desiree, and Ford. I never, *ever* lied to you about the present. The letters are the past, Shelby. My love for you is the present and, I hope, the future."

His halting words sounded so fine. She had never wanted to believe anything more, but she couldn't. She took a deep shuddering breath. "The letters aren't the past, Clay. You and I both know that they impact on the present."

He gazed at her for a long second. "I think the transfer will hold up after all these years," he said in a low voice.

"But you're not sure, are you?"

"A bunch of love letters as evidence? I doubt —"

"But you're not sure, are you?"

He glanced at the heavy bag. "No."

"Then why don't we find out? I have Bryant's home phone number. He said I could call him anytime."

Clay's face turned still and grave. "You obviously want to."

With unsteady fingers Shelby picked up the phone on the coffee table and called her lawyer. Luckily Bryant was in, having just sat down to breakfast. He listened without comment to her story and then confirmed that, if the facts she stated were correct, the forgery made the transfer invalid. The letters were hearsay evidence, but the original transfer could be looked up at the county courthouse and the signature of the father compared to another document with his real signature. This would be hard evidence. Before she hung up, however, he left her with a warning.

"Shelby," he began, "pursuing justice after all these years will be costly. All the people who bought parts of that land and the people who bought parts from them aren't going to want to renegotiate. The Trasks are a powerful family with connections in the judiciary. They will fight this. I can't guarantee you what the results will be."

Shelby thanked him and hung up. "The deed is invalid."

Clay barely reacted. He just kept looking at her, waiting. She realized that it didn't matter what the facts were—no scandal would happen if *she* didn't pursue it. Well, some things could not be forgotten—or forgiven. Desiree's heartbreak had to be avenged. Desiree—Shelby's one true family. Taking Clay's love and forgetting the letters would be tantamount to abandoning Desiree and the memory of all she went through. Shelby could not do that. She felt a debt of love to her frail, tragic aunt who'd risked everything for the love of Ford Trask and had lost.

And what of Shelby's own betrayal by Clay? Could she forget that? She'd been lied to continuously by him. From their meeting in Bryant's office when he'd said that her land would be a mere "prudent" buy to telling her that his grandfather just wanted some old love letters back, Clay had misled her from the beginning. Both Langstaff women had suffered at the hands of the Trask men. It had to stop. In a voice seared with pain she said, "See you in court."

He closed his eyes. His head lowered slightly as if under a great weight. Shelby quickly grabbed the bag of letters and started to leave. As justified as she felt, she still couldn't bear to see the face that bewitched her so in such distress. Why couldn't she hate him? Part of her did. He'd lied to her, played her for a fool, and more contemptible than that, he still said he loved her.

But part of her still loved *him,* and that scared her. Loving someone meant letting your guard down and lowering all of your defenses, a terrifying risk for Shelby. There was only one time in her life when she'd allowed herself to be that emotionally exposed, and that was yesterday, with Clay. Now she was confused and heartsick. Had her old cautious impulses been right all along?

He caught her arm at the door. She didn't want to look at him but had no choice. A mistake, for there were tears in his eyes.

"You now have what you've always wanted," he said in a hoarse voice, "perfect revenge against the rich. You can destroy the family that caused your aunt so much pain." He exhaled a shuddering, wrenching breath. "I guess I can't blame you."

Shelby stopped, surprised at his words.

"I would probably feel the same way if our situations were reversed," he said. "But, Shelby, will this suit really be about Desiree? She said she was at peace in her letter. She finally forgave my grandfather."

"I can't forgive."

"Who? My grandfather, or me?"

"You never loved me! To you, I was just dollar signs and acreage, to be wooed with your infamous charm. And I fell for it like so many have since high school."

He let go of her arm. "I told you I wasn't perfect! Love isn't perfect. If what you really wanted was the Prom King, then I don't believe you ever loved me!"

"What?"

"Yes, you were just satisfying your own insecurities so that you could say, finally, that Clay Trask wasn't good enough for you!"

"That's not true! I do love you!"

The admission brought tears to her eyes. Clay touched her shoulders with trembling hands. His face had never seemed so vulnerable, so open. The enigmatic Clay Trask stood before her with no secrets. "Then let's go on, Shelby! Let's start anew, away from the past. You can choose where you belong, and I'm asking, choose the future, with me! I'm sorry for all the pain I've caused, but I've never deliberately hurt anyone I've loved. And I do love you so. If you were to walk out that door, it wouldn't be losing Park View or the Tramarts that would haunt me. It would be losing you. You've given my life new meaning."

The sentence echoed in Shelby's brain. " 'My life has no meaning without you,' " she said. "That's what your grandfather wrote to Desiree. He asked her to trust him, have faith in him. She broke laws for him, and then he abandoned her."

"History won't repeat itself!"

"No, it won't." She opened the door and left the room.

Chapter Eleven

Clay felt cut in two. *She's gone,* he repeated to himself in a torturous litany. *I've lost her.* He tried to make his feet move, but he couldn't. The throbbing ache of regret kept punishing his tired mind. *It's my fault,* he thought. *With all my lies and evasions, how could she finally trust me?*

What had it all been for? The great Trask name? *We don't deserve our good fortune after what Grandpa did to Desiree,* he thought. *Our whole empire, our very identity is based on land we had no moral right to keep. Grandpa, why didn't you come back for her?*

Clay began to walk to the stairs. His grandfather could no longer remain silent. Clay needed answers, or he felt he would go crazy. *I must have been mad to sacrifice the love of my life for a myth—the myth of the successful Trask family.*

He climbed the stairs slowly, remembering how shattered Shelby looked when she left. Clay just couldn't stop thinking about her. He decided to call her after he spoke with his grandfather just to see if she got home okay. She'd probably hang up on him, but at least he'd know she was all right.

If only he could see her again and really know that all love was gone! Surely the fire they had couldn't be extinguished so easily. Then he remembered he would see Shelby again—in court.

Shelby drove her car without really knowing where she was going. When she hit the Ohio River, and momentarily considered driving in, she knew she'd better go home. *Home,* the word made her heart ache thinking about it. For a fleeting afternoon yesterday she thought she'd found her home, the one place where she truly belonged, with Clay. Now all that hope was gone, and she was desolate.

The hope had vanished, but not the love. She'd allowed Clay to come into her life, breaking her cardinal rule against letting herself need anyone. His absence from her life would be a wound difficult to heal.

She'd had no choice but to leave Park View. He'd sacrificed her trust for his family. That couldn't be forgiven, could it? Shelby replayed their final words like a broken record. "History won't repeat itself!" he'd cried. He wouldn't take her land and leave her, as Ford had done to Desiree. Why couldn't she believe him?

The question tormented her. She didn't want

revenge; she wanted love. She wanted to be the most important person in one man's life. Perhaps that's why she left Park View. Clay had never put her first.

She parked in front of Desiree's house. The phone rang as she walked in the door. That damn phone! "Hello!"

"Shelby, this is Logan."

"Oh . . . hi, Logan."

"Are you okay? Did you call Bryant?"

"Yes."

"I called the old poop myself to ask him what recourse you had with the letters, but he wouldn't talk to me."

She almost laughed. "He told me that the forgery made the transfer invalid."

A long silence ensued, so long that Shelby thought the phone had gone dead. "Hello? Logan, are you there?"

"Uh, yeah, I'm here." He whistled. "You're looking at a fortune, honey."

Why did it always come down to that? "I don't want the money! I never wanted money! I wanted . . ."

"What, Shelby?"

She couldn't say it out loud. It hurt too much. Tears spilled over her cheeks. "Logan, I can't talk anymore."

"Are you crying?" he asked softly. "Oh, honey, I'm sorry. Look, my mother had a sovereign remedy for stress. She mixed a nice pony of bourbon with some hot mint tea and a dash of honey."

Shelby wiped the tears with her fingers. "I think that's called a toddy."

"She called it deliverance. Hey, whatever you want to name it is fine by me. Just *try* it, and then get some sleep if you can. You'll need your strength to take on the Trasks."

Her strength? Before this summer, all her strength had come from her anger. Loving Clay, however, had emptied much of that turmoil from her heart. Now those insecurities had been reactivated.

"I guess you're right. I'll try it."

He clucked approvingly. "Maybe there'll be some justice around this town for once."

She hung up and went in search of his mother's sovereign remedy. Shelby rarely drank, and never in the afternoon, but right now she just wanted a balm for her troubled mind. And sleep, she wanted desperately to sleep.

Desiree's liquor cabinet tended toward liqueurs that looked like amber glue, but Shelby unearthed a dusty bourbon bottle. She rounded up the other ingredients and mixed all three according to Logan's advice and her mood.

The toddy sent a warm wave through her, especially on an empty stomach. So pleasant was the initial jolt that she decided a second toddy—maybe a little bigger—would be just the ticket to slumberland.

The alcohol mercifully dulled all thinking. She

was contemplating a third nip when the phone rang again.

"Shelby?"

It was Clay. The pain of hearing his voice cut through the blanket of toddies—almost.

"I don't wanna talk now."

"Are you all right? You sound funny."

The drinking brought out her fighting spirit. "Too bad for you! You're gonna be sorry for what you did!"

"I am sorry."

"Oh, yeah? You . . . you. . . ." She couldn't think what to call him. All the words that came to mind weren't bad. How could she still love him?

"Cad," he suggested.

"You're geddin' warm."

"Liar."

"Yes! You lied about everything!"

"Not everything," he said with a ferocity that pierced her hazy brain, "and you know this in your heart, if you'll just believe, not in me, but in yourself! I love you. Are you so sure that labels mark us forever, that we can't transcend the images of our high school days? I don't, but *you've* got to believe!"

"I don't believe anything anymore."

"Don't say that, Shelby, it scares me. Listen, I talked with my grandfather and—"

"This isn't about him!" She hung up, unable to bear his voice any longer. She knew she'd sounded slightly muddled, but she didn't care. The thought of Clay calling back, however, prompted her to unplug all the house phones. Then she collapsed on her bed, still wearing the jeans and blouse she'd thrown on that morning, and fell into a shallow sleep.

She awoke to the muffled sound of movement downstairs. Still a little groggy, she doubted her ears at first. Had she remembered to turn on the surveillance system when she got back? Considering how distracted and heartsore she'd been, the possibility existed. Her clock told her that she'd slept for about ninety minutes. The afternoon sun had clouded over. Wincing a little from a toddy-induced headache, she hauled her body off the bed and plodded to the open door.

Her bedroom was the closest one to the staircase on the second floor. The hall was darker, more shadowy than the other rooms because it was windowless and the light was off. Shelby listened for the sounds that had pulled her out of blessed unconsciousness but didn't hear anything.

Satisfied, she turned toward her soft, comforting bed when she heard a creak and then another from the first floor. One creak sounded like a window being raised, and the other, weight being applied to ancient, warped floorboards. Suddenly she heard a tinkling sound, like pebbles bouncing off a wood floor. Shelby knew immediately that someone had entered her home, and not in the conventional way!

Clay had warned her that the windows were the vulnerable spots in her security system. It sounded like they were in the front parlor. Of all the brazen nerve, she thought, until she realized that Desiree's house was still isolated. There was no one to witness the break-in.

Fear sobered Shelby right up. Her heart began to pound. She figured if she could get to the second-floor telephone, she could call the police. Damn it, she thought. The phone would have to be plugged in again, but that would take no time. She just had to get to it without being noticed.

The hall rug muffled the creaks produced by her weight. The phone was close to the stairs. Shelby made her way in the murky light.

She tiptoed to the small table where the phone rested. Quickly she bent to reconnect her phone. As the cord made a glorious click, she heard a soft padding sound, like feet carefully stepping up a worn staircase carpet. For a millisecond Shelby debated whether to try to call 911 or run. But run where? The stairs were blocked. Frantically she stood and reached for the receiver, when suddenly a black figure in a ski mask appeared on the landing, not six feet away. The figure carried a gun, and it was pointed at her head.

Instinctively she ducked as a bullet singed her hair. The intruder advanced, aiming again. Shelby lunged at the black figure, catching the hand before the insidious revolver could be fired again. Behind the mask she saw two icy-blue eyes.

Fear gave her strength. She tried to wrestle the gun away but couldn't loosen the grip of her attacker. Furthermore, she had to keep the gun from pointing at her. She realized, however, that the assailant didn't match her height. That gave her a fighting chance. They stumbled on the landing as each tried to kick the other's legs while still grappling for the gun.

They were almost to the stairs. Shelby heard footsteps downstairs and knew with increasing terror that there would soon be two against one. She had to get the gun. With all the force she could muster, she crashed her body against her attacker, propelling the black-clad body against the top stair's railing.

The blow stunned her assailant sufficiently to allow Shelby to pull the gun away, but her victory was short-lived. The intruder quickly recovered and made a mad grab for it, sending both of them sprawling perilously close to the stairs. Their heavy fall caused Shelby to lose her grip on the revolver. She could hear it tumbling down the steps. Now there were only fists to fight with. Shelby struggled to defend herself against the black-leathered punches. One blow brought blood from her nose. Another hit her ribs, causing a sharp pain.

She grabbed her attacker in a body lock. They rolled practically to the top step. Shelby felt the drop with her foot. She prevented her assailant from pushing her down the stairs by simply not letting go. In the melee she pulled the ski mask off.

It was Heather Scott! Stunned, Shelby screamed out her name. Being discovered made Heather momentarily lose her focus. Shelby pinned her down, causing Heather to utter a piercing cry of "Help meeeee!"

In the hazy light of the staircase Shelby saw a man, also dressed in black clothes and ski mask, at the bottom of the stairs. He was carrying the gun.

"Shoot her!" Heather commanded.

The man tried to speak, but the ski mask muffled his voice. He pulled it off, apparently giving up the need to remain anonymous. Logan Langstaff fingered the mask. "Um," he said, his smooth voice timid and high-pitched, "that wasn't the plan."

"The plan has changed," Heather said through gritted teeth. "You have to do it."

The gun wavered, as Logan did. He took several steps up, still pointing the revolver at Shelby, but his face registered unease.

"Logan, please," Shelby said. "Please."

He looked ill, as if he couldn't believe he'd been stuck with the dirty work. His discomfort seemed to be less over the fact that she would die than that he was the one who'd have to kill her.

"I can't," he said.

"Eeeeeyaahhh!" Heather screamed.

Shelby had never heard such rage. She was no match for the strength such anger gave Heather, who overpowered Shelby's weakening arms. The fury of her attack on Shelby, however, combined with the tangled positions of their bodies propelled them both down the long, wide staircase. Their descent was stopped midway by Logan, who'd rushed up the steps to prevent them from falling any farther. Between him and Heather, Shelby didn't have a chance of escaping. She found herself pinned against the stairs.

Heather took the gun from Logan. He made no protest. "We have to make this look good," Heather hissed as she smacked Shelby across the face with her hand. Shelby tasted blood.

Logan winced. "Just do it."

Heather aimed the gun at Shelby's head. Shelby knew she was going to die. No bargains could be struck with someone holding a revolver so resolutely. But she couldn't die without knowing why!

"Why, Logan, why?"

He answered simply. "For the money."

"But I have no money!"

Heather smiled, a chilling, mean smile. "But you will, Shelby, darling. With the letters and the land, you'll own the Trasks. And after your unfortunate death, it'll all come to Logan, your only living relative."

Shelby's windfall. The land and the letters. Logan would get his revenge against Clay, and Heather would get her rich meal ticket. Shelby had once thought that her inheritance would free her. Now it would kill her.

She made one last attempt to get out of their clutches. Screaming and flailing, she tried to break free. It was useless.

"Keep her still!" Heather commanded. She aimed. Shelby closed her eyes.

She heard the gun go off and a scream. Oddly, it wasn't her screaming. She opened her eyes to see Clay Trask holding Heather's trigger hand in the air. With all the tumult he must have come in undetected. His grip was so tight that his knuckles showed white. Heather screamed in pain as she struggled to free herself from his other arm, wrapped tight around her torso.

Another roar filled Shelby's ears. Logan cried out, his voice a mixture of fear and anger. He released Shelby with an impatient shove and immediately attacked Clay.

Encumbered by Heather, Clay was an easy target. Logan punched him across the jaw. Clay's head snapped back, and he hit the wall. Dazed, he clung to Heather's trigger hand. The gun went off, and then again. Shelby went as flat against the stairs as she could, waiting for one of the bullets to hit her. Heather was insanely trying to shoot anything.

The few seconds that Logan scrambled to avoid Heather's line of fire gave Clay the chance to recover. He crushed Heather's wrist so hard that she had to give up the gun. But just as he grabbed it, Logan attacked him again, sending the gun flying over the banister.

Free now, Heather started down the remaining steps. Shelby assumed this was to find the revolver, so she lunged for Heather's legs, catching one foot and causing Heather to fall against the railing and hit her head. Moaning, Heather collapsed on the stairs.

Clay and Logan were now locked in a duel of fists. Dragging her battered body up, Shelby debated whether to help Clay, who seemed to be doing pretty well without her, or find the gun. Then she saw Heather start to sit up, and the decision was made. No doubt in seconds Heather would be strong enough to help her lover against Clay or go looking for the revolver herself. Shelby had to find it first. Quickly she wedged her body past a still-groggy Heather and fled down the rest of the stairs.

Shelby had to act fast, but where was the gun? Desperately she searched near the staircase and the adjacent parlor. She spotted the gun halfway under the fringe of a footstool. Turning, she saw that Heather had joined forces with Logan against Clay, but the tide seemed to have turned against them. Clay had Heather in an arm lock with one hand and was trading blows with Logan with his other. He looked as if he hardly needed Shelby, but she picked the gun up and fired into the ceiling. All parties froze.

"That will be enough," she said in a voice harsh with pain and determination. She pointed the revolver at Heather and Logan. "Trust me, I'll shoot."

The two stunned people sagged to the stair carpet. Clay gazed at Shelby, his nose and mouth bleeding. He was gasping so hard that he couldn't talk, but his eyes conveyed relief and love. As he walked to her, Shelby saw his face slowly change from exhaustion to triumph. He deserved to be proud, she thought. He deserved a celebration, a parade! But when he lightly pressed his cheek against hers, he whispered, "My heroine." Shelby closed her eyes for a brief second in a silent prayer of thanksgiving.

Clay took the gun from her and motioned to Heather and Logan to come into the parlor. "I'll baby-sit," he said. "You call the police."

Shelby agreed, but she had to ask one question first. "Was this your idea, Logan, or Heather's?"

Heather merely laughed as she sat on a slightly sprung love seat. Collapsing next to her, Logan put his head in his hands. He moaned within the depths of his arms. "It wasn't fair," he said in a muffled voice. He lifted his head. *It wasn't fair!* Why, *why* should you be the one to inherit the house? You didn't even want to be rich."

"Shut up, Logan!" Heather warned, but he seemed to want to justify himself.

291

"I didn't want to do it, Shelby," he said with absurd sincerity. "I always liked you."

Clay let out an incredulous laugh, but Shelby wanted Logan to continue talking.

"I liked you, too."

"I would even have let you keep this barn if I just could have found those letters."

"Shut up, Logan!"

Shelby dabbed at her mouth. "So you were my intruder. I should have known with all those sympathetic phone calls urging me to get out of the house, and—" She almost laughed. "How's your heavy breathing, Logan?"

Logan blinked, his dazed mind beginning to understand. He quickly glanced at Heather. "What are you talking about?"

"Nice try," Clay said, "but Shelby suspected that her mysterious caller was a woman. I bet both of you took turns."

Heather pulled off her leather gloves. "You'll never be able to prove that."

"No, we'll just have to be satisfied with attempted murder."

"If it's any consolation, Logan, I found the letters by accident," Shelby said.

His ego flared up. "I'd have found them if I'd had more time to look."

She nodded. "Perhaps, but I rarely left the house. You must have dropped your teeth when you saw me at the picnic."

"You said you were leaving just as we saw

you." Tears of self-pity welled up in his eyes. "I never get a break."

"Poor baby," Shelby commiserated. "I suppose it would be cruel to tell you that there was one other time I went out."

Defeated, he looked at her with loathing.

Shelby couldn't resist asking Heather, "Why Logan? If you wanted a rich man, why didn't you go for Buzz or Clay?"

Heather lost a little of her cool. "I do love Logan," she said. "We're . . . a lot alike. Besides, I saw the handwriting on the wall this summer. Buzz wasn't going to marry me. He told me he wanted someone younger." She looked at Clay with chilling hatred. "And you were never going to marry me.

Clay nodded. "I wanted someone nicer."

The police came quickly. Under their questioning, Logan broke, but lawyers were called. Shelby and Clay managed to piece together the general story. Heather and Logan had planned to make her death seem like the aftermath of a robbery. Then with her tragic demise, Logan could claim her estate as her only living blood relative.

The plan was logical. Shelby had reported a prowler after she'd been hit on the head—by Logan as it turned out. He'd suspected that the letters might be a gold mine the minute Shelby had first told him about them at the Fairview Country Club. While she watched Clay play tennis, Logan had broken into her house to find them. Anything to do with the Trasks bore looking into.

Shelby assumed that they hadn't tried to kill her before because they hadn't known what the letters might reveal. After she blurted out the whole story to Logan that morning, however, they knew that with her out of the way, they would be on easy street. Forget the few piddling dollars that Desiree's land would fetch. They would have the letters, and thus the Trasks, in their power. That meant millions.

Logan's compassionate suggestion of a toddy— "my mother's sovereign remedy for stress"—was calculated to render her easier to kill. He hadn't counted on Clay, however.

Neither had Shelby. All these months she'd doubted his integrity, while missing the snake in her own family. She thought she'd never see Clay again, except possibly in court, and yet he'd come today and saved her life. Why?

With the police inside her house with Logan and Heather, Shelby suggested moving to the front porch. Clay readily agreed.

They walked stiffly to the porch swing and sat down. Shelby gazed at Clay, his face still handsome despite the puffy eye, cut lip, and purple bruise on his cheek. Shelby had no idea how she looked. Their injuries had been mostly cuts and bruises, which Clay expertly bandaged using

Shelby's first-aid supplies. The mirror could wait.

"Clay," she said, "thank you for saving my life."

He took her hand in his. Both showed cut and swollen knuckles. "You saved mine."

She shook her head. "No, I don't think so. You pretty much had Heather and Logan under control by the time I found the gun."

"So *you* say."

"It's just that saying thank you doesn't seem like enough. Not nearly enough. I don't know how I'll ever repay you."

He gently touched her wounded face with his fingers. "You're alive. That's payment enough."

"I could destroy the letters. Forget that—"

"No!" Clay got up so quickly that he winced in pain. Shelby put her hand out to him, but he avoided her touch.

"Isn't that what you want? Isn't that what your family wants?"

He wouldn't look at her. "We have no right to ask you to do that."

"But I thought . . . then . . . why did you come here today?"

Clay slowly walked to the front of the porch. Dusk had settled, the long, lovely Louisville dusk, when a summer's day simmers down to a pleasant warmth. He took a deep breath and turned around.

"After you left this morning, I went to my grandfather. I told him that the letters had been

295

found and that I had read them. I was angry—at myself mostly, but also at him—and confused. My grandfather is the most important influence in my life. He understands me in a way my parents never have. They love me, but they adore the Prom King."

Clay closed his eyes for a moment, overcome, it seemed, by the magnitude of his illusion. "He told me that one day I would meet the right woman, and I was to let nothing stand in my way. He didn't tell me that *he* would get in the way, that I'd be forced to put my fears for him over love."

Shelby's mouth went dry. "Clay, I'm beginning to understand why you did. Up until I read the letters, Desiree had been a remote, puzzling figure to me. Now I see her as a real person. A person I can love. With that much love in my heart, I can't say to what lengths I would go to protect her reputation."

"Providing the reputation is worth saving," Clay said. He leaned against the porch wall, grimacing as he rubbed his left arm. Shelby wondered if his physical pain could match the emotional turmoil she was seeing.

"I asked my grandfather how he could live a lie all these years. Why hadn't he come back for Desiree? Why had he kept the land?"

"What did he say?" she asked softly.

Clay looked at her with the saddest eyes. "My grandfather didn't come back to her because, at first, he couldn't. He was in prison."

Shelby inhaled sharply, a move that caused twinges of pain in her rib cage. "What for?"

"Robbery. He wanted to come home to Desiree with a little nest egg, but every time he'd get a few dollars ahead, his job would end or he'd be laid off. The Depression made it hard for men like my grandfather, farmers with little skill besides farming. He didn't want to ask Desiree for money, and he was so close to Louisville when it happened. Really, he was coming back to her when he stole some food in Indiana just to survive. Unfortunately he was caught, and with food and money so scarce in those times, the public outcry against thieves was great.

"He was too ashamed to tell her. This shame, combined with the killing of her father, made him feel unworthy of Desiree. He thought if he didn't write, she'd marry someone better. When he got out of jail, he thought about not returning to Kentucky, but the land was all he had. He met my grandmother, and they married. He never tried to contact Desiree because he thought she wouldn't want to see him, but his anguish at not keeping his vow to her has eaten away at him all these years."

Clay looked as if he hadn't the strength to stand.

Tears sprang up in Shelby's eyes. "How they both suffered," she said.

"I . . . I was so angry . . . in the beginning,"

he said, "but despite what he's done, I can't hate him, Shelby. I can't."

"No, of course you can't," she said as she got up and went to him. She put her arms around Clay. With a sigh he pressed his face against hers. "You were right," she said, "we have to forgive."

"Oh, Shelby, when you love someone—"

"You just love them, for what they are. I know that now."

"Even if they're not perfect?" His voice sounded choked.

She felt his heart racing. "Who is?" she said. "I trust only imperfect people."

His bruised arms wound tighter around her. "I had to come back today, to tell you about Grandpa. And to say. . . ." His voice dropped off; he seemed drained.

"What, Clay?"

He pulled back and looked into her eyes. "That I understand now that love means sacrifice. When I asked you to choose where you belonged, I realized that *I* hadn't committed. Oh, I said I loved you, but still I wanted the land and the letters and my family's good name, too. I wanted you to put my needs first, but I hadn't put you above everything else."

He put his hands gingerly on her cheeks. His thumbs checked the tears streaming down her face. "I came today to tell you that you're more important to me than anything, certainly more

298

than money or a few Tramarts. I can't live my life for my parents, or for the greater glory of the Trask name. Do what you want with the letters. If coming to terms with the past means that *we* might have a future, then I'm ready to start over in a cabin.

"Shelby could hardly breathe. Every muscle in her body ached, yet she felt thrilled, joyous. She was finally the most important person in someone's life. "I'll live anywhere with you," she said with a radiant smile, "but if it's a cabin, I think we should build a newer one. I mean, I like that brass bed, but there's no room for *my* office."

Clay's eyes widened as a deep sigh escaped from his lips. Impetuously Shelby rushed to kiss him, but her impact on his cut lip made them both fall back in pain. They grimaced in more discomfort as they started to laugh.

"We won't be kissing for a while," she said.

Clay massaged her wild, curly hair. "Oh, no, we just have to be more careful." He bent and gently pressed his lips against hers. She responded with a slow testing of pressure until their mouths fused in a kiss of love and forgiveness. Shelby finally understood that with love, real love, forgiveness is automatic. Clay still loved his grandfather, despite what he'd done. She loved Desiree, even though the old woman was never able to reciprocate. By always standing alone, Shelby had never had to compromise. She'd missed so much.

If she wanted perfection, she could remain the caustic reporter of the rich, judging others, but not letting herself get too close to be judged—or rejected. If she wanted to be loved, however, she'd have to risk exposing her vulnerabilities. Well, she was ready. As their kiss ended, she pulled her head back. "I love you, Clay. All my life I've been looking to belong, while publicly spurning it. I told you that people don't belong to people, but I was secretly hoping for an invitation."

"I'm asking."

"Then I say yes, yes! Earlier today you accused me of not believing in your love because I didn't believe in myself. You were so right. I couldn't because I was hanging on to the past, afraid to let go of old hurts and prejudices. I even intended to use Desiree's legacy to exact justice for these slights."

"I told you the letters—"

"Will be burned. And the land will be sold. I know now that Desiree's true legacy to me is that the past should remain the past. I'll leave revenge to people like Heather and Logan."

"Are you sure?"

"Absolutely. After all, how do I explain to our children that Mommy sued Daddy."

He laughed. "Some financial agreement will be drawn up."

"Clay—"

"No, I insist. There should be some justice in

this."

She smiled and buried her head in his chest. "You know money doesn't mean that much to me."

She felt his lips on her hair. "You told me that money could have positive effects· if it's in the right hands," he said. She looked up. He took her hands. "Here they are."

Her throat felt tight. "I'll be rich."

"It's just a label."

The day finally caught up with Shelby. She started to sag. Clay caught her and they walked back to the porch swing. She leaned against him, his arm around her, as they started to slowly rock in the old chair. The moon was beginning to show faintly in the sky.

"I'm so happy, Clay. I want everyone to be happy, too."

He smiled. "That's a tall order."

"Well, perhaps one person. I'd like to meet your grandfather."

She felt his hand tighten on her shoulder, but he was silent. She pulled herself up to see tears in his eyes. "He would like that," he said hoarsely.

She snuggled in his arms. "I guess I'll even have to get used to Mapes. How did he manage to elude all your safety precautions when he broke into my house for your grandfather?"

"He did all his searching before Logan attacked you. The house was easy then."

"I never suspected a thing."

"He prided himself on that." When Shelby let out a derisive sigh, Clay said, "You might like Mapes more if you knew how guilty he's felt all these years over what happened. He never prospered. In fact, he was nearly penniless when he asked my grandfather for a job at Park View."

"It's strange that your grandfather hired him. After all, Mapes ratted on Ford and Desiree."

Clay nodded. "Yes, he did, but remember that my grandfather also did something that he regretted for the rest of his life. Mapes was his comrade in guilt—and fear. Both men thought that one day the past would come back to hurt them. Mapes even confessed that your aunt tried to call my grandfather a few weeks before she died, but he intercepted the call because he thought that, finally, the ax was about to fall. How did he know that she wanted to forgive?"

Shelby sighed. "They lived their lives in limbo, the past choking any hope for a future."

He looked into her eyes, and Shelby saw the quiet integrity, the goodness that she would love all the days of her life.

"That won't be us," he promised.

In the peaceful summer twilight Shelby looked to a new future, with Clay.